MURDER FOR PENNIES

The Complete

Cases of the Parson

1937–39

JAMES DUNCAN

illustrations by Arthur Rodman Bowker

cover by J. George Janes

BLACK MASK

2024

Table of Contents

Double Trouble

Havana becomes a port of call for
sudden deaths and all the passions

THE PARSON, AN under-sized man, surveyed the soft-lighted dining patio with dark muddy eyes, hands in his coat pockets, a cigarette slanted from his lips. Then with a jerk of his chin, he said, "O.K., Vince."

Vincent Guard strolled to his customary table with light, flowing steps, sat down. The Parson, dainty as a doll in his suit of black, took a chair at his right where he could watch the door. Then Guard glanced to his left. It became an open-eyed, transfixed stare. When the soft-shoed waiter with a deferential, *"Buenos noches, Señores"* came for his order, Guard was still in a trance.

He stayed that way while the Parson ordered. The party on his left was large—seven or eight people. There were three girls and five men. Guard wasn't sure of the number. His gaze was riveted on one girl.

She sat at the head of the table as by divine right. She was the most beautiful being he had ever seen, at once fragile yet firm. Her dress was white, satiny stuff; it didn't cling but appeared molded as part of her rich, glowing skin. Her deep athletic tan was the more striking for the sheer blondness of her hair. Over the hair she wore a coronet of blue stones but her eyes were bluer than the stones.

She couldn't be more than five feet in all but gazing into the moist depths of her eyes, feeling the impact of her personality, Vincent Guard fell madly, hopelessly in love with her.

And at that moment the electric in their glances sparked.

The Parson growled something. At the big table, a man leaned over and touched the girl's arm, spoke to her. Naomi Frost looked startled.

Vincent Guard flushed. He could guess what had been said. His eyes dropped to the shimmering table-cloth. When he looked at the Parson, there was a breathlessness about his eyes, his nostrils were wide and he drew in a deep breath like a man who had been running hard.

"Ixnay, ixnay," the Parson muttered. "No janes, kid. Eyes front!"

From his pocket the Parson took a scrupulously clean, scented handkerchief and wiped his palms dry. They were always sweaty. He liked a dry finger on a trigger.

Vincent Guard smiled. His head was whirling and his heart pounding. He pushed back his chair and stood up.

"I gotta talk to that girl."

The Parson stiffened, jerked like a beady-eyed squirrel but did not stop him. Guard floated across the tiled floor like a sleep-walker. He didn't know where his nerve came from, but the words were there, inane enough, but ready.

"I should like to dance with you."

She did not nod nor speak, but she stood up and seemed to

lean toward him in an almost imperceptible surrender. There was a hushed, stunned silence at her table but Guard would not have known if they had shouted. He had eyes only for Naomi Frost. They moved together to the dance floor around the broad L of the patio. He put his arms around her very carefully, very tenderly and they began to dance.

It was past ten when Vincent Guard and the Parson went up to their luxurious suite. The Parson, rarely angry, slammed the door.

"Now you've done it. Just wait'll the boss hears!"

Guard sank into an easy chair. "Parson," he said quietly, "go to hell."

The Parson stared at him hopelessly. An expression of amusement flitted across his face. "Did you date her?"

Guard could contain his elation no longer. He towered from his chair, flinging his arms upward in sheer jubilation.

"Did I date her? Did I date her! Breakfast at the Creole, lunch at the Biarritz, the whole blamed afternoon at the track, dinner on her yacht. Parson, you're a free man tomorrow."

"Damned white of you to think of me," the Parson said bitingly. Then, "O.K., kid, have your fun."

AFTER TWO DAYS of heady, whirlwind courtship, Vincent Guard and Naomi Frost ran up to Varadero Beach for the day. The water sparkled in the hot, white sunshine like an immense burnished sapphire. Flame appeared to flicker and dance on the salt-white beaches in contrast to the palm groves at the foot of the jade-green hills.

Vincent and Naomi frolicked in the surf like any other pair of kids and ate lunch in a miniature *bahio*. They laughed a great deal. As the afternoon waned, they trudged back to the car Guard had hired for the return trip to Havana. Their feet whispered into sand. Birds called and screeched in the lime-green shadows, echoed in the gorges. Vincent and Naomi were very happy.

A car was moving very slowly on the road. Guard saw it but did not particularly notice its snail-like pace. The road was built up two or three feet higher than the beach. The car came to a stop. Naomi and Guard were fifty feet from their own car when a series of *pop-pop* explosions whacked out and threw up fine sprays of sand at their feet.

Naomi suddenly screamed, fell to her knees; but she was frightened, not hurt. Guard pushed her behind the shelter of a hummock. Lead hissed again and again into the soft sand. Guard's face was white to the lips. It took him a second to make sure the girl was unharmed. But by that time the shooting had ceased. The car, moving fast over the concrete, zipped out of sight.

Guard made a troubled movement of his head. A chill blue light coursed through his eyes. His heart was pumping fast. Naomi inhaled, then let her breath out slowly. She was frightened, angry and bewildered at one and the same time. She stared at Guard with a stricken look.

"Vincent, wh-what happened?"

He felt her body shaking against the arm he placed across her shoulder. "Some mistake. Must be."

"It was no mistake. Vincent, those men wanted to kill you."

His lips tightened. "Come on, we'll drive back to town."

Troubled eyes looked appealingly into his. "Vincent, I—I just can't...." She broke off and after a split second tried again. "Why won't you trust me? Don't be afraid to tell me anything."

His face was suddenly older as his cheeks furrowed with lines. The chill in his eyes became ice. "There's nothing to tell," he said.

"You don't trust me," she said quietly.

They had neared their car. A speedy looking roadster was parked behind it, motor purring. A woman stepped out of it and walked toward them. She held a bottle in her hand. Her sudden appearance checked Guard's reply.

"Hello, Vince."

She was pretty, but beneath the flash of her uncommonly good clothes was a streak of vulgarity. Her throaty voice jarred Guard. He stared at her uncomprehendingly. He had never seen her before, yet she knew the name.

"You don't know who I am? Yeah, sure. Maybe you're ashamed of me! I seen the boys gun you. Next time they'll take more time." Her eyes glittered strangely as his astonishment mounted. She said with burning sarcasm, "You and your dead pan! You almost got me believin' I ain't me!"

"Who are you? What do you want?"

Her eyes were burning in her head. A jerking shoulder said nerves. There was a twitch to her lips. "You forget Sally Walsh pretty damn quick, don't you?" She cackled. "A lot of other guys don't."

"I—" He stopped speaking and stared at her in sudden alarm. "What's in that bottle?"

"Naomi Frost!" The woman nodded and smiled. "So that's your latest! You're aimin' high, Vince."

"What's in that bottle?"

She gave Guard a ghastly, wicked grin. "Beauty lotion."

"Beat it!"

"You're mooching right up to the Social Register. Not bad for a—"

"Vincent," cried Naomi, "what is it? What's in the bottle?"

"Acid!" He flung the word at her, took a step toward the woman. "Throw it away, you damn witch!"

"Sure! Oh, sure!"

"Naomi! *Look out!*"

The woman had suddenly flung the contents of the bottle at Naomi's face. The liquid described a flat trajectory in an upward slope. Guard leaped. His hand flung out, threw Naomi violently aside. Some of the liquid splashed against his wrist. He screamed in involuntary agony; his whole arm felt on fire.

The woman was laughing hysterically. Her eyes bulged and there was madness in them. Her blood-red mouth was ugly with strain. The jerking of her shoulder had communicated itself to her whole body. She turned and slipped into the roadster, jarred the gear into place, jammed down on the accelerator. The car made a sweeping U-turn, sped away. It was over as quickly as that.

Naomi, half-blinded with tears, was at Guard's side, shudders scurrying up and down her spine. For two minutes she was in such a disordered state he was afraid she was going to have hysterics. But the grimaces of pain he could not hide shook her out of herself. She took his arm in both her hands. His hand hung loose at the wrist, limp and detached.

"V-Vincent, you're badly hurt!"

"Nope." A shadow passed over his face. He couldn't pass it off blithely. "She aimed the stuff for your face. She was all hopped up. You could see it in her eyes."

Blood was pouring back into Naomi's face, but horror still whitened her lips, left its mark in her eyes.

"It doesn't seem real—the shooting and then that woman!" Confusion kept her speechless for a second. Then, "Vincent, look at me! Who was that woman? What is she to you?"

His face was stern, set. "Do you want the truth?"

"Of course!"

"I never saw her before in my life."

Naomi stiffened, stabbed him with a searching look.

"But her name—Sally Walsh. And she called you by yours."

He shook his head. "I'm telling you I never saw her before."

"And the men who tried to kill us?"

"I don't know who they are, either."

There was brittle silence for a second or two as they stared into each other's eyes. Naomi said, "I'll get some wet sand to ease the pain. Does it hurt very much?"

She ran off to hide her tears.

A DOCTOR DRESSED the seared wrist. Then Guard dropped Naomi at the Yacht Basin in Vedado and watched as a launch taxied her to her yacht. He drove to the Imperial Hotel. When he came into the suite, the Parson was there waiting, arms placed akimbo.

"The last time, see?" the Parson said softly. "That skirt is running you ragged. Out all night, out all day." Then he saw the bandaged wrist. "What happened to you?"

"I'm quitting, Parson. Tonight!"

"What happened to your hand?"

"Oh, that. A woman tried to throw acid on Naomi's face."

"What woman, sap?"

"She called herself Sally Walsh. But that ain't all. Three men in a car threw lead at us. First bullets, then acid!" His voice changed, hardened. "Who is the Walsh number, Parson? Gosh, she was hopped to the eyes all right, all right."

The Parson's thin shoulders tightened. He said nothing.

"O.K., I get it." Vincent said. "But do I have to take that, too? I tell you I've had a bellyful!"

The Parson took a cigarette from his pocket without producing the pack. He worried it between nicotine-stained, doll-like fingers, put it in his mouth and snicked a match on his thumb-nail. Smoke trailed wispily from his paper-thin nostrils.

"So she's here," he said at last. "And the tommy-gun artists are here. I've been expectin' them sooner or later. That's why I wanted you to have your fun first." He added irrelevantly, "Now ain't that something!"

"I'm quitting!" Guard snapped suddenly. "I'm going to tell Naomi all about myself."

"Don't be a jack. You're pullin' down a grand a week."

"For what? So I can be shot at! So Naomi can have acid thrown at her! I don't care for myself but—would you know what it meant to be in love?"

"Yeah."

Guard, brought up short, widened his eyes ingenuously. "You? In love?"

The Parson jerked a gun from a shoulder holster. "With li'l' Gwendolyn." He caressed the weapon.

Guard laughed in nervous relief. "And me figuring you might be human after all!"

"Relax, boy. Take a drink. Take two drinks. You need 'em."

"No. I'm quitting this lousy business. No more front."

Knuckles rippled over the door panel. The Parson's right

hand went swiftly to his gun. He moved to the door, opened it with a sudden lurch.

A voice said, "Mr. Guard? Vincent Guard?"

The Parson grunted, moved aside, but his hand remained near his gun. A lean, distinguished-looking man entered, swept Guard with keen appraisal.

"I'm Andrew Goodwin, United States vice-consul for Havana. I've just come from Naomi Frost's yacht."

"Oh! Have a seat, Mr. Goodwin."

"Thanks but what I have to say won't take long. Are you staying long in Havana, Mr. Guard?"

"Er—why, I don't know."

"Will you open gambling houses here?"

"Gosh, no!"

"I must warn you that I'm not here in an official capacity. I'm a friend of Miss Frost's, a friend of her father. Miss Frost has many friends in the American colony here. Naturally, they've been very worried over her association with you."

Guard's jaw muscles strained.

"I've already heard what happened at Varadero," Goodwin went on. "I'll be plain. Naomi Frost is a fine girl. You ran a string of gambling houses in New York and were part of a money-lending racket. Federal agents made it hot for you and you slipped out of New York with several millions and an announcement that you were through with—ah—illegitimate enterprises. Cuban authorities are not likely to extradite you, but if you make yourself unpleasant you could be deported as an undesirable alien."

"I—say, wait a minute! Repeat that!"

"I thought I was making myself plain. Miss Frost's friends are determined that you should let her alone. Federal agents are waiting in Miami for you to show your nose. I trust we understand each other, Mr. Guard."

Guard's fists clenched. "The hell we do!" He laughed recklessly, crazily. "Are you in love with Naomi?"

"I don't see what that has to do—"

"This: You want Naomi and you're trying to freeze me out!"

"—with the fact that you're no fit companion for her."

"All right, you've recited your piece. Get out!"

Goodwin turned, felt the Parson's eyes on him. "Suppose I do not choose to?"

The Parson's hand slid upward. "Do you want to stay?"

"No," Goodwin said.

The Parson removed his eyes. "Well, get out, then."

The consul moved with dignity to the door. It closed behind him.

The telephone jangled. The Parson crossed to it, jerked the receiver off the hook, mumbled a terse, "Hello."

He nodded sagely and listened without comment. Then finally the words ceased rumbling in the receiver diaphragm and he said, "At nine-thirty, boss. O.K."

He hung up, glanced oddly at the young man. "It's all around town how you were shot at in Varadero. Also Sally Walsh's acid-throwing act. The boss wants to see us at nine-thirty."

"Swell! I'll tell him to his face I'm quitting."

"You don't," the Parson bent his head to one side, "know the boss."

" 'No fit companion for her'—remember his saying that? Why the stiff-backed ——."

"Huh? Oh, you mean Goodwin! Forget it, kid. After all, he's right!"

At nine-twenty, the Parson and Vincent Guard left the hotel and took a cab. Twice they circled the Prado and then rode out along the Malecon. The Parson kept an accurate check. They were not followed. They turned into a side street. The Parson reached forward and touched the driver on the shoulder.

"Right here will do," he said.

The Parson and Guard walked back to the Malecon. Almost immediately, they stopped another cab and climbed in. Swinging around a corner the car headed back past Cabaña Fortress. The ride was short. The streets became narrow, unclean. Drab, ancient buildings formed an unbroken line on either side. Pedestrians were few. It was the old quarter of Havana.

They got out of the cab, again the Parson paid and they walked. They had trouble locating the house, all the streets looked so much alike. Then they went past the anise-smelling bar on the corner and knew they had hit it right. The house was to the left of it.

HUGE BRASS-STUDDED DOORS opened onto a patio that was more like a courtyard. It was dirty, paved with irregular flagstones. A parrot hung in a cage in front of a recessed window. Other windows stared blindly down at them from all four sides. The inevitable guava tree, leaves streaked with pigeon droppings, grew in one corner.

They moved to a door. The Parson rapped sharply in a code signal. The door opened a crack. "Come in."

They went in. A squat man with bowed legs and chest like a beer barrel regarded them from under bushy eyebrows. His linen was soiled and wrinkled. "Theesa way, *por favor.*"

They followed him through a draughty hall that was narrow

and smelt of rancid olive oil. He opened another door, stepped aside. The Parson stepped in. Guard followed immediately behind. It was a low-ceilinged room furnished with heavy table and equally heavy chairs. The walls were white-washed. An unshaded bulb hung from the ceiling.

In one of the chairs sat a man who could have been Vincent Guard's twin. He had the same copper brown hair worn close-cropped, blue eyes, straight, thin nose. Only a closer examination would reveal any difference. The seated man's lips were thinner, curled in a sneer. He looked older, his hair actually was several shades darker and his eyes were cold, uncommunicative.

The Parson said carelessly, "Hello, boss."

The man grimaced. "Take a chair." The grimace widened. "You, too, Dolan. Sit down!"

The man known in Havana as Vincent Guard but addressed now as Dolan abruptly sat down. "Look here, Mr. Guard," he began in a rush, "I've come to tell you I won't—"

"Take it easy, Dolan."

The young man bit his lip.

"What he's tryin' to say is—"

"Parson! Suppose you go into the next room and keep Monk company. He's lonely."

The Parson looked at his boss with eyes like glass. Then he rose, quitted the room.

"Good. Now, Dolan, what happened this afternoon?"

"Nothing, just nothing at all. Some guys opened a chatter-gun on me from a car. I had a girl with me and…."

"H'mm!"

"What?"

"Go on with your story."

"There is no more. They didn't shoot good. Maybe the range was too long." His brow wrinkled earnestly. "No sooner were they gone than a dame named Sally Walsh chucked a whole bottle of acid at the girl with me."

The man smiled. "Is that all?"

"Except they thought I was you."

"Isn't that what we wanted them to think?"

"You didn't tell me that when you took me on for this job!" the young man named Dolan exploded. "You said all I had to do was loll around hotels and the race track, be seen by everybody and let 'em think I was really Vincent Guard."

"But I'm payin' a thou a week."

"Not after I get sieved you won't!"

"You mentioned a girl before—Miss Naomi Frost?"

"Yeah." A deep flush suffused Jerry Dolan's neck and cheeks.

"Planning to get married?"

Dolan was surprised. "How'd you know?"

"Never mind. I know. It's O.K. with me, see? But with a girl like that a fella needs dough, important dough. Hang on to your job a little longer. I'll raise the ante to two grand. Whatta you say?"

"Nothing doing. I'm gettin' out with a whole skin while I can."

"You got the Parson with you for protection. He's my best gun."

"The Parson's just color in case anyone doubts my identity. He's been around you so much people expect you every time he shows." Dolan looked at Vincent Guard. "That Sally Walsh—was she your girl?"

Guard smiled ruefully. "She thought she owned me body and soul. So what?"

"Nothing, except that you must've given her a dirty deal. And those men who shot at me—do you know them?"

"Slightly."

"Sort of a shooting acquaintance, huh?"

Guard's grin widened. "A sort of give and take." His grin faded and he was silent a second. "Does anyone know your real name here?"

Jerry Dolan shook his head.

"You didn't tell Miss Frost?"

Dolan snorted. "But I'm going to."

Vincent Guard shook his head. "No, you won't."

A dull red color was pushing through from under Dolan's collar to emblazon his neck. He said very slowly, "I'm going to tell her the truth."

"You're getting tough."

"No, I'm pulling out. And when I do, she'll know my real name and all there is to know about me."

"Including me?"

"Including you."

Vincent Guard shook his head. "That's no way to talk, fella. You don't want to get me sore. If you so much as breathe a word to her about me, now or any time, you'll be steppin' on my toes. Get it?"

Dolan was looking at him with a chill stare.

"I can check up," Guard went on. "If I hear you've been shootin' off your mouth—well, you know, something could happen to your girl." He looked at Dolan. "Something very unpleasant."

Dolan gripped the table with both hands, leaned across it. "You can't scare me."

"I wouldn't bother with you," Guard said, preoccupied. "I'd concentrate on your girl."

Dolan straightened with a snap. "You make me sick! If it wasn't for Naomi, I'd have blown out of Havana a long time ago. I've been fed up with your rotten job a long time. I'm walking out of here as Jerry Dolan, see? I *am* Jerry Dolan! You want a front—get someone else. I'm through!"

"Stay where you are!"

A blued gun appeared suddenly in Vincent Guard's fist.

"You don't think I can afford to chuck this business, do you? I've been hiding in this hole for two weeks. I'm staying here!" The gun was held firmly. "You're sticking at your job. If you don't things'll be happening—not to you, to Miss Frost."

"You and your crummy threats! Put that rod away!"

Guard looked at Dolan curiously, respect mingling with astonishment. "Maybe you're forgetting I've got the rod—not you." He rose to his feet.

"You're too yellow to do your own shooting, Guard."

He was inching forward as he spoke. Suddenly his head snapped around to see who was coming in the door. No one was in the door, but the move inevitably forced Guard's eyes to stray. Dolan whirled back, leaped.

A clenched fist smashed into Guard's face. Guard fell back, stunned. Dolan caught the gun hand, twisted sharply. The weapon fell to the floor. Instantly Dolan pounced on it and as quickly was backing to the door.

"And I suppose you thought you were tough," he muttered.

Vincent Guard lay on the floor. Dolan turned and ran.

A second later the side door leading to an inner room flung wide and the Parson flitted through followed by a stocky, gorilla-like man. The Parson's eyebrows lifted. The real Vincent Guard rose slowly to his feet, holding his jaw.

He shook his head ruefully. "What a sock!"

"What happened?"

"I pulled a gun on him and he—well, he took it away! Hit me like a ton of brick. And me with a gun in my fist!"

The faintest shadow of a smile wreathed the Parson's lips. "The kid's got guts," he said. "Damn if he ain't!" He looked very pleased.

The stocky, gorilla-like man grunted. "Does he get mopped up, boss?"

Vincent Guard looked thoughtful for a moment, then shook his head.

The Parson walked around to the table, toyed with an ash-tray. "Hey, boss," he remarked casually, "is the dough O.K.?"

"Sure."

"It's still here, huh?"

"Yeah. What's eatin' you?"

The Parson did not raise his voice.

"It ain't here."

"The hell it ain't!"

"I took a look at that hole in the floor."

"Afraid of a double-cross?" Guard sneered.

"Not exactly. You wouldn't be dumb enough to cross *me*. There was two valises crammed with bills. When this thing is all over I want my cut."

Guard's voice subtly altered, grew silken. "Parson, you're a card! Monk, show the Parson the new hiding place."

Monk ambled across the floor to the table, pulled away the cloth. "Underneath," he grunted.

The Parson bent down, whistled. Two pigskin bags were strapped to the underside of the table. With the cloth in place they were entirely out of sight.

"Every cent just as we left New York with it," Guard said. "If you want to hide something don't put it where folks can't find it. Put it where they won't look." He winked. "Want to look through 'em?"

"Cripes, no! O.K., I'll blow."

"About that Dolan kid—keep him away from the girl."

"Is that all?"

"You know what I mean."

"I know."

"And, Parson, keep an eye out for Poggi and his boys. The next time Poggi orders a shooting, they won't miss like out at Varadero."

The Parson muttered something, went out, slamming the door.

Guard looked after him, lips pursed thoughtfully. "The Parson is getting like Sally Walsh used to be—hard to handle."

"It's just his way," Monk remarked. "Know what he was talkin' to me about? About how much he liked that Dolan kid! Can you imagine the Parson likin' anybody!" Monk dropped into a chair. "So Poggi's here," he said.

"Yeah. We expected him, didn't we? Poggi wouldn't twiddle his thumbs when he's lost three-quarters of a million." His laugh was a sharp, derisive bark. "Poor Poggi! Shooting at Dolan!"

"What if he finds out Dolan is Dolan and not Vince Guard?"

"How's he goin' to find out?" Guard demanded. Then, "How would you like to be splittin' our dough say tomorrow or the next day?"

"Huh?"

"Listen! If Poggi thought I was dead, what'd he do? Toss in the sponge and quit! O.K. Supposing he's made to believe I croaked, we could crawl outa this hole and go to Europe and spend our pile."

Monk stood up, crossed to a cupboard, came back with a bottle of Bacardi and a glass. He poured himself a drink, downed it, said, "Great!"

"Look, Monk! It's up to you. That Dolan kid is a dead image of me. When he's standin' in front of me, it's like looking into a mirror."

"What do I do?"

"Go down to the Yacht Basin. Dolan will show there. He's head over heels in love with the Frost dame. He can't stay away long. When he shows, you bop him. How do you like that?"

Monk grinned crookedly. "I like that fine. The Parson won't like it a nickel's worth."

"To hell with him!"

"Yeah." Monk poured another drink, smacked his lips. "So I think maybe we ought to include the Parson in the bopping." He looked up casually.

Guard did not meet his eyes. "That's occurred to me, too."

Monk finished his drink, went and got his hat. He put it on and said, "Be seeing you, boss," and went out.

Vincent Guard stood motionless for a long minute, transfixed in thought. Then he glanced down at his watch: ten-five.

AT TEN-FORTY, JERRY Dolan was speaking to a negro boatman at the Yacht Basin. For a dollar he was rowed out to where the *Sea Witch* was anchored. A light breeze ruffled the surface of the water. Mosquitoes moved in clouds. A dusty haze came up from the slack water around the wharves, blurring the lights along the curved sweep of the water-front.

The boatman drew alongside, reached out and held fast to the landing stage with one hand. Port-holes of the *Sea Witch* were cheerfully agleam with yellow light.

Dolan said, "Wait," and climbed the railed ladder to the deck. A uniformed sailor popped out from nowhere. Dolan asked for Naomi Frost. The sailor touched his cap and disappeared. He returned a few moments later. "This way, Mr. Guard."

Dolan frowned at mention of the name, but followed readily enough into a corridor. A door was open. The sailor pointed to it, withdrew. Dolan knocked. Naomi called out, "Come in."

The room was intimately her own, vaguely perfumed by the scent of her own person. Dolan had never been in it before. Naomi held out both her hands to him. He took them in his strong brown ones.

"Vincent!" she said, smiling. "I'm so glad you came back. I really didn't expect you."

But beneath her gay tone was anxiety. There was a snap to his eyes that told her he had hurried, that he was in a hurry now.

He dropped her hands abruptly, strode to the port-hole and looked out. "Naomi, darling, don't ever call me Vincent again."

"But it's your name!"

"It—" He broke off as a vision of Vincent Guard's face floated before his eye. "I'll explain later. In the meantime, don't use that name!"

Her eyes grew round. "Certainly, darling." The vehemence of his tone had startled her.

He whirled about suddenly, blurted, "Naomi, would you

marry me now—tonight?" And before she could answer, "I'm leaving Havana. A Dutch freighter sails for Curacao at midnight. I've spoken to the captain. He'll take us both."

Her concealed alarm leaped to the surface, was written large on her features. She held out her arms to him and they gave themselves to each other's embrace.

Then she held him at arm's length, eyes searching deeply into his. "You're in trouble! You're been in trouble ever since I've known you." Her mind leaped on ahead to tangibilities. "Those men at Varadero who tried to kill you!"

He shook his head, tried to laugh. "It's not that at all. I don't dare tell you now, but on the boat when we leave Havana…. Will you come?" His brow furrowed. "I'm asking you to come with me on trust."

"But I can't simply drop everything and run off. The yacht… my father… my guests."

"Naomi, dear, just the two of us."

"What about packing?"

"There's no time. We have to get aboard. We can be married at sea. The boat stops at Kingston in two days. We can get clothes there."

"But your bags! You know, the ones—" She stopped, frowning at him slightly.

"Everything gets left behind, darling. We start from scratch."

She cocked her head prettily on one side. "All right, I guess I can keep our secret. You said I wasn't to mention it again even to you and you certainly meant every word of it."

Dolan was barely listening. He gulped as he took her hand again. "I know I'm asking a lot of you. You're taking me on trust for what I can't explain. You've been swell. But if you don't want to go…."

Her brows lifted in protest. "Oh, but I do want to go!"

"You really will?" He laughed suddenly. "You don't mind sneaking off this way?"

She laughed. "It's what I've always wanted—an elopement!"

His face became suddenly very grave.

"It's that and more. I couldn't leave Havana and know you were alone. Someone might try to hurt you."

Her nose wrinkled and her mouth screwed up in a pout. "If you'd only stop talking in such riddles!"

"Never mind! You'll know soon enough."

She moved toward the door. "I'll be back in a minute."

He barred her way. "No. I won't let you out of my sight until we're aboard the freighter."

"But I've got guests aboard for dinner!" she cried. "Goodwin, the consul, Marilyn, the Wylies. I must tell them something!"

"You can radio from the ship so they won't worry. Let's go! I've got a rowboat waiting to take us to shore."

But she held back. "You're certain you won't want your bags? I mean aren't they terribly important?"

He shook his head impatiently. "I told you we can get clothes in Kingston if we—"

She kissed him silent. "I'm ready if you are."

The sailor was not in sight when they hurried down the ladder to the rowboat. An excited hub-bub of voices rising from the aft portion of the yacht reached their ears. Naomi was inclined to wait to find out what had happened, but Dolan hurried her into the rowboat. "We haven't a second to lose."

The grinning negro shoved off, bent gleaming muscles to the single oar astern. Over the water, the voices from the *Sea Witch* rose in a definite clamor. Looking back, they saw a figure rush to the rail. A voice shouted, pointed an outflung arm at them.

"What can be the matter?" Naomi asked.

"Don't know and don't care," Dolan murmured happily in her ear.

There was always a line of cabs on the concrete drive leading into the Basin. One darted out of line, toward them. The driver hopped out to open the door.

"Maquinas Pier," Dolan told him and helped Naomi into the open tonneau. His own foot was raised to follow but suddenly he turned, more by instinct than anything else. But he hadn't time to get a word out of his mouth, nor time to snap out the gun he had acquired from Vincent Guard.

A gun crashed twice.

Dolan flung down against the side of the cab. Naomi, on the far side of the leather cushion, sat transfixed, frozen with fear. The driver ducked and slewed his body, squealing like a stuck pig. Dolan corkscrewed around the rear of the machine and brought out his gun. But he did not fire.

A voice behind him said quietly, "Let me take him."

Dolan's mouth emitted a pent-up, explosive breath. His whole body tightened as he jerked around and saw the Parson. The black snout of a Luger was in the Parson's hand and it was pointed at a clump of shadows lost in blackness against the side wall, overhanging the Basin. Packing boxes on which nets had been laid to dry stood there in dim outline. Out of the dimness, a streak of orange light stabbed through accompanied by a muffled roar. Lead flattened into the metal of the car with a dull *wh-ack!*

The Parson's movements were cool, unhurried. He raised the Luger and it responded with a single sharp cough. There was a queer, strained silence. Then the sound of a body falling, the scrape of boxes on the ground. There were no more shots.

The Parson melted around the far side of the car. Dolan called after him, but he did not answer. Then Dolan saw him sliding toward the empty packing boxes, dim, wraith-like. He disappeared behind one of them.

The cab driver found his voice, was yelling, *"Madre de Dios!"*

"Shut up. Get behind your wheel." Dolan slid into the tonneau, took one of Naomi's hands in his. He felt her trembling. "It's all over, darling."

"I'm so frightened for you! You're not hurt?"

He laughed. "Not even scratched."

Other cab drivers were shouting, gesticulating. The Parson sidled back, leaned in the open door, one foot on the running board.

"It was Monk," he said in a quiet, conversational tone. He eyed Naomi gravely, impersonally, taking stock of her personality. "He's dead, bullet through the heart."

Naomi gasped at this, but before she could speak, Dolan said, "Monk! Good Lord, he was trying to kill me!"

The Parson's mouth got tight and he said sardonically, "If he wasn't, he gave a damned good imitation, anyway."

There were two reddish spots on Dolan's cheek-bones. His knuckles were white. He said thinly, "Guard, huh? But why should he want to kill me? Why?" He saw Naomi straining to hear every word he uttered. His teeth clicked together. Alarm was growing in her face. Her eyes were puzzled. He said abruptly, "You followed Monk, huh?"

The Parson nodded at the shrewd guess. "I figured a double-cross was about due."

The taxi driver was yelling and a crowd was collecting. The cabbie was hopping from leg to leg, telling everybody how many shots there were and how many *Americanos* had been killed. The number kept increasing with the size of his audience.

Dolan grabbed the Parson's arm, and yanked him in. "You're riding with us," he explained. He leapt out, plowed through the crowd and laid both hands on the sweating driver. "Maquinas pier! *Sabe! Muy pronto!*"

The cabbie looked as if he were going to go up in smoke. When he finally exploded, "*¡Señor, el policía!* Eet ees forbidden to run away. *¿no es verdad?*" The Parson appeared at Dolan's side, playing with the gun. The driver rolled his eyes heavenward, implored the protection of his patron saint and slunk behind the wheel.

As the cab jerked forward, Dolan looked back. A launch, speeding over the water from the direction of the yacht, was almost to the dock. The cab bowled through the narrow streets at a steady clip.

At the Maquinas pier, the driver was dismissed with a ten-dollar bill. The Parson held out his hand. "I'll fade."

Dolan's eyes were shining. "I won't forget you long as I live, Parson."

"Hell, far as I'm concerned you're the home team, kid." He drew Dolan aside. "Just one thing. Tell the girl who you are, if you want to, but no one else until you're well clear of here, see? Because if they turn up Vince Guard, they'll turn me up, too. I can't afford to have him turned up account of he's holding a stake for me. Get it?"

"Sure. Trust me. Good-by!"

There was a siren somewhere, coming toward them, getting louder.

"S'long."

The sirens were suddenly swooping down the cobbled street. "The Spic cops ain't so slow after all," the Parson said bitingly. He slid away to the shadowed darkness of a near-by parked car.

Headlights glaring, two automobiles appeared at the mouth of the cobbled driveway, jarred to a stop. Uniformed men tumbled out of the first one. From the second appeared Goodwin, the consul, his face gaunt, strained, a sailor from the *Sea Witch* and a woman who rushed to Naomi, put her arms around her and immediately began crying. The uniformed men were police. Naomi freed herself from the woman, paled visibly, clung to Dolan's arm.

Goodwin strode forward importantly. The cops formed a triangle behind him. He pointed at Dolan, said crisply, "Is that the man?"

The sailor peered with lips parted, head cocked in a gesture of profound study. Dolan saw that he was the same fellow who had been stationed at the landing stage aboard the *Sea Witch*. He leaned forward, then nodded. "That's him," he said.

Goodwin spoke sharply in Spanish to the police. Two of them instantly ranged themselves on either side of Dolan, grabbed his arms. He looked too surprised to offer resistance.

But Naomi flared, "Andrew! What does this mean?"

Goodwin grimaced, looked momentarily confused. There was a load of dynamite ready for but a spark in each of her eyes. He cleared his throat heavily, said, "My dear, I'm saving you from a horrible mistake!"

Her nostrils thinned, her jaw got stiff. "I merely planned to get married!" she retorted. "If you call that a mistake—"

"Naomi! Don't be silly!"

"What's silly about getting married to the man you love?"

"If you'll come with me quietly," Goodwin said with dignity, "I think we can save a lot of embarrassment all around."

"What do you mean?" There was a definite fighting set to her jaw now.

"It's a police case." Goodwin was stern as with a child who refuses to understand. "But perhaps I can keep your name out of it."

"You'll tell me what this means, Andrew Goodwin, or—"

"Naomi, we tried to call you from the yacht but you wouldn't stop. When we heard the shots, we thought something had happened to you, but the boatmen told us you were unhurt and headed for the Maquinas pier."

She stared at him with a disgusted look. "If you mean the shooting on the pier, Vincent had nothing to do with it. So there!"

Goodwin let his breath out. "A man was killed at the Yacht Basin, yes. But Mr. Guard can explain further, if he will."

"I damn well can't!" Dolan said watching Goodwin narrowly. "And furthermore, don't call me Mr. Guard!"

"That's your name, isn't it?"

"It—" Dolan bit his lip, checked himself. He felt ashamed. Blood poured flamingly into his face. His voice got a bit thick. "Anyway, Naomi is right. I didn't kill that guy at the Yacht Basin. He fired at me, tried to murder me, sure! But I didn't even shoot back."

Goodwin's voice was velvety. "But that isn't the charge against you."

Confusion gagged Dolan, kept him speechless. He could only stare.

"What is it, what is it?" Naomi demanded in panic.

Goodwin could not conceal evident triumph. "A woman murdered aboard the *Sea Witch*. She was found stabbed to death in one of the unoccupied cabins and identified from letters in her handbag." He paused, his eyes hard and glittering. "Her name is... was Sally Walsh!"

RAFAEL PEREZ WAS fat and sleek and handsome. He was an attorney with the biggest practice in Havana. He spoke English faultlessly. Naomi Frost and Andrew Goodwin sat in his office and listened to his purring voice. From the window, the gilded dome of the *Capitolio* was visible as if in a frame. Perez smoked a fat, oily cigar.

"It would be better if Mr. Guard would talk," he was saying. "His stubborn silence can serve no good purpose. The facts are too much against him. Our Cuban courts are not exactly partial to an American."

Goodwin looked angry. "Frankly, I believe he's guilty, Mr. Perez. Miss Frost insisted on my securing the best attorney and naturally I selected you, but I wish I could wash my hands of the whole affair."

Naomi's eyes were dark with wrath. "You can leave us, Andrew, if you like. After all this is none of your affair any more."

Goodwin flushed a brick-red. "I'm sorry, Naomi. I can't help expressing what I feel."

"And I know that Vincent is innocent. I asked him and he told me!"

"Don't be a child! The word of a gangster, of a killer! Of

course he'd tell you he was innocent. Playing on your credulity, he thinks he can—"

"I think you've said enough, Andrew!"

Perez laid his hands on the desk, leaned forward, speaking rapidly to cut off Goodwin's retort. "We have to consider the facts, Miss Frost. At the moment they are our primary concern. Sally Walsh was murdered some time between eight and eleven p.m., death caused by a knife wound through the heart. Mr. Goodwin, here, found the body because the cabin door was slightly ajar and he had the curiosity to look inside. He called Emil Lundborg, the sailor on the deck watch.

"Lundborg immediately confessed that the woman had bribed him to get aboard the yacht. She had given him twenty dollars, told him she was a newspaper writer, come to interview you, Miss Frost. It was about a minute after eight when she came on the deck. Lundborg told her the location of your cabin and watched her disappear down the corridor. That was the last he saw of her alive. And you, Miss Frost, did not even know she was aboard your boat."

Naomi nodded dumbly, face white and strained.

"That's clear enough," the attorney said. "Now we come to Mr. Guard. At twenty minutes past eight, he stepped onto the *Sea Witch*. The sailor, Lundborg, immediately recognized him from pictures in newspapers in the States. Mr. Guard said he wanted to see you, and, according to Lundborg, seemed rather agitated. Lundborg went to speak to you about his arrival. When he returned, Mr. Guard was not on the deck. Lundborg didn't think anything of that. Mr. Guard appeared suddenly in the corridor coming from the direction of the cabin where, later, Mr. Goodwin found the woman dead.

"Now the weapon. It was a letter opener that had been lying on a desk in the cabin. There are several such aboard the *Sea Witch*. No fingerprints were found on the handle but the blade was stained with blood, making it without question the fatal weapon.

"Mr. Guard returned to the yacht at a quarter of eleven. You, Miss Frost, and he left at about five to. But at about the same instant that Mr. Guard came aboard the second time, Mr. Goodwin discovered the corpse of Sally Walsh.

"The motive, Miss Frost? This Sally Walsh was known to have been intim— ah, close to Mr. Guard back in the States. The incident of her throwing a bottle of acid at you is known to the police and the prosecutor. In other words, she was jealous of Mr. Guard's attentions to you. Possibly, she came aboard the *Sea Witch* to do you some bodily harm, although no weapon of any sort was found on her person."

"And you honestly believe Mr. Guard killed her?"

Perez shrugged. "I have merely woven a web of circumstances. And there are the letters which enabled us to identify Sally Walsh. They are rather damaging to Mr. Guard. There were three altogether. Each bore the same message. Mr. Guard was tired of her, was going on a trip and hoped she wouldn't trouble him any longer."

"And there's still one thing," Goodwin put in. "I've wired Washington for instructions. Even if Guard should be acquitted, Federal agents will be on hand to accompany him back to the States. I've seen to that."

Naomi's eyes bit him with a loathing stare. They widened; her lips trembled and her hands shook. For just a moment she held the pose; then she stood erect, slim and straight as a boy.

"Andrew Goodwin," she said in a voice that shook just the least bit, "you're hateful!"

Perez said blusteringly, "But surely, Miss Frost, surely...." He leaped up and moved toward her. "Surely, you can't speak of Mr. Goodwin in a manner to—"

"I'll speak as I please! That goes for you, too, you—you octopus!"

The door slammed shut behind her.

The taxi in which she had been driven to Perez' office was still at the curb. She flitted across the sidewalk and got in. A confused cry of alarm ripped past her lips. A dim figure was seated on the cushions beside her.

"Don't yell," the figure said disgustedly. "It's only me."

"Parson!" She had peered closer and recognized him.

"Yeah. I watched 'em take the kid to the *juzgado*. Then I followed you here. I been waitin' nearly an hour. What's the low-down?"

"Parson, you're Vincent's friend! You'll help him, won't you?"

"What's the low-down?" His voice was chilling.

Rapidly she sketched the details of what had happened. "And he won't talk or say a word in his own defense," she finished with a catch in her voice.

"Why?" He spat the word at her.

"I don't know. They won't let me see him."

The Parson's eyes glinted. "Damn that kid! I'll tell you why he won't talk. I told him not to say a word that might incriminate me in—in another matter."

She caught at his arm with eager frenzy. "Are you sure?"

He shrugged, looked straight at her for a long second. "How good is your heart? Can it take a mild shock?"

"Why, what do you mean?"

"The guy you know as Vincent Guard ain't Vincent Guard. His name is Jerry Dolan. The real Vincent Guard is hiding some place here in Havana, afraid of his shadow, of Sally Walsh, and a gent named Poggi."

If he had poured cold water over her, he could not have achieved a more sensational effect. She gaped at him, open-mouthed, eyes childishly wide, pupils dilated in wonder.

"Pretty soon the real Vincent Guard will be afraid of me."

"But it can't be possible. It doesn't—"

"That's the whole of it, lady. Not Vince Guard but Jerry Dolan!"

Woman-like her mind leaped backward to the point that had been troubling her most. "Then Vincent—I mean, Jerry was telling the truth!"

"About what?"

"That woman—Sally Walsh. At Varadero Beach, he said he'd never seen her before."

"Sally was a total stranger to him."

"But how did it.... Why did he take Guard's name?"

"You kinda like the guy, huh?"

Her face was flushed, lips moist, eyes gleaming. She nodded happily. "Tell me. Do they look very much alike?"

"Like two peas. That's why the act has gone over so well. When Poggi shot at you two at Varadero, he thought he was shooting at Vince Guard. Sally shoulda known Vince and *she* was fooled! Y'see, the real Vince Guard, well... he's had to lay kinda low. It was me who picked up Jerry Dolan on a park bench. No clothes, no money, no job. I dragged him to a barber, got him shaved and brought him to Vince. You couldn't tell 'em apart."

"Who is this Poggi?"

For a fleeting instant, the Parson almost smiled. "Poggi is the guy who got the short end of the stick," he said. "He was Vince's partner in a string of houses. It was his dough that got Vince started. We added a money-lending racket to the gambling business. Then the Feds tightened up. It looked like Alcatraz. Vince pulled a fast one. He skipped with nearly two million in cash. Poggi's been tearing whatever hair he had left since."

"And here in Havana, Jerry Dolan has gone by the name of Vincent Guard to fool Poggi?"

The Parson nodded. She looked searchingly at him. "And what are you getting out of all this?"

He didn't look at her. "A cut of the big dough. Me and a guy named Monk, we're supposed to share with Vince."

"Monk? The man shot at the Yacht Basin?"

"You catch on, huh? Yeah. That leaves only me and Vince." He leaned forward and tapped the driver's shoulder. "I'll get out here."

Naomi looked confused. "Where are you going?"

The Parson's face was lazy, without expression. "The kid didn't put the chill on Sally, did he?"

"No! No!"

"Someone did. It wasn't a Dutch. O.K. The kid's got one chance. Find the punk who framed the kill."

"Then you know who did it?"

The Parson scratched his head. "Lady, I didn't say that." He started to get out.

"Wait!" She caught his hand in her own. "Let me go with you."

"Not where I go."

"But I can help, Vin—I mean Jerry would want it so." Blue eyes looked beseechingly into his own.

For once in his life, the Parson was nonplussed.

"Please, you'll let me go with you! You can't refuse!"

"So now I'm a sucker for baby blue eyes!" he said disgustedly.

"They're s-sky blue." She was trying to keep her chin from trembling.

"Huh? Well, O.K.!" He gave the driver directions and settled back in his seat.

"Thanks," Naomi said humbly. She held herself prim and straight and bundled up small so he wouldn't think she was in the way.

The Parson was annoyed with himself. To his own mind it appeared he was losing his grip. He had never done a favor for a woman before in his life. He drew out his neatly folded hand-kerchief and wiped his hands. He wiped them very carefully.

GUARD'S HOUSE SAT in a dark, deserted, shuttered street. Only an occasional arc-lamp lighted the way. Naomi kept close to the Parson, shivered despite her best efforts to be calm. The Parson did not speak.

They had dismissed the cab two blocks down and walked the rest of the way, heels ringing on the narrow sidewalks. As they stopped before the house, the Parson spoke for the first time. "You'll be in the courtyard. Stay there until you hear from me. Get it? I don't want anything to happen to you and no interference."

The door from the street opened, he led the way to the patio. He motioned her to stay where she was and he went on to the single door. Instead of knocking as he had the last time, he simply stared at it. It was slightly ajar.

There were lights in the lower story windows, but no sound coming through them. The Parson drew a Luger from a shoulder holster, dropped it into a side pocket, went on in. In the hall, he stopped.

An unpleasant odor crinkled his nostrils. It seemed to permeate the house, pungent, distasteful. He drew the gun from his pocket, cocked it, held it loosely, carelessly in his right hand. He moved over to the door on his left, turned the knob and shoved it wide.

He moved in very fast behind the gun, but nothing happened. The room was empty. But the odor here was stronger. Eyes dark, watchful, he tiptoed across to the inner room, froze on the threshold.

A man lay on the bed, arms outspread, tied to the bedposts. A gag covered his mouth, the lower part of his face. It was Vincent Guard.

A small, wickedly sharp hatchet lay on the floor beside the bed. It was blood-soaked. The hatchet had chipped away at Guard's knee-cap. The whole foot dangled loosely, the trouser leg ripped open to the thigh. A tourniquet had been bound around the leg above the knee to cut off the flow of blood. The bedclothes were wet, crimson.

The other foot was bare. Its sole was a huge blister or a series of blisters. It had been burnt. That explained that heavy odor—burnt flesh.

The Parson drifted into the room slowly, face tightened and ugly. He stood at the side of the bed and looked down at Guard. Then he touched his wrist, fumbled at his heart. The heart action was slight. Guard's nostrils pumped breath stertorously. His chest rose and fell. The Parson turned, and as he turned a voice said, "Hello, Parson. Long time no see,"

The Parson stood stock-still, like a graven image. The door swung shut. Behind it had been concealed three men. The foremost of them had spoken. He was short, stocky, bald-headed. An army automatic was in his hand, held low. The other two men held .38 revolvers. The bald-headed man took a half-step forward.

"Lift 'em high, boy," he said.

The Parson did not move. But his lips parted enough to say, "How's tricks, Poggi?"

Poggi grinned, tight-mouthed. "Keep the guns on him, boys. Eddie, you get to the left of him. That's fine! Slug, you stick by me."

"What's the matter? You afraid of me? The three of you stand around like you was afraid of me!" The Parson put his eyes on Poggi.

The bald-headed man kept grinning. "We can take you any time you want to try, guy. This ain't New York." But the grin, nevertheless, kept getting thinner and thinner until it faded altogether and became a scowl. "Just try something."

The Parson's eyes were unconcerned, without expression. He looked over to where Vincent Guard stirred faintly. "What you been doin' to him?"

"A heart to heart talk. Only he kept passing out on us. And he didn't talk. Maybe we'll have more success with you."

The Parson registered neither surprise nor fear. If anything, his face, his eyes were more uncommunicative. He muttered at last, "You're pretty bright at that, Poggi. How'd you nose out

Vince's hide-out?"

Poggi shifted his weight warily. "We get around, y'know. This evening I ran into Sally Walsh. Coincidence, wasn't it, meeting her in Havana?"

"I'll say." His eyes flickered. "But she didn't know where Vince was."

"Ha, that's right! But she told me Vince was stuck on a dame who owns a yacht. So what do we do? We park by the Yacht Basin and watch all comers. Well, we didn't see him go on, but we caught him coming off. Then all we had to do was follow him here. Easy as that."

"Nice work."

"That's right," said Poggi good-humoredly. "You always appreciated finesse, didn't you?" In the same tone, he added, "Slug, you relieve Mr. Parson of his hardware."

The Parson stood relaxed. Poggi had not insisted again on his raising his arms. Slug moved warily toward him, was reaching out with his left hand to snatch at the gun when suddenly the door flew open, hit Poggi a terrific whack. He cried out in sheer alarm, stumbled to one knee. The Parson saw Naomi Frost outlined in the doorway.

At the left of the Parson, the man called Eddie swung his gun in a swift arc. Naomi dropped to hands and knees. The gun blasted and a slug passed harmlessly over her head.

Poggi had been scrambling to his feet. The Parson's body corkscrewed about, the gun appeared in his fist and he fired from the hip. Poggi slammed down to the floor again, looking bewildered, uncertain of himself.

The man called Slug thumbed a swift shot at the Parson. Lead tugged at the brim of his hat, continued on upward to the ceiling, jarred loose a small hailstorm of plaster. But the Parson, himself, did not move. His movement was confined entirely to his gun arm. It raised, the gun spoke with a dull, sharp cough. Slug started going backward like a man who has been straight-armed. His spine jarred against the door jamb and he slid to the floor in a sitting posture.

Eddie lined the Parson's body with his muzzle, squeezed the trigger. The Parson took the bullet in the shoulder. He heard a scream—Naomi's scream—whirled with the impact, cold-faced, cold-eyed, held up his gun and fired. Eddie turned side-wise, slowly and cautiously, looked as though he were going to wave a hand in farewell. His face twisted up and he fell across the bed, head loose, arm outflung. He did not move.

The Parson ran a small tongue over dry lips, moved over to Poggi. The bald-headed man was through. His eyes were glassy, open. Slug's body was still jerking, but that was only muscular reflex. After a while the jerking stopped.

Naomi appeared at the door, haggard, skin the color of ashes. She had a hand to her cheek, the nails digging into the skin. She was swaying slightly, swallowing with apparent difficulty.

The Parson looked at her as if he did not know her. Then he crossed the room and slapped her face hard with an open palm.

Color blazed in her cheeks and she straightened, gasped like a swimmer coming out of cold water.

"For the love of Gawd don't faint!" he bit off.

"No, I—" Her lashed lids were brimful of tears. "I'm all right."

"Kinda tough on you to see all this," he said quietly, with unexpected gentleness. "The first killin' always turns your stomach."

She had recovered far enough to see the blood streaming

down the sleeve of his coat. "You're—hurt!"

He looked annoyed. "Naw! Lemme alone." The gun was hot in his hand. He looked down at it. "Li'l' Gwendolyn," he murmured, almost happily.

He left her abruptly and went to the bed. Vincent Guard had stirred. Naomi took a single look, turned away, white and shaking again. The Parson undid the gag, removed it, then untied Guard's wrists. His eyes did not linger on Guard's bloodied knee, nor on his blistered foot. A panicky feeling took possession of him when he did, a feeling of loathing and horror that both surprised and shocked him. It was new to his catalogue of emotions.

Roughly he shook Guard's shoulder. Slowly the eyes opened, stared sightlessly into his own. The lips were moving. He bent close, caught the slow trickle of words. It was uncanny that those lips made sound at all.

"… hell with… you. Never find…."

"Vince!" said the Parson. "Vince, can you hear me?"

But the eerie whispering went on regardless.

The Parson straightened, looked at Naomi. She whispered, "There were two of them. I understand now. Vincent Guard and Jerry Dolan."

The Parson nodded. "Both went to your yacht tonight—at different hours."

"And he," Naomi wouldn't look at the bed, "killed Sally Walsh."

The Parson looked down at Guard, then bent over him. "Did you hear that, Vince? She says you killed Sally Walsh. Did you? Sally Walsh is dead. Dead. Did you kill her, Vince? You gotta tell me. Was it you, Vince? Did you knife her?"

The half-open eyes widened. "Sally... saw Sally on... yacht."

The Parson looked at Naomi with his cold doubting eyes. They dropped back to Vincent Guard. "You killed her!"

"No... no. Saw her... Sally—stabbed... saw her myself. Sally dead... good ole Sally."

"You killed her!" the Parson came back.

"No... no...."

A rush of blood from the lips cut off further speech. Guard's body jerked. The whites of his eyes showed, cross-veined, yellow-white blobs.

The Parson straightened. He touched Guard's wrist briefly, turned away with a shrug. "So much for that."

"But we're no nearer helping Jerry!" The name, still new to Naomi's lips, was used hesitantly.

"He wasn't lying," the Parson said, looking down at the stiffening form of Vincent Guard. "Look, kid, we gotta get outa here in—" An expression of wonder flitted over his face. "Gee-sus! I nearly forgot!"

He rushed into the larger room, yanked the cloth off the table, knelt and breathed a deep sigh. The two pigskin valises were strapped to the underside of the table just as he had last seen them. Hurriedly, he undid the thongs which held them in place, eased the bags to the floor. Naomi watched his every action with widened, astonished eyes.

Swiftly he unstrapped the valise. Without opening it, he unstrapped the second. Then he flung back the covers simultaneously. His nape bristled, his eyes slitted. Speechlessly, he pointed down into the open bags.

They were crammed with newspaper, neatly cut into bundles and neatly tied.

STARTLED PEOPLE IN night-shirts and robes looked down from balconies in morbid curiosity. They jabbered to each other in Spanish. It amused the Parson more than anything else. There was no policeman in sight. The jabbering rose to a shrill cry of alarm as the Parson and Naomi appeared on the street, but no one attempted to halt them.

They walked six blocks rapidly to a main artery. In front of an open-air café stood a taxi. The Parson shook the driver awake. They were driven to the Yacht Basin.

A power launch was tied to the dock, manned by a sailor from the *Sea Witch*. He touched his cap respectfully to Naomi. "They've been worried for you, Miss Frost. Mr. Goodwin is aboard and a cop, too."

"Yes? Thank you, Williams."

The Parson followed her into the launch. He looked gaunt, thinner. His left arm was aching badly, though the bleeding had stopped. But he could not think of the pain. He was thinking of paper, painstakingly cut to the size of currency bills. Bundles and bundles of it. It was still back there in the two valises in the room adjoining the one where four men had met death.

Sally Walsh was dead and Monk was dead. And the valises contained not money but paper. Far away he heard the low of an outbound steamer.

The launch made fast to the landing stage. The Parson followed Naomi up. There was no one on the deck. She said, "In my cabin."

The Parson matched strides with her down the corridor. She opened the door, clicked up the lights. He followed inside. Immediately she went to the bed, knelt and dragged forth two valises from under it, similar to the pair which had contained the bundles of paper. Then she stood to one side and eyed the Parson uncertainly.

She said, "I didn't suspect—there were two. Perhaps now that I know maybe I couldn't be fooled. When he came in here and asked me to keep the valises, I thought he was the man I loved."

The Parson said, "Sally Walsh couldn't tell 'em apart."

"I thought his manner strange—yes. But I knew he was in trouble—some kind of trouble. He told me to guard the bags, not to tell anyone he had brought them, not even to mention them to him again unless he spoke about them first. I can remember just what he said. 'This is our own little secret. Promise me no one else will know.' Of course, I promised."

The Parson looked at the bags as if waiting for something to happen. "Vince always played a clever game," he said finally. "There was no safer place for the bags than with you. He figured that out, knew he could get at 'em any time day or night."

He touched the locks. The locks were brass, half-inch thick. He glanced around the room, then drifted out into the corridor. A fire-ax rested in a stanchion attached to the wall. He took it down, hefted it, went back into the cabin. Two judicious blows opened the first and a single blow forced back the lock of the second. Very carefully he laid the ax down. Then he knelt and threw back the lids of the bags.

A grim, triumphant smile lighted his features, the only outward evidence of the excitement that seethed within him.

The bags were the real McCoy, jammed full with money.

"Vince wasn't so bright at that," he muttered. "He wanted to double-cross both me and Monk, keep all the dough for himself."

Two bright spots showed themselves in Naomi's cheeks. "How did he dare trust so much money to me?"

The Parson grinned. "He counted on your loyalty to his double. I can see his whole plan now. Get Monk to kill Jerry and me; he would rub out Monk himself. That would leave the money for him alone. And with Dolan's death, Poggi would be thrown off the trail. But if in the meantime Poggi did get to him, there'd be only that newspaper for Poggi to get."

"But this doesn't help Jerry Dolan any!" Naomi said suddenly. "I don't care about the money. I don't even want to think about it."

The Parson riffled a packet of bills. "Money," he growled. "Well, maybe we can buy off the prosecution."

"Do you really think that's possible?"

"Worth a try, if everything else fails."

She looked at him. "Why can't we go to the police and tell them about the real Vincent Guard? Jerry Dolan didn't come aboard here until about a quarter of eleven. It was Vincent Guard who came at about eight. We can prove that now. It was he who killed that woman!"

The Parson snapped a look at her. "In the first place, Vince didn't kill Sally Walsh. In the second place, to prove that Dolan isn't Vincent Guard would drag me in. The Cubes won't exactly cotton to a guy like me. There's the killing of Monk, Poggi and his two boys. No, there must be another way."

"But we must do something quickly!"

"I'll think of something. Maybe I'll blow outa Havana and then you can tell the cops anything you want. Anyway, we'll see in the morning. I'm going home."

"And the money? Won't you take it with you?"

"Leave it. If Vince could trust it with you," he grinned, "so can I."

"I'll see if the launch is waiting."

The corridor was cut in two by the recessed door opening onto the narrow deck. At the further end of the corridor a door was open a little and voices could be heard plainly. One was a deep, placating rumble, the other high-pitched, angry. It was the second voice they heard.

"So now I'm under arrest. That ain't worth no hundred bucks. What if it means my A.B. papers, where'll I be, huh?"

"Quiet! Quiet!" the deep voice grated earnestly. "You've got nothing to worry about. I'm backing you up. Your arrest is just a legal form."

Naomi stiffened perceptibly. That was Andrew Goodwin's voice. Wide-eyed she turned to the Parson. "D-did you hear that?"

He nodded somberly. "Maybe we ought to take a look."

He led the way this time. She caught his arm. "But you don't want to be seen in any part of—"

"Come on!" he said gruffly.

He didn't knock on the door. He just shoved it wide with the flat of his hand. Naomi, behind him, saw Goodwin standing in the center of the cabin. Facing him and to one side stood Lundborg, the seaman. In a chair against the wall, sat a blue-uniformed Cuban policeman, smoking lazily. At sight of the pair in the doorway, he jumped to his feet and his hand moved to his holster.

"It's quite all right," Naomi said quickly. "I am the owner of this boat."

But evidently the man understood no English, for he only

glowered truculently. Goodwin said something in Spanish. A light of understanding broke out over the cop's face and he sat down again abruptly, with an apologetic shrug.

After a second without moving, Goodwin said, "I was quite worried about you, Naomi." But he was looking at the Parson narrowly, watchfully.

She said, "Is Lundborg under arrest?"

"Technical arrest. He's an important witness. They're taking no chances on his skipping away."

"You mean there'd be no case without him?"

Goodwin frowned slightly. "Not much I guess." He was still sighting at the Parson. "Who's your friend, Naomi?"

She ignored the question. "Lundborg, if you've been hiding something from the police, now's the time to tell it."

Lundborg looked sullen, frightened. But his long nose twitched nervously. "I dunno what you mean."

Naomi's voice rose. "We just heard you say something about getting one hundred dollars. Who gave that sum to you? For what?"

Goodwin spread his hands. "What's this, Naomi?"

Again she ignored him. "We heard you, Lundborg. You could be liable as an accessory after the fact. That's as bad as having done the murder yourself!"

A sweat broke out on Lundborg's blunt, red face. "Hey, lay off, Miss Frost."

"Naomi, are you trying to frighten the poor fellow?" Goodwin asked casually enough.

"More than that; I'm trying to get him to use some sense!" she snapped.

"Now, child, you're being rather ridiculous, you know." But he wouldn't take his eyes off the Parson.

The Parson had a handkerchief out and was wiping dry the fingers of his right hand.

"I'll give you a last chance, Lundborg," Naomi cut in.

"Jeeze, I didn't do nothin'. Honest! I don't wanna be mixed up in no murder."

"Who gave you the hundred dollars?"

Lundborg swallowed hard, looked furtive, hunted. "If I tell you, will you—" His voice cut out and there was an instant of tight silence. He ran a finger between his collar and neck. "Jeeze, I'm gonna talk. I knew I'd get into trouble. I...."

"Lundborg, don't be a damn fool!" Goodwin cried.

"To hell with you! I'm lookin' out for number one. Listen! Mr. Goodwin here gave me the hundred. For what? So's I'd tell the cops that woman bribed me to come aboard the boat. Well, she didn't bribe me. It was Goodwin, who—"

"Lundborg, for the last time, I'm warning you...."

The Parson's voice cut in very quietly, "Suppose you shut your trap!"

Goodwin spluttered but couldn't get any words out.

"Go on," said the Parson to Lundborg.

Lundborg spoke rapidly. "Goodwin brought her aboard. He gave me twenty to keep my mouth shut. Later he gave me eighty more to say I'd been bribed by her. He told me if it got around he'd brought her on board he'd get in trouble. He swore he had nothing to do with her murder. He said Vincent Guard had killed her."

Naomi cried, "Vincent Guard is dead! We can prove it. We can prove, too, that you—" She stopped short as if something momentous had just occurred to her. She paled. Her breath caught spasmodically. "Andrew, it wasn't— You didn't!"

"He did it!" the Parson ripped out. "He murdered Sally Walsh."

"No, I— Why should I do anything like that?"

The Parson shrugged. "You did it."

"No, I gave Lundborg that money. I'll admit that. I smuggled Sally Walsh on board."

"And killed her!"

"No!" Goodwin's voice was strangled. "No!"

The Parson put his eyes on him. "I know Sally Walsh. I know how her mind would work. She went to you, Goodwin, because she'd snooped out the fact that you were in love with Naomi Frost. She figured you'd be just as sore as she was about Naomi takin' up with Guard. She figured you right. You brought her on board to get her to speak to Naomi. Then something happened and you killed her. At the same time you saw a chance to frame Guard. It was an almost perfect plan. Circumstantial evidence tied in so nicely with Guard's visit at eight that you—"

"No!" His voice broke. "Naomi, you don't believe I…." Insanity blazed in his eyes. "Yes, you do! I can see it! You do!"

He darted suddenly to his right so quickly that the policeman was caught napping. He had been listening to the conversation, distractedly seeking to understand what was being said. Goodwin made a wild grab, snatched the heavy gun from the man's holster.

The Parson did not shoot. His right hand had dropped into his coat pocket, rested on the butt, but he kept his trigger finger rigid.

"Don't move, anybody!" Goodwin's face was tight, desperate. "I won't be arrested. I won't go to trial. Do you understand?" There was a fine madness about him. "I killed her!

Sure I killed her! But I killed her to save you, Naomi! Can you understand that? I threw away my career, everything to stop her from killing you. That's what she wanted to do. She had a gun...."

He didn't go on right away. And it seemed as though all the others in the cabin were not breathing while they waited, soundlessly.

Then words came again, thick, hot, tumbling from his corded throat. "She came to me as that fellow says. She gave me the whole history of her relationship with Guard. It was pretty sordid. I knew a recital of it would sicken you, turn you against Guard. That's what I wanted. And that's why I smuggled her aboard the yacht. I hid her in the unoccupied cabin to await a moment when I could get you to see her alone. I left her for perhaps ten or fifteen minutes. When I came back, she was changed. She was half-hysterical, noisy, reckless.

"She looked as if she'd just taken dope. She said, 'You think I'm going to talk to that damn bim. O.K., that's what you think.' Then she snatched a small caliber gun from her hand bag, said, 'I'll talk to her with this. I'll teach her to steal my man!' I tried to argue with her, tried to get the gun from her. She turned it on me. I snatched up the letter opener from the writing desk. She was pretty strong, but the blade went through her heart."

"Sure," the Parson said soothingly. "You murdered her to save your girl."

"It was self-defense!" Goodwin screamed. "She'd have shot Naomi!"

"What'd you do with her gun?"

"I threw it overboard. Then I saw Guard come aboard. I saw

my chance! Yes! I framed him. I whistled down the corridor. His attention was attracted. He walked down to see who it was. I had left the cabin door open. He saw the body. It nearly overpowered him. When he backed away, Lundborg happened to see him."

"All right, drop your gun," the Parson said.

"Andrew!" Naomi screamed. "Oh, don't!"

Goodwin had the muzzle at his ear. There was a sudden ear-shattering explosion. Three drops of blood splashed in the shape of exclamation points against the wall. Goodwin crumpled slowly.

"Andrew! Andrew!"

The Parson laid a hand on her shoulder. "Relax, kid. He had no other out. When he grabbed the roscoe, I knew he was going to do the Dutch. He had that look in his eye. That's why I didn't plug him."

His unruffled calmness soothed her strangely. Her head drooped and she let out a long-drawn breath. "You know so much about death.... Oh, I'm tired."

"Chin up, kid. Can you sling Spic lingo? O.K.! Explain to bluecoat before he breaks a blood vessel. Then you worry about gettin' the boy friend home." He whirled on Lundborg, words like rapier thrusts. "You're the witness to everything said here, see? Don't you forget it; It's your only chance to save your own skin."

Shadow-like, he slipped through the door, was gone.

HARBOR LIGHTS OF Havana, a cluster of diamond points, receded steadily as the *Sea Witch* lifted her nose high to the Gulf swell and its blue waters.

A steward came to the rail, coughed discreetly. Jerry Dolan, his arm still tight about Naomi, turned.

"Order to deliver this when we passed the breakwater sir. That's all, sir."

It was an envelope. Jerry ripped open the flap with an impatient thumbnail, took out a folded sheet of paper. It said:

Read you were to be married before you sailed. Luck to both of you. I took Vince Guard's bags with me. It wasn't two million—that was just build-up. Only about hundred and fifty grand in all. I'll be in Montevideo or Buenos Aires or some hole like that. Guess I'll just run through the dough and have a good time and I guess that's all.

The Parson.

Jerry Dolan looked up. "Gosh, lovely, you're crying! And over a mugg like the Parson!" He was grinning, eyes sparkling.

Her mood buoyed to his. "Meanie!" she said. "Anyway, he—he wasn't a mugg!"

He looked down into her eyes a long second. "No." He held her closer. "I guess maybe he wasn't."

The Parson Tells a Lie

The Parson does some straight shooting and some fast thinking

THE *MARINOCO* PITCHED and rolled in the heavy swell. The sickening rainy heat set in the second day out of Curacao but now with the Trinidad blue beckoning across the water, the rain let up. But it was still hot. The Parson lolled in his bunk, watched the Boca through the port-hole as the islands loomed up one by one in green, ferny masses of foliage. He smoked endlessly, pinching the cigarettes in his delicate, doll-like fingers.

In the afternoon a brassy sea-going tug waltzed out to just beyond the headlands, cuddled close against the *Marinoco* and warped her toward the wharf. The swell was left behind; the bay was a motionless sheet of blue-green glass.

The Parson completed his packing, went up on deck for the first time since he had come aboard. His jet-black hair was crisp, tight against his scalp. His face was delicately modeled, each feature chiseled, and he had acquired his nick-name from this and from his deceptively delicate manner. His eyes were chill, austere knobs of black when they were concentrated on thinking, but otherwise they were mild, disarming. He wore a black suit, a white shirt and a black tie.

Flying fish skimmed away from the ship's side, their arched spines glistening in the sun. Cariba, "the little Paris of the Caribbean," lay just ahead, a geometrical arrangement of white houses with red roofs under majestic cocoanut palms. A band was playing on the wharf. The offshore puff of wind carried snatches of melody to the ship. The corners of the Parson's mouth turned downward. Another port.

"Parson! Hey, Parson!"

The Parson jerked about as if pulled by a string. A tall, square-shouldered man in gray golfing cap and light gabardines stood at the rail a few yards away. An expensive-looking cigar was stuck in his mouth, unlit. A smile broadened his handsome, square-jawed face as he strode forward on long, straight legs. But there was a hard, questioning stare in his slate blue eyes.

"Hello, Nicoll," the Parson said. "Didn't know you were aboard."

Cole Nicoll stood back, surveyed the slighter man from head to foot. "Well, well," he drawled, "the Parson in the flesh. What the hell you doing in Cariba?"

The Parson shrugged. "That's what I've been asking myself ever since I got aboard this tub at Curacao. But one spot's as good as another."

"Umm. You've been away from New York a long time."

"Plenty long."

"I guess the boys back home don't miss you much."

The Parson looked up. "Why not?"

"Well, for one thing," Nicoll said slowly, "you used to be a pretty dangerous gunman."

"Whatta you mean—used to be!"

Nicoll shook with noiseless laughter. "O.K., boy. I was only kidding."

They had known each other back in New York, had been friends after a fashion. Nicoll was an official with the Cullen Steamship Lines. Rough mannered, boisterous, but on the square, he had been a frequent habitue at the gaming tables the Parson had run for the Vince Guard-Poggi syndicate. That was some years back. A lot had happened since then. The skirmish in Havana when Poggi had killed Guard and the Parson had eliminated Poggi. The money which Guard had tried to squirrel and which the Parson had appropriated and spent. All that and a lot more. And now another port.

"Sue is in Cariba," Nicoll said. "Remember her?"

The Parson looked up. Yes, he remembered. She had been a singer in one of Guard's swanky clubs—a swell kid. Cole Nicoll, he remembered, had waged a very determined campaign before she had consented to say yes. But they had not been a very well matched pair.

"How is Sue?" the Parson inquired.

Lines were being heaved over the bow of the *Marinoco* as she drifted close to the wharf. The band was braying. Sweet cockney West Indies voices were heard above the din.

"She doesn't expect me," Nicoll said slowly. "She's been here a month—getting a divorce."

When the Parson looked at Nicoll, he saw he was smiling. But the smile was only superficial. Nicoll's jaw was tight, his slate-blue eyes sighting hungrily among the people down on the wharf.

"She wants to get rid of me. She hates the very sight of me." He laughed. "Ever hear of George Masterson, the private dick? Well, he's been down here keeping an eye on her. She'll never get that divorce." He shook his head, shrugged. "Never put your money on women, boy. The odds are always against you. And when they fall in love with another man...."

The Parson did not speak.

"... you're sunk. Takes the starch out of you." He leaned forward. "But I'm not through fighting. There's an ace or two up my sleeve. The man she wants is broke. He used to be a second mate on one of my own ships. Can you imagine that? Well, he stood a chance of making some big dough. As a matter of fact, he still has that chance if I say the word. Get it?" His icy blue eyes snapped and crackled. "*I can make him a rich man with just a single word.*"

The Parson put his eyes on him. "You're leading with your chin."

Nicoll laughed, baring teeth. "Hell, no! I'll just say to him, 'I'll make you a millionaire if you'll give up Sue.' Then I'll go to her and tell her, 'Sue, your lover left you for money. I bought him off. But you can have him if you'll take him poor.' Then I'll watch 'em both squirm. I'll watch 'em crawl and suffer as I—" His lips remained open as if he were going to say more but no more words came for a while. Then, "It's right here, boy." He tapped his breast pocket. "Everything that goes to make Sue's man rich or poor." The ladder was being lowered and lashed by four husky blacks. "Come along, I'll drop you at your hotel."

They were cleared through Customs in short order. Nicoll moved with long-legged self-sufficiency. The Parson bobbed at his side. Outside the wharf gates, a crowd of spectators milled. Two men, hurrying, nearly bowled over Nicoll. He righted himself, shouted at them. They hurried on. The Parson had noted them; a thin-faced, sharp-featured man and a stocky, broad-faced one. They had seemed to bump against Nicoll deliberately, but Nicoll was too self-absorbed to be more than irritated.

Nicoll signaled the first cab, had the bags stowed into it. The driver was a young Chinese who wore horn-rimmed glasses and spoke English with a precise Oxford accent; he looked like a college student. He scurried around to the side of the machine and settled behind the wheel. Nicoll was just getting into the cab when the shots were fired.

There was barely any noise, just three pop-pops close together. The Chinese driver yelled something in Chinese and ducked low in his seat. Blood had spattered his glasses. Not his blood. Nicoll, foot on the running board, started backward as if he were being pushed. The Parson caught him. There was another pop. Nicoll's body jerked in the Parson's grasp. The cloth of his coat jumped. He slumped to the ground. Life went out of him before he hit the white coral road. The Parson was under him.

Something plunked to the ground from out of Nicoll's pockets. It was a huge wallet. The Parson rolled clear of the man's dead weight and fell on it. When he got to his feet a second later, the wallet was no longer where it had been.

People were screaming and the tootling band came to a slurring stop. A brassy trombone was the last to be heard. High-pitched Negro voices grew in volume. A heavy hand touched the Parson's shoulder. He turned as a thick British voice said, "What's this? Now what's this?"

The Parson looked at the helmeted, beefy policeman, grunted, "*This* is murder."

The Britisher looked shocked as if the idea had just occurred to him. "Murder? Blimey! Friend of yours?"

"In a way, yes."

"What's his name?"

"Cole Nicoll."

The beefy face of the cop showed the effort he was making to think. "Nicoll. Why, 'e's the bleedin' chappie Mr. Cullen of the Cullen Lines was wytin' for." He stared down at Nicoll. "Why, 'e's an hofficial of the Cullen Lines, 'e is. Is 'e dead?"

The Parson turned away, disgusted. "Don't take my word for it."

The Chinaman was wiping his glasses with a pocket handkerchief, explaining to three other Chinamen in sing-song Cantonese how the glasses had come to be spattered. But he was still hunched behind his wheel as if wedged there. The Parson took a pack of cigarettes from his pocket, lit one. He offered one to the shaking driver, who instantly cut off his flow of Cantonese and said, "I am deeply indebted to you, sir. I am not indulgent to nicotine."

The policeman was writing in a notebook with a thick stub of a pencil. More policeman came—on bicycles. The Parson looked on and marveled. The crowd grew thicker. Nicoll lay on his back, eyes no longer questing but closed as if in sleep.

They found the gun. It was done so quickly that the Parson was a trifle bewildered. But he had to concede the efficiency of the English-trained policemen. Their minds were a trifle slow but they moved fast. And even their minds—well, they acted dumb but in reality had a full grip on the situation.

IN THE NEAT, well ordered office of the Inspector, the Parson heard him painstakingly relate how the gun had been found. Forty yards from where Nicoll had been killed, stood a deserted house. The shots had been fired from a broken window on the attic floor. A bobby made a routine investigation of the house and found the gun lying on the floor. It was a Luger from which four shots had been fired. Prints had been smudged on the stock and trigger so that they were beyond identification.

But the cops had not stopped there. Within a hour, they had traced it to a gun shop in the city. It had been sold to an

American named David Gaynor. Twenty minutes later David Gaynor was formally arrested and charged with the murder of Cole Nicoll.

The Parson was detained merely for routine questioning. But he didn't mind staying. He had a hunch that Gaynor was the sailor Nicoll had mentioned as the man Sue Nicoll had fallen in love with. Gaynor was brought into the office between two bobbies.

"Do you know this man?" the Inspector asked the Parson.

"No." But his eyes rapidly scanned the fellow's face.

Gaynor was standing at ease, staring coolly and somewhat contemptuously down at the Parson. There was something firm and fine about his face that you couldn't help but like. He was tall, rangy, with high cheek-bones, rusty brown hair that curled thickly behind his ears, and eyes like twin chunks of blue ice against the deep tan of his face.

There was the barest shadow of a smile on the Parson's lips. If this was the man Sue had picked, she'd picked a good one.

The Inspector put aside his pipe, measured Gaynor with a keen unwavering stare. "We hang men for murder here and we hang 'em quick. None of your long-drawn trials. You've got a chance to speak, Gaynor. Tell us what you know."

"I didn't kill Nicoll."

"Can you identify this gun?" The Inspector pointed his pipe at the Luger on his desk.

"Yes, it's mine."

"It was found in a deserted house near where Nicoll was killed."

"Then it was planted there!" Gaynor flamed. "It was stolen from me and planted." He took a deep breath, swallowed. "Listen, why should I kill Nicoll?"

The Inspector shrugged. "The motive. You worked on one of the Cullen boats, didn't you?"

Gaynor nodded. "Second mate on the *Allabad*."

"You met Mrs. Nicoll, Mrs. Sue Nicoll, aboard her?"

"No, I met her in New York."

"When?"

"About six months ago."

"And when she came to Cariba some four weeks ago, you dropped your job on the *Allabad* and took up residence here. You've been seen together a good deal. Did you know that Mrs. Nicoll was suing her husband for divorce?"

"Yes."

"Did you know that Mr. Nicoll was contesting the suit?"

Color leaped to Gaynor's cheeks. "What has that got to do with it?"

The Inspector stood up. "This. He would've won his case. Mrs. Nicoll would never have been free. Do you understand? You killed Nicoll to marry his wife."

Gaynor towered, his fists clenched, nostrils twitching. "It's a damn lie! I'm being framed!"

The Parson watched him with a speculative eye. This was the young man Nicoll wanted to see crawl. Well, he wouldn't crawl. Nicoll would have been disappointed if he had lived. Gaynor didn't flinch or cringe—that much could be said for him. And the Parson admired nerve—guts, he called it. It was one of the few traits of character he had any respect for in another human being.

"You don't deny ownership of the gun," the Inspector said. "Do you deny being in the vicinity of the wharf when Nicoll was killed?"

Gaynor folded his arms. "O.K., I was there. I went down to see the boat come in. No crime in that, is there? But as she was made fast, I went away. I didn't even know Nicoll was aboard." The Inspector kept his keen inquisitive stare bent on Gaynor. "I'm not going out of my way to make you look guilty. But do you blame us for arresting you? You were seen as the *Marinoco* came in. Then you went away. A few minutes later Nicoll was murdered by bullets from a gun you admit is yours. What else is there to it?"

"I tell you it's a frame-up! The gun was planted!"

"Yes, you mentioned that before." The Inspector waved his hand. "Take him away."

The Parson stood up, peered down at his knuckles. "Know what? That kid's innocent."

"What!" the Inspector jumped.

"Where's your proof?"

"No proof. It's just something you sorta smell. The truth, I mean. That guy Gaynor's on the up and up. He needs a break."

The Inspector relaxed. "You had me worried for a moment. It's just what you Americans call hunch, eh? Well, thank you, Mr. Ormond." Ormond was the name the Parson had given. "We need not detain you any longer. Will you stay in Cariba for some time?"

"Long enough to get acquainted."

HE HAD NOT been more than five minutes in his room when the wall telephone rang. He lifted the receiver, said hello.

"Mr. Ormond? Thomas Cullen is my name. I've just spoken to Inspector Brickell. I understand you were the last person to see Nicoll alive. I'd see it as a great favor if you'd come over for a chat. The Cullen Lines. Yes, the building is on Bolivar."

The Parson was suspicious. "How'd you know my hotel?"

"I called every one in town. Will you come?"

"O.K. Say, in half an hour."

He didn't unpack. He went to the door, turned the key. Then he sat down at the table and drew from his pocket the wallet that had fallen from Nicoll's pocket. It was longer than the ordinary wallet and was choked with a sheaf of papers. The heading read: Engineer's Report on Lake Manuelo. In smaller letters was the word: Confidential.

He tried to read through the report, but it didn't make much sense to him. There was a rough, hand-drawn map on the last page. He studied it. It showed a river surrounded by swamp on both sides. At the end of the river was a small patch with fine criss-cross lines through it, labeled: Lake Manuelo. Half-way along the lines indicating the river there was a curve and a break. Here there was lettering which read: Manuelo Falls. He went back to the first page and tried to read it again, but it was too full of technical engineering references to mean anything to him. He put it aside, stared at it with a scowl.

Nicoll had said he could make David Gaynor a millionaire or keep him poor. The Parson stood up. The whole blamed thing was beginning to get thick and he didn't like it that way. He took a cigarette from his pocket without producing the pack, stuck it between his lips, then forgot to light it. Perhaps this was not the paper Nicoll had meant. But it had to be!

A timorous knock sounded on the door and he turned slowly and looked at the panel. The knock was not repeated. He gathered up the sheaf of papers, replaced them in the wallet. He moved quietly to the door. "Who's there?" he called.

No one answered. He put one hand on the knob and the other on the key. He turned the key and flung open the door. At the same time, his hand snaked up to the automatic resting under his arm. A man stood on the threshold. He was the thinnest man the Parson had ever seen and one of the tallest. Bones stuck out in his face, in his neck. His skin was yellow, the corners of his mouth tobacco-stained. He wore a white drill suit that was no longer white and which was several sizes too small for him. His eyes were bright and eager, but the whites were furiously yellow. He wore no hat. His hair was matted, dirty.

He looked at the Parson with a glance at once secret and alert as though he were waiting for a signal to begin laughing. Bird-like, he craned his neck through the door with an air of gleeful secrecy. Then he nodded his head as if he were glad there was no one else present. A chortle started deep down inside him. He leaned forward, whispered, "Manuelo."

The Parson blinked, but said nothing.

"Manuelo," the old man said again, impatiently, as if he were uttering a password.

"Who in hell are you? What do you want?"

The old man smiled indulgently, shook his head. "Manuelo will make me rich. I bought it for twelve hundred dollars. Everybody laughed at me. Worthless, they said. But I can laugh at them. Can't I laugh at them? *You* know."

"Know what? What're you talkin' about, you fool feeb?" Then he remembered the sheaf of papers. Manuelo Lake and Manuelo Falls.

His arm lashed out, snatched the old man's wrist. It gave him a creepy feeling. It was like touching a corpse. "What about Manuelo, huh? Come on, tell me."

A crafty look came over the man's face. "You don't know?"

"You know damned well I don't."

"Leggo my wrist! You hurt!"

The Parson released him. There was such an air of pipe-stem frailty about this walking scarecrow that the Parson was afraid his bones would snap off under any kind of pressure.

"If you don't know about Manuelo why did you steal Cole Nicoll's wallet?" the old man said with a sidelong smirk.

Nothing changed in the Parson's face, save that his lips drew together a little tighter.

"Aye." The man nodded like a child hugging a secret. "I saw you. I saw the wallet fall from his pocket. I said to myself, 'It contains the engineer's report. Now I'll be rich.'"

"You saw me pick up the wallet?" the Parson said slowly.

The man made a sound like a giggle, nodded.

"How did you know what was in it?"

"I just knew!" he whispered. "You get like that when you've waited a long time. You get to smell things like."

The Parson moved casually. His intention was to put hands on the man and drag him inside the room. Privacy was indicated. But he backed away warily inch by inch.

"Did you ever see Manuelo?"

"No. What's there?"

"Money." The old man laughed hysterically, banged against the wall.

The Parson leaped at him, but the man sidestepped nimbly, pivoted and ran down the corridor with amazing speed despite his shambling, bear-like gait. The Parson did not run after him. His voice came back in a crazy, cackling laugh. Then the corridor was silent.

BOLIVAR IS A narrow street on the fringe of the commercial part of the city. The buildings are old but whitewashing twice a year gives them a spic and span look. From the top of the hill the sweep of the harbor can be seen and farther out Viejo Light. The opposite view takes in the island. The offices of the Cullen Line are at the very top.

The Parson arrived in a cab, the driver of which had not stopped honking his horn for one moment during the short ride. Bright-plumed West Indies cocks fluttered out of their path and they had just missed hitting a ruminating goat.

A bright-faced young clerk said, "Ah, Mr. Cullen is expecting you," and showed the way to an inner office. He stood aside as the Parson entered and announced, "Mr. Ormond, sir."

A man, standing at the window with hands folded behind his back, turned as the Parson came in, said, "Ah, Mr. Ormond," and waved to a chair. He was about thirty-eight or forty, but his eyes were youthful, his manner brisk. He wore a suit of fine linen and white shoes. "Cigar? Drink? The cigars are particularly good, if I may say so. Made especially for me, you know."

The Parson shook his head. "What's on your mind, Mr. Cullen?"

Cullen bit off the end of a cigar, stuck it in his mouth. The paper band around it was white with a big C printed in a black Gothic letter. His eyes meanwhile were coolly appraising the Parson. Quite abruptly he said, "Cole Nicoll was my right-hand man. We worked together in the Cullen Lines for fifteen years. We were like brothers."

The Parson shot him a brief look. "Well?"

"Inspector Brickell told me you were a friend of Cole's, that you met him abroad the *Marinoco*. You were right beside him when he was shot to death. Now here's the funny thing about the whole business. Cole had in his possession an engineer's report, a confidential report that happens to be extremely valuable. The engineer died a week or so after the report was made—a natural death, by the way. And as it happens, there was only one copy of his report in existence. Cole had it with him when he stepped aboard the *Marinoco*. But when we searched his effects after he had been killed, we couldn't find it."

The Parson took his eyes from the ceiling, put them on Cullen. Cullen looked up; then he moved again to the window. He said, "Cole radioed me from the ship en route so I know for certain that the report was on his person. Yet when he was dead, it wasn't there."

"Have you informed the police?" the Parson asked solicitously.

Cullen cupped his chin in one hand and made a slow circuit of the room. He placed each foot gently and his footfalls were noiseless. He talked as he moved.

"This is not exactly a matter for the police."

He moved around the room again, his chin still cupped in his hand. He sat down, leaned back in his chair comfortably. It was very quiet and cool in the office. He said very thoughtfully:

"Or is it?"

"I wouldn't be the judge of that," said the Parson.

Cullen put his palms flat on the desk and leaned forward. There was a quizzical look in his face.

"Your name's not Ormond. You're the man known as the Parson. I've seen pictures of you in the papers back home. You've got a reputation for being a straight crook—a man who'd cheerfully fleece a fellow crook but just as cheerfully die for a friend."

The Parson fixed a hard, stony stare on him. "Are you going to make something out of that?"

"No, I can be your friend, just as Cole was. There's no sense telling the Cariba police who you are. They'd just ship you out as an undesirable alien. I want you around."

It didn't take the Parson long to make up his mind. "How much is that engineer's report worth?"

"In money? Plenty. In time? Even more."

"I'll try some rum if it's thick and black."

"Nothing here but the thickest and the blackest." Cullen produced a dark, opaque bottle and two tall glasses. "Ice? Limes?"

"As is, will do." He took the proffered glass, drank.

Cullen drank. He wasn't looking at the Parson when he said, "I'll bid five thousand."

The Parson inspected the liquor beads on the inside of his glass. He shook his head.

"Seven."

"Do I hear any more?"

Cullen grinned. "Ten. That's tops."

"Nuts."

Cullen spread his hands. "After all, I don't know why I should pay for something that legitimately belongs to—"

"Don't you want to pay?" The Parson started to get up.

"Wait a minute. Fifteen. By Harry, that's all!"

"Do you have the cash?"

"No, but...."

Cullen fretted his lower lip, his eyes grew moist. But he

retained an air of gentlemanly detachment. "I can have the cash tomorrow morning."

"Delivery tomorrow then." The Parson looked sidewise at the window. "Someone out there playing Jack-in-the-box?"

Cullen rushed to the window. Venetian blinds were drawn half-way. He drew the window up, stuck out his head. He looked up and down the street before he closed the window again. "No one there," he said. "Did you see anybody?"

"Maybe I imagined it. Well…."

There was a knock on the door. The young clerk put in his head. "Mrs. Cole Nicoll, sir."

"Show her in."

The Parson said, "No, tell her to wait a minute."

The clerk hesitated, looking doubtfully from the Parson to Cullen. But Cullen nodded curtly and the door shut.

The Parson said, "Do you know a lanky, wild-looking guy of about sixty, sixty-five? Nothing but bones and eyes."

Cullen's brow contracted, then cleared. "Oh, you must mean Jim Hull. Everyone in town knows Jim. He's not quite right in his mind."

"Crazy?"

"Well, I wouldn't go so far as to say that. But actually I suppose he must be. He's been in Cariba twenty years or more. What about him?"

"Nothing. I'm just curious. Was he connected in any way with Cole Nicoll?"

Cullen looked up sharply. "Huh? I don't know what you mean."

"Did he know Nicoll or did Nicoll know him?"

"Possibly. You see, Nicoll used to come to Cariba on business a great deal. Just as I do. Sort of shuttling back and forth from New York, you know. Cariba's the terminus of our line."

"Hmm. You can let Mrs. Nicoll in now."

"But you haven't finished about Jim Hull. I'm curious…."

"I've finished," said the Parson, but he didn't get up.

SUE NICOLL CAME slowly into the room. She was a honey blonde with blue eyes and eyebrows and lashes that were amazingly dark. Her features were far from perfect and taken separately she was not beautiful. But the total effect was of striking, unusual beauty, just the same. There was a tired, drawn look about her face now, the look of a person over whose head storms had broken with such fury that the capacity for feeling pain or happiness has been dulled.

She looked through and past the Parson with utter indifference as Cullen was taking her hand in both his. Then sudden recognition flared in her eyes and she looked startled. Two spots of color bedaubed her cheeks, heightening her beauty.

She hesitated as if she did not quite believe her eyes. "Parson," she said softly.

He stood up. "Yeah," his flat voice said. "Hello, Sue."

"Parson." She came toward him. "I didn't know you…." She stopped, looked at Cullen. "Then it was you with him at the last. You're the Mr. Ormond the police told me about."

He nodded. It was five years since he had seen her. She had been lovely then, a songbird of eighteen with a voice that made things crawl up and down your spine in response. Now she was more mature, an exotic, breath-taking beauty. And there was still magic even in her speaking voice.

Cullen hovered over her. To anyone with eyes it was obvious that he was crazy about her, dog-like in his devotion, as only an older man can be who knows his love is hopeless. He got her to sit down while he stood by her chair. The Parson remained standing.

The gentleness of the Parson when he permitted himself to show it was an odd phenomenon. It showed in his eyes, softening their patent-leather gleam, in the set of the lines about his mouth. He never wasted words ordinarily, but now he was completely silent.

Cullen cleared his throat. "Then you two know each other?" He spoke as if he didn't quite relish the idea.

"The Parson and I are old friends," Sue said with half a smile. She looked at him. "I didn't think I'd ever see you in a place like this."

"Times have changed."

Cullen coughed. "Sue, if you only knew how terribly I felt over the whole thing. If there's anything I can do to help…."

She touched Cullen's arm. "Thanks, Tom. You can help." Her face drained of color and her blue eyes again became dull, stricken. "It's Dave Gaynor." She spoke the name softly, almost slurringly, as if afraid emotion would betray her. "Dave didn't kill my husband. He was framed, Tom. We've got to help him."

"But, Sue dear, the police are certain he was the murderer. Surely, you won't stand up to defend the man who coldbloodedly ki—"

"Tom! Please!" She was on her feet, her lips shaking, her face white as chalk. "It's a lie—a lie! Dave didn't kill Cole."

"But, Sue dear, how do you know?"

"I know! I spoke to Dave. They let me see him. I asked him. Oh, can't you understand? Dave wouldn't lie to me."

The Parson smiled ruefully. He said, "Sure, the kid was trapped."

Both Sue and Cullen looked at him. "What do you mean?" Cullen said.

"He was framed. The gun was stolen from him, used in the kill and deliberately planted where the limey cops would be sure to find it."

Sue nodded, said brokenly, "Yes, that's the way it was. It had to be that way."

Cullen looked bewildered, unsure of himself. "But can we prove it?"

The Parson shrugged. "I think not—at present."

"Then what *can* we do?"

"Muddle along, hope for a break."

Cullen sank into a chair, lost in thought. "Look!" he said suddenly. "There's a private detective living in Cariba, name of Masterson. I've had occasion to use him before in service of the Line. I'll set him to work. If anyone can get at the truth, he can." His brows went up speculatively. "Of course I don't share your belief that Dave is so innocent. But still for your sake, Sue, I'll do everything I can." His voice lowered. "Cole would have wanted it that way."

"Cole...." Her voice tightened, clotted. "Cole and I were so unhappy. Nobody knows how much." She was remembering aloud, talking as if to herself. "When he was alive—I thought I hated him. Now I know it was just my unhappiness." She moved to the door. "Parson, will you come to see me? I'm at the Plaza."

The change in her voice was abrupt, startling. From tragic overtones to a casual invitation. The Parson nodded. "I'll be around."

When the door had closed, Cullen whipped on the Parson. "Do you really think Gaynor was not the killer?"

The faintest shadow of a smile creased the corners of the Parson's lips. "Well, I don't know, but did you ever see a bunch of platers come shufflin' outa the paddock—and then outa the lot of them is one that catches your eye because his head is high and he's prancin' and looks like he's all horse? You make a rush for the window to get down your bet."

Cullen fixed him with an irritated, caustic stare. "What in heaven's name are you talking about?"

"Dave Gaynor."

"Umm." Cullen's lips tightened primly. "I guess I understand what you mean. Gaynor's a swell boy, the tops. But hell, all I can say is that for a chap who's known as a crook you're a funny kind of crook."

The Parson frowned. "What's funny about fifteen grand?"

WHEN THE PARSON walked into the squad room of the city prison, Dave Gaynor was seated beside a plain, mahogany table and a guard was standing near the window. It had taken the Parson ten minutes to convince Inspector Brickell that he had a right to see Gaynor. Gaynor looked up at him with a kind of questioning indifference, his straight eyebrows making a barely perceptible movement. There was a chair beside him and the Parson slipped into it.

"I've just been talking to Sue Nicoll," he said by way of breaking the ice. "I'm a friend of hers."

Gaynor brightened a bit. "Did she send you here?"

"Yes, in a way. We're trying to get you clear of this mess—Sue, Cullen and me."

Gaynor's brightness faded out. "Yeah," he said dully. "I didn't kill Cole Nicoll. Is that what you want to know?"

The Parson got out a package of cigarettes. "Did you ever hear of Manuelo?" he asked. "That guard is going to sprain an eardrum trying to hear what we say. Have a smoke?"

Gaynor took one of the cigarettes and the Parson held a match to it. Smoke spirals intertwined. Gaynor watched them curl upward. "What did you say your name was?"

"Ormond."

"Can the guard hear us?"

"I don't think so."

"Why should I tell you anything, Mr. Ormond?"

The Parson shrugged slowly. "I don't know, except that I may be able to help you—and myself. I'm practically flat. A big piece of change would go nice. A guy offers me fifteen grand for a lot of papers. That makes me think it's probably worth much more."

"That would depend on the papers, wouldn't it?"

"Suppose you have a look at them. That'd be one way of proving to you I'm on the up and up." He spoke a trifle louder. "I can lease the boat for a year. That is, if these papers are in order."

He got out the wallet that had fallen from Cole Nicoll's pocket and drew forth the sheaf of papers. "Look 'em over, pal."

Gaynor dropped his eyes, took the sheaf in his hand. Color flamed in his cheeks as he skimmed rapidly through the sheets. After a long minute, he nodded. "Looks like it's a good enough boat. Of course, the jib boom will need trimming down. Too much spread for her narrow beam. Take a good-sized blow down here and her bow would drag under water." He threw the papers on the table carelessly.

The Parson said, "Oke," and put the papers away. The guard had ceased his vigilance and gazed placidly out of the window. "Well?" said the Parson.

"Where'd you get that?"

"The report? From Cole Nicoll."

"Who offered you fifteen thousand for it?"

"Cullen himself. Now what about it—will you let me in on it?"

"What do you want to know?"

"What makes this worth fifteen grand? What's at Manuelo?"

Gaynor was staring at him with burning eyes, as if he were trying to make up his mind. "It's worth all that and a lot more to Cullen. It belongs to his Lines, really. You see, an engineer made that report. It took him two years to complete it. It cost around fifty thousand, maybe a little more. If this report is destroyed, it would mean two more years of work and another fifty thousand. The engineer who did this job died."

"Cullen told me about that. What did you say made Manuelo so valuable?"

Gaynor was still sighting at him. "I didn't say."

"But if it ties up with Nicoll's killing, why keep it from me? I'll find out anyway sometime. Maybe too late to help you."

Gaynor made a troubled movement of his head. "You think Manuelo is behind the murder! By God, you may be right at that."

"Is Manuelo a man?"

"No, it's a lake."

"Then how can—"

"The report," Gaynor snapped, clicking his teeth. "They wanted it. Keep it to themselves until they could force—" He stopped short.

"Who is *they?*"

"A group of men; three, maybe four of them. I don't know who they are, but I've been followed by them. They never tried any violence though."

"There's always got to be a first time," the Parson said. "What did they try?"

"Oh, my room was searched two, three times. So was the old man."

"Old man, eh?" The Parson sighed. "He wouldn't be a bony scarecrow, would he?" he asked slyly. "Name of Jim Hull or something like that?"

Gaynor looked startled. "How do you know?"

"That doesn't matter. Now let's case this from the beginning. If we're going to get you outa here, I've got to be in the know." He looked down at the floor. "And if there's dough in it, I'd like to make myself a cut of something substantial."

Gaynor nodded. "O.K. Cullen will be willing to pay us a little more. That will take care of you. I don't know why I trust you," he said impulsively, "but I do!"

"That's swell, boy. Now let's have it."

"It's thirty-two years ago. They were just beginning to use asphalt extensively. You've heard about the Pitch Lake in Trinidad. They've taken millions of dollars out of it in asphalt. Well, there's another such lake—a natural bed of asphalt, thirty miles down the river. A company was formed in England to work it. It went bankrupt in a couple of years. That was thirty-two years ago."

"Then we can chalk them off," the Parson said.

"Yes," Gaynor said. "The big problem was how to get the pitch out. From here to Manuelo Lake there's twenty-four miles of swamp. To build a railroad or any other kind of road would cost a lot of millions. The river isn't navigable because there's a seventy-foot falls plunk in the middle. The thing was just no good. There stood the lake and no way to get its product to a market. So the English company went bust. Two smart young Americans thought there was still a chance to salvage something out of the concern. They bought the company's shares and a lease for nine hundred and ninety-nine years. They paid around twenty thousand for the whole shebang—and went broke. There wasn't a nickel to be made out of the business."

"Where are they now?" the Parson asked.

"One of them died a few years later. The other is still kicking around."

"Jim Hull."

Dave Gaynor nodded slowly. Then he went on:

"The other was my old man. Working on the Cullen boats, I saw Jim a good deal whenever we put in here at Cariba. Then about a year ago, I took a leave of absence and we went up to see our property. Jim had never lost his dream of riches. I went along more to humor him than anything else. I never thought Manuelo would ever bring in a copper to either of us. But on that trip I got an idea. I saw something that opened my eyes. When we got back, I went to Cole Nicoll and put the idea before him. He liked it so much he talked Cullen himself into spending all that money to hire an engineer for a survey."

"What," said the Parson, "was the idea?"

"Didn't you read the report?"

"Yeah, but it's all a lot of Serbian to me."

"Its main idea is simple, though. It contains a report on how to smash the falls, build a short, interlocking canal and make the river navigable for oceangoing steamers."

The Parson leaned forward a little.

"You're beginning to get the idea, huh?" Gaynor said. "With that falls dynamited out of existence, Cullen boats can jockey up smack to Manuelo, load pitch on the spot and carry it out again. Instead of being cut off by swamp and a waterfalls, Manuelo Lake could become a money-making mint."

The Parson leaned back, eyes dark and fathomless. "It sounds better than good."

"It's the truth," said Gaynor earnestly. "Will you sell Cullen the report? I mean you won't hold out on him, will you?"

The Parson sighed. "Not if you cut me in on the big deal."

Gaynor nodded. "That's a bargain."

The Parson looked down at the floor again. "I want to ask you something a little personal. Is Cullen in love with Sue Nicoll?"

"Why, yes, I guess he is from what I've seen of them together."

"You sound as if you didn't mind."

Gaynor smiled ruefully. "I mind plenty, but what good would that do? After all a woman like Sue can make up her own mind."

The Parson dropped his cigarette to the floor, stepped on it. "Could Cullen have had the chance to steal your gun?"

"Why, I dunno. Yeah, he could but…" He looked suddenly at the Parson with very level eyes. "Do you mean to tell me Cullen knocked off Cole Nicoll?"

"I'm not telling you a thing, boy. But it's just a good idea to sorta check up."

"My God, that's impossible! You don't know Cullen. He's an ace."

"I know, I know," the Parson muttered. "And maybe it isn't my business but it occurred to me that with Nicoll killed and you up for his murder, Cullen is in a swell spot to do some high-class wooing."

Gaynor grimaced, shook his head. "You don't know Cullen," he repeated. "I can't believe it."

The Parson smothered a yawn. "For a guy supposed to be in love, you're funny. I should think you'd hate Cullen's guts."

"Why should I? We're both in the same boat."

The Parson watched him narrowly. "What do you mean?" He had forgotten about his yawn.

"Well, Sue's one of those girls—you know, you never know where you stand. So Cullen and me, we're philosophical about it. We take turns consoling each other."

"But I thought Sue was crazy about you?"

Gaynor laughed sarcastically. "That's news to me. Oh, I've been around her a lot. We've gone out together now and then and danced and looked at the moon. But so has Cullen."

The Parson stood up, staring narrow-eyed into space. "First thing, we've got to get you out of here. Second, sell the Manuelo stock to Cullen." He grinned crookedly. "After all, I'm in this for the dough."

The door opened and a uniformed guard stuck in his nose, said, "Mr. Masterson to see the prisoner."

The head withdrew and a man walked in, closed the door. He stood spread-legged before it, a cigar in his mouth. His black hair was straight, glossy. His long face held a cold, imperious look. His eyes were blue.

The guard at the window came over. "Now, myties, one visitor allowed at a time."

The Parson said, "O.K., Gaynor, be seein' you."

Gaynor nodded. "Do you know Masterson? This is Mr. Ormond. Mr. Masterson."

"Hello, Ormond. Cullen's been telling me about you." There was a good-humored smile on his face. "Cullen thinks you may have been framed, Gaynor, and that I can help get you out of this pickle. Well, all I can do is try. That's all any private detective could do."

IT WAS DARK when the Parson walked out on the sidewalk. The tropic night had fallen suddenly. The prison gate clanged shut behind him. There was no cab in sight; he walked. An orchestra was playing on a dais placed in the midst of an open-air café. The gourds rattled, glasses clinked. This was Cariba's vermouth hour.

A cab rolled up, stopped at the curb near him. Automatically, the Parson moved toward it. It was a touring car, curtained in the rear. He opened the door and had a foot on the running board. He jolted to a halt.

"Don't try to run," said a voice from the rear seat. "There's a gun pointed at you—a silenced gun."

It was a long enough ride, the Parson thought. He rode in the back seat with a gun pressed against his ribs. His own gun had been lifted from him by the driver. Also the contents of his inside breast pocket. Cole Nicoll's wallet.

Anger smoldered deep inside him but he kept it buttoned up. He'd been taken for fair. There was no use losing his head over it now. The gun had been pointed at his heart. He had altogether too healthy a respect for the persuasive powers of a gun to have resisted. He had simply stepped into the car and they had driven off. At first they had made no attempt to search him. Then the driver stopped the car a few blocks farther on, got out and went through his pockets.

He had had a chance to glimpse their faces then and he'd recognized them. The two men who had brushed against him on the dock when he'd landed with Cole Nicoll. Somehow their faces had stuck in his memory. The thin-faced man and the stocky, thick-chested one with the hooked nose.

They were past the city now and riding on a white coral road. There was no traffic and only an occasional house skirting the highway.

"Hey, Abe," said the hooked-nose man to the driver.

"Yeah." The man didn't turn his head.

"Viejo Point. Where the cliff is."

"Right."

"Do you know Viejo Point?" said the man to the Parson.

"No. What's there?"

"It overlooks the water." He seemed to be enjoying himself. "And in the water is sharks and barracuda."

Abe growled, "Aw, lay off, Fred."

The Parson said nothing. The road was bumpy and the car bounced but the gun moved with his body. A dozen plans flitted through the Parson's mind but he set them down as pipe dreams. That gun in his side would go off at the first false move he made. The miles clicked by steadily.

"What's it goin' to get you—droppin' me over a cliff?" he said.

Fred, beside him, laughed gutturally but he didn't answer. The driver, Abe, squirmed a little in his seat. The Parson put him down as a guy with nerves and no stomach for a job of this kind.

"Listen, fellas, you got what you went after—that wallet. Why add murder to the score?"

"Save it," said Abe, "for the sharks."

"All right, look at it this way. The police know I'm in town. I'm a witness to Nicoll's murder. Maybe someone noticed you picking me up back there near the prison. Then I'm missing. The cops will put noses to the ground and maybe they'll smell you out. Then what happens? They'll pin the Nicoll kill on you."

"To hell with that kinda crap! We had nothin' to do with the Nicoll kill and nobody saw us pick you up."

"But you got the wallet!" the Parson repeated. "Yeah, come to think of it, you boys are bright at that. How'd you know I had it?"

Fred laughed again, self-satisfied. "Oh, we hear things here and there. Some guys, y'know, some guys they don't know how to button their kissers."

From the front seat, Abe snapped, "Well, learn to button yours, dope!"

"Now don't get in a lather," Fred said, his voice silken and even. "The mugg here gets the business. Anything I tell him sticks with him."

"It was Jim Hull," said the Parson in brittle tones. His eyelids narrowed over his brightly gleaming eyes. "Jim Hull saw me."

Fred prodded the gun a little harder and said, "Sure it was Jim Hull and what you gonna make of it?"

There was a trace of amusement in the Parson's tone. "Damned if I know. That guy ain't as crazy as a lot of people think."

The car slowed. The road came to an abrupt end. Through the windshield, the Parson could see the dark sea. From a point to the left a light winked out over the water, disappeared and then came on again at regular intervals. That would be Viejo Light. It was somberly quiet when Abe shut off the motor.

"Outa the car," said Abe. "Any bloodstains and there might be trouble."

"Yeah. O.K., you, outa the car. Open the door and step out." The Parson didn't move.

"Out! *Out!* Can't you hear?"

"I'll take it like I am, and I hope blood smears all over the damned cushions."

"Ah, get out, lunk!" Fred rasped.

The Parson stayed put. Slowly the gun was withdrawn from his side. With his left hand, very cautiously, Fred reached behind him and opened the door on his side.

"Get your cannon in action, Abe," he snapped. "Don't let him move. I'll go around to the other side and drag him out."

Still the Parson didn't stir. Fred slipped out. Abe held a gun on him, eyes enormously wide in the semi-dark. The Parson figured he wasn't up to it. Not for this kind of a job. Abe wasn't a gunman—he merely carried a gun around.

Fred had run around the rear of the machine, and now flung open the door on the Parson's side. He stood there spread-legged, chunky, a gun in his fist, making a squat, ugly shadow obliquely away from him.

"Chop him, Abe," he barked. "If the lug won't move, we'll drag him out feet first."

Abe got up on his knees in the front seat the better to reach the Parson. His right arm was upraised. His lips were working with nervous impatience, baring his teeth in a horrible grin. His right arm started downward. The Parson fell sidewise down on the cushion. The gun swished by his head. Outside Fred was dancing and shouting.

The Parson twisted his body abruptly and with both hands caught Abe's forearm just above the wrist. The sudden twist brought a scream of pain from Abe. His body hurtled over the seat, bounced down in a heap. The Parson fell down with him to the floor boards and at that moment Fred began shooting. There was flame but little sound.

Slugs splatted into Abe's body, jerking it. He screamed shrilly. Then he was on his knees in front of the Parson, shielding the Parson with his own body. He was coughing, blood dribbled from his lips down the corners of his mouth. The Parson reached around and grabbed his gun, twisting it from his grasp. The movement threw Abe down. He went down slowly, his head and knees touching the floor as if in a salaam.

Fred started shooting again as he moved backward. Lead sang against the metal of the car. The Parson fired twice in rapid succession. Fred turned and began to run. The Parson took careful aim, fired again. Fred slammed down as if he had been tripped by a rope. The Parson couldn't see him very well in the surrounding darkness.

Then flame in a sharp, angry spurt appeared about twenty yards from the car where Fred had fallen. The Parson drew a careful bead on it and fired. A blurred shadow jerked up and settled down close to the ground. The Parson waited. It was very quiet. The soft lap of water below could be distinctly heard. The shadow did not move. The Parson got out of the car and moved around the rear of it. He fired and leaped back. No shot came in answer. He circled back of the car a few feet and made a circuitous advance.

But Fred was through shooting. He was through living. The Parson knelt beside him and went rapidly through his pockets. He retrieved the wallet that had been taken from him, patting it grimly as he put it back where it belonged. There was another wallet, apparently Fred's own. It yielded about fifty dollars. The Parson regarded the roll of bills gravely, then stuck them into his pocket with a shrug. There were no papers. In another pocket he found a pocket comb which he put back. The last pocket held a bunch of keys. The Parson went through them. Attached to one was a flat metal tag, on which lettering had been stamped. In the darkness, the Parson smiled to himself.

He went back to the car and dragged forth the thin-faced Abe and overhauled him. His pockets contained a handkerchief, a package of American chewing gum and thirty-five dollars. The Parson tossed the handkerchief away, leisurely broke open the package of gum and stuck two sticks into his mouth. He looked down at the corpse of Abe, then turned his glance to where Fred lay. After a while he climbed into the car. He'd let them lie as they were. He turned over the motor and drove back toward the lights of Cariba, looming beckoningly in the distance against the tropical night sky. He was quite satisfied with himself.

He had retained the wallet containing the report on the pitch lake of Manuelo and his gun. He had acquired two other guns, about eighty-five bucks, a package of chewing gum, a car and a key.

CHING'S WAS THE biggest bar in town. Its mahogany length stretched nearly half a block. Six bartenders were on duty twenty-four hours a day. The Parson went in past the out-of-door tables. A heaped-up counter on the left purveyed mountainous sandwiches. He stopped there and got two ham sandwiches, brought them to the end of the bar and perched on a stool.

The bartender was a broad-faced, grinning Chinese with yellow buck teeth and eyes twinkling cheerily from among rolls of fat. The Parson munched on the food and ordered beer. The beer was cold and good in its frosted, funnel-shaped glass. A man on his left was talking loudly in Spanish to another man and using his hands a lot. From time to time he sipped anise and wiped his mustache with the back of his hand. It took a long time for him to finish the tiny glass. Then he and his friend went out. The Parson ordered another beer.

"Have one yourself," he said to the barman.

"Hello, hello, hello," he said in a high, falsetto voice. "I dlink."

The Parson hunched over the counter on his forearms. "Big place you got here, John. All white men in Cariba come here, huh? But I don't see Jim Hull."

The grin threatened to crack the face of the Chinese wide open. "Jim, he come. Not he' now. He come."

"Do you know where he lives?"

"I likee Jim. He goo' fella. Him fliend you?"

"Good friend. Best friend I got. Old-time back-slappin', do-or-die pals. Where is his house?"

"Hello, hello, hello."

"Damned parrot!" the Parson muttered to himself. "What street did you say it was on?"

"I ask."

He moved down the length of the bar with a waddling, duck-like shuffle. The Parson finished the sandwiches, drew out a cigarette and lit up. In a few minutes the barman was back, breathless but beaming.

"Hello, hello, hello. He live Rivadiva, 22. You know?"

The Parson was laconic. "I find."

He had left the car two blocks down. He had no further use for it. He stood for a moment on the sidewalk, thinking things over. A cab came along. He signaled it, climbed in and said, "Go to 22 Rivadiva."

The cab swung in a U-turn and headed southward through the city. The broad, gaily lit thoroughfares were left behind. The streets became narrow, dark and mean. Even at this early hour there were few pedestrians. Fifteen minutes later, the cab poked cautiously into Rivadiva. The Parson got out, paid. He said, "Wait, buddy."

Unused docks that had rotted with time were only a block away. Beyond them, the placid waters of the bay shone like molten pitch. The houses were tumble-down cottages, set rather far apart and fenced in. A dog ran out desultorily at the Parson's approach, uttered one indecisive bark and plodded back, its duty done. Negro voices lingered in the air, but no one appeared anywhere. The Parson searched for numbers. There were none. Then near the head of the street, number 20 was chalked on the rickety gate. He turned in at the next house.

A light showed from one of the windows. He went up sagging steps to a creaking, narrow porch and knocked on the door. He waited. No one answered. He knocked again, rattling the door. The faulty catch slipped and the door swung open. The Parson stepped into a narrow hall. There were two doors, one at the further end of the hall and one directly at his left.

There was light underneath the nearer door, lying in a slanting shaft along the floor. He tried the knob and went in.

Jim Hull lay on the floor with his head smashed.

His dirty white hair was red with blood. A few drops of blood were on the floor. He was still warm. A bottle that had contained rum lay a few feet from him. There was blood on the white and green label and a few hairs stuck to the glass. There had not been any kind of a struggle apparently. None of the rickety furniture had been overturned.

The Parson's eyes wandered over the room, then steadied. On the floor near the rattan table was a cigar. The end had been well chewed, but it had not been lighted. The narrow paper band was white. On it was printed a big C.

He let himself out of the house, walked slowly to the cab down street, his head lowered. High-pitched voices followed him. He climbed into the cab and only when he had slammed the door roused himself. "Let's go," he said.

The Chinese driver bobbed his head. "What is your destination, sir?"

"Huh? Oh, make it the Plaza this time."

It was one of the best hotels in the city. Though only four stories high, it embraced a square block. Landscaped grounds fronted the broad, low veranda. There were a lot of people about, sipping iced drinks and strolling. The place was popular with tourists, but also accommodated quite a number of permanent guests. The British colonial buildings were hard by, dotted with tennis courts. The Parson paid and tipped his driver. A number of the veranda sitters eyed him curiously as he walked into the lobby. His black suit made him conspicuous. All the other men wore white linen.

He did not stop at the desk but walked straight to the elevator. "End of the line," said the Parson to the uniformed attendant. The elevator was one of those openwork affairs that jounced up and down when it stopped. The Parson walked down the corridor, watching the numbers on the doors.

He stopped before number 402, knocked gently. Nobody answered it. He tried the knob. The door was locked. He reached into his pocket and drew out the bunch of keys he had lifted from Fred. He selected the key with the metal tag attached, fitted it to the lock and let himself in.

He clicked up the lights. It was a luxuriously furnished room. The furniture was an ivory color and cool looking. There was a table to one side on which stood a portable typewriter and a mass of papers. Back of the typewriter was a small correspondence file. He tried the doors first. One showed a closet, another the bathroom and a third, connecting with the next room, was locked. He went to the table. A box of letterhead paper was to the left of the open typewriter. On it was printed: George Masterson, 11 East 40th Street, New York, Confidential Inquiries.

He picked up the file box. It was constructed of steel and was locked. None of the keys on Fred's ring fitted it. He took it to the window ledge and banged judiciously against the masonry work. Then he used a penknife. The lid snapped back. There were only a few papers within. Each was headed Confidential Report. They were carbon copies. Below the word Report was typed: Re-Mrs. Cole Nicoll. He read the papers through. They were pretty much alike in content though they varied in dates.

They were a detailed account of Mrs. Nicoll's movements for the past month. The Parson had seen enough reports from private detectives to recognize the snooping touch. Sue had lunched here, played tennis there, had gone swimming, dancing, riding. The date and the hour were carefully given. But only one man's name appeared alongside hers—David Gaynor's.

Quite suddenly the Parson laid the papers down and stood listening, rigid as a pointer. There was someone moving close by but he couldn't tell exactly where. For a full minute he did not move. Then he tiptoed to the locked door that connected the room beyond and put his ear against the panel. The noise of someone moving had stopped but now there was another sound, faint, muffled and barely perceptible, like a person moaning in pain. He knelt to the keyhole and peered through. Within the narrow orbit permitted him, he could see a quarter-section of a bed.

A man lay on it fully clothed, but only the upper half of him was visible. A handkerchief gagged his mouth. From the way he lay, the Parson could tell that his hands and feet were tied. The face was partially averted but the Parson had no trouble recognizing it. It was Thomas Cullen.

For an instant he knelt there immobile. Then he straightened slowly, his lips sucked in against his teeth and in his eyes was a dangerous glint. He took a handkerchief from his pocket and methodically wiped the fingers of his right hand. He liked a dry finger on a trigger. Then he took a Luger from his shoulder holster.

"Hold the pose!" said a voice from the hall door.

The Parson's nerves jerked at the cold menace in the voice. He turned his head slowly. Masterson stood in the open door with a pocket automatic in his hand.

He sidled into the room and closed the door. He swallowed

hard, opened his mouth to speak but instead of words a funny squeak came from his throat. His handsome face was very set but pale, and his eyes looked wary but uncertain.

The Parson said, "You look frightened, my friend. Don't get frightened."

"You—you— Drop that gun!"

A bleak grin spread itself across the Parson's face. "I don't think I will. Suppose you drop yours first."

"Listen. You're trespassing. You broke into my room." Masterson was getting excited as he talked. "I can kill you for that and the law will be on my side."

"But I didn't break in," said the Parson tranquilly. "I used a key."

"A—a key?" The big man was uncertain. "A key?"

"Yeah. The one you gave Fred. Remember Fred… and Abe? You sent them to rub me out but they messed up." He added tauntingly, "Guess where they are now!"

"Wh-where?" said Masterson almost involuntarily.

"Over at Inspector Brickell's office, spittin' out their guts. They couldn't talk fast enough. They were tripping all over each other when I left."

Masterson made a grotesque effort to smile. He wet his lips. He said hoarsely, "You're lying! You can't get away with it."

The Parson smiled ruefully. "What's the sense of denying everything now? Fred and Abe were working for you. You were after the Lake Manuelo shares. They said so. You knew that Cole Nicoll had the engineer's report on him. You killed him to stop Cullen from going ahead and buying out Dave Gaynor and that crazy old gent, Jim Hull. You framed Dave Gaynor. But you didn't get the engineer's report. *I* got it. Jim Hull saw me, but not being right in his mind he couldn't keep his mouth shut. You found out about it from him and you sent Fred and Abe after me. But Jim Hull not only saw me get the engineer's report, he saw the person who fired that gun and killed Cole Nicoll. So you killed him to shut his mouth."

Veins stood out on Masterson's forehead, thick cords pulsed in his throat and his face purpled. He was shouting, "No, no! You don't understand! I didn't kill… kill anybody. Jim Hull isn't dead!"

"As dead as a salt mackerel!" the Parson snapped. "And don't choke up on the word kill!"

"As God is my witness, I never killed anyone in my life!"

"Nerts!"

"Listen, you gotta believe me! Good God, why should I k-kill? I'll admit I was after Lake Manuelo. I tried to keep Cullen from getting the shares before he realized how valuable the property was, but I had nothing to do with the m-murder of Cole Nicoll. Nothing, I tell you!"

Again the Parson smiled ruefully. "You forgot old man Hull."

Masterson's voice was clotted. "I don't know anything about him. I didn't know he was dead until you told me a minute ago."

"But you found out from him that I had the engineer's report."

Masterson's eyes did things in his head.

"You've been pretty smooth," said the Parson quietly. "How did you find out about Manuelo?"

Masterson choked. "That was back in New York. Gaynor came to Cole Nicoll and told him all about it. Nicoll was skeptical at first. It was I who persuaded him to send the engineer to make a survey."

"And Nicoll sent you here to Cariba to watch Sue, didn't he? Oh, I've read your reports. They were just to blind Nicoll to your real job down here." His voice cut like a whip. "Then if you didn't kill Nicoll and Hull, you know who did!"

Masterson's face whitened slowly, his lips opened and stayed apart.

The Parson said, "Who has the room next to this one?"

"I—I don't know what you mean."

"Well, there's a guy lying on the bed in there." The Parson jerked his left thumb to indicate the connecting door. "He's tied hand and foot and gagged. And he looks a hell of a lot like Tom Cullen!"

"I… Cullen! No, no! It can't be!"

"It is!" said a voice behind the Parson.

The Parson didn't stir. He had heard the lock click back a split second before but he had waited. A gun bored into his back.

He said, "O.K., Sue. I was wondering how long you could stay behind that door without coming in."

"Don't move!" Her voice was shrill, ragged with a tinge of hysteria.

But he turned very deliberately. She did not fire. The cold contempt in his half-lidded eyes seemed to paralyze her. She shrank back a half-step. A little Webley revolver was in her fist but it was pointing downward.

"A connecting door!" The Parson's voice cut her like a rapier. "You and Masterson, huh? Very, very intimate. And all the time back in New York your husband was getting reports from Masterson. He was supposed to be spying on you but instead you played house together."

Color crept slowly back into her cheeks. All at once she

looked defiant. "I don't have to explain to you. What do you know about a woman's heart?"

The Parson grinned crookedly. "You've been a fool, Sue. Now you'll both hang. I don't think there's any prejudice against hanging a woman in Cariba."

The fingers of her left hand flew to her mouth, choking off an outcry. Her eyes dilated wide with sudden horror. The hand moved upwards and the back of it pressed against her forehead. She swayed a little. Then, breathlessly, "George! He's the only person who knows. I heard everything he said through the door. He was probably lying about the police. George, that plane you said you chartered— We can fly to—"

"You won't get far," the Parson clipped. "Radio is faster than your plane. You'll be brought back both of you to face murder charges. You'll hang...."

"George, don't listen to him! Do something! George, as you love me—"

"Yeah!" Masterson's voice was a piping squeak. "You got me into this. Now I'm getting out while I can. Listen!" He took a breath, swallowed air. "I had nothing to do with the murders, see? *My* hands are clean! She killed her husband. She—"

"George!"

"Ah, you make me sick! I won't hang. I'll tell the cops the truth."

"George!"

There was a new inflection in her voice that stilled him. He looked at her in utter fright.

He mouthed, choked on his words. "Sue—don't—I—"

The Webley in her hand was steady. The shots crashed once, twice, almost together. Masterson slammed backward. His lips contorted. There was a look of ghastly incredulousness on his face. His eyes were terrible; they were fixed on her face, the eyes of one already dead. Only he was not dead yet, but dying, dying in agony.

In the sudden lull, the Parson twisted to one side and flung himself at her wrist. Her gun hand twitched as he caught hold in a pure reflex movement. Flame blinded him as gun-powder sprayed into his eyes. Hot lead seared his shoulder, plowing through the cloth of his black coat, and hot blood bathed his arm. He had her gun. He twisted viciously, but she clawed at him, screaming like a mad woman, scratching at his face with the nails of her left hand.

He jerked away, pulled her with him. She tore away from his grasp. He heard her gun fall to the floor. But there was heavier thunder reverberating in the room—the sound of Masterson's .38. There were three shots close together. Then it was very quiet. The Parson marveled that Masterson had found strength before he died to kill her.

The Parson dug at his eyes with the knuckles of his fists. Slowly vision came back as the shocked optic nerve began once more to function. Sue Nicoll lay crumpled on the floor, one hand under her left breast, the other outflung, like a child sleeping.

It was a full minute before he became aware that there was a great deal of shouting in the corridor and that someone was knocking on the door. It was hard for him to tear his eyes away from her. He moved like a sleepwalker to the door, shivering despite himself. He was amazed to find himself so unnerved.

The man who had been knocking on the door fell back when the Parson opened it. "Wha-what happened?" he stammered.

The Parson stared at him. "Happened?" he repeated, steeling his face for the lie. "George Masterson was the man who murdered Cole Nicoll. I forced him to confess. Nicoll's wife heard him and came in with a gun. She shot him. He shot her. That's all."

He turned abruptly and went into the room where Cullen lay, straining at his bonds. He knelt over him and untied him. When he unfastened the handkerchief from about his mouth, Cullen exhaled with a loud, "Whew!"

The Parson said, "You heard everything that went on in there?" he jerked his thumb toward the other room.

Cullen nodded, wide-eyed.

"You heard what I told them at the door?"

"Yes."

"Which story are you going to tell the cops?"

Cullen nodded somberly. "You can trust me. I'll say it was Masterson all the way through. I'll insist that he was the person I saw murdering poor Jim Hull. I'll say I followed him to his room and accused him to his face; that he slugged me unexpectedly and tied me up. That's the way you want it, isn't that so?"

THE HIGH-HULLED *MARINOCO* throbbed a whistle in accompaniment to the tootling band. Slowly she slipped away from the pier, motors drumming. Dave Gaynor was up on the deck, waving. He looked out upon the neat geometrical arrangement of white houses and red roofs. He turned away abruptly from the rail as if the sight were more than he could stand. The Parson grunted something under his breath, but when he looked at Cullen beside him there was a tight grin on his lips.

The Parson's left shoulder was bulky under his coat with bandages. The wound still pained him, but his grin was one of relief.

"Ah, me," he drawled. "Love's wonderful. That kid will worship the mental image of Sue the rest of his life. And to think she used his gun to kill Nicoll, knowing the police would find Gaynor's motive."

Cullen's lips tightened. "But in many ways she was a wonderful woman."

"You're telling me." He swung in beside Cullen's long stride. "So you saw her do the job on old man Hull, huh?"

"Yes."

"Tell me about it."

Cullen was silent for a long minute. "Hull had told me he had seen you pick up Nicoll's wallet. And he had hinted he had seen a lot more. I mentioned it to Sue. It was only much later that I understood what he meant—that he had seen the murderer, too. Hull had seen Sue enter the deserted house before the boat docked; seen her leave after the shots were fired. Sue knew he knew. So I went to Hull's house to talk to him. Someone was there already. I tiptoed up to a window. One pane was broken so I heard what was said.

"Sue was trying to buy him off so he'd keep quiet, but the crazy old man jeered at her. He told her he was going to the police when he thought the time was ripe. I suppose childishly he was proud to be the possessor of so important a secret. Then… she picked up the bottle and crowned him—hard….

"I was so stunned, I couldn't move or make an outcry. Before I was fully aware of what was happening, she had slipped out. I went into the house to help Hull, but he was beyond help."

"You dropped your cigar there."

"I suppose so. I was dazed. I stumbled out of there, half crazy myself. Only after I'd walked for a long time did I think of going up to see Sue. Going to the police never occurred to me, not even after I knew that she had killed Cole."

"Yeah," said the Parson dryly, "people in love do funny things."

"Sue murdered because she was in love," said Cullen. "Cole would never have given her a divorce. She knew that and saw no other way to get rid of him. And when I went up to her room and told her I'd seen her commit murder, she snatched a book-end and struck me."

The Parson sighed audibly. "And all because of a tin-horn sport like Masterson. He didn't give a hoot for her. All he cared about was using her to get close to Nicoll so he could grab off the Lake Manuelo stock."

"The people you fall in love with," said Cullen bitterly, "you don't pick them; it just happens. Like a flood—like an earthquake."

"Yeah."

"By the way, Gaynor cut you a slice of the money I paid him for his stock, didn't he?"

"Yeah. Why?"

"Oh, I was just wondering how you were fixed for dough. How much did you get?"

The Parson looked pleased with himself. "We settled for fifty grand. I figured I earned that much." He laughed. "You got yourself a lot of pitch for your money."

They walked on in silence. "There's still one thing I want to know," said Cullen after a while.

"Go ahead."

"This business of your covering up Sue and fixing it for Masterson to take all the blame."

"He was cold meat anyhow," the Parson said. "And, well, I used to like her a lot once. Then there was Dave Gaynor. It would kill him if he ever found out the truth."

"But weren't you in love with her, too? Even a little bit?"

The Parson looked at him, dark eyes glinting with amusement.

"Me, in love? Hell, that's something for you to figure out!"

Cullen said, "I said it once and I'll say it again: For a crook, you're a funny kind of crook."

Delayed Snatch

The Parson cracks his Luger at double-crossers

THE MONTECITA CLUB on upper Leeward Road is the one spot in Cariba where you can find half the male population on any given night. Its horseshoe cabaret floor is always crowded, always noisy with conversation in three or four tongues, alive with the clinking of bottles and glasses and the scraping of chairs and feet; the blurred rhythms and dark, primitive gourd rattlings of the *cubañola* orchestra. It is a place meant for pleasure.

Once each week a ringside table was occupied by the beefy British resident-General and his stringy, horse-toothed British wife. Caste lines are lax in Cariba, "the little Paris of the Caribbean," and Lee Fong, the plump smiling Chinese proprietor of the Montecita, stood at the glass curtain which is the street entrance and warmly shook the hand of each patron—black, yellow, white and the in-between color variants.

A warm landward breeze was setting the glass curtain into gentle motion that night in May when it was thrust aside and the Parson entered, dainty as a doll in his suit of midnight black.

Lee Fong was not the person to lose his composure but his smile was merely mechanical and polite when he said in his high-pitched, cackling voice, "Much welcome, my goo' fliend."

The Parson gave a harsh, dry laugh. "Hi yuh, Confusius."

He stood running his somber-lidded eyes the length and breadth of the circular room. He first saw Soo Gee, Fong's bodyguard. Soo Gee was looking upstairs. Lee Fong ran gambling rooms upstairs above the cabaret. The Parson had played once or twice. An adept at games of chance, he had caught Lee's croupier switching dice. The Chinaman had smilingly fired the croupier but glinting shafts of malignity shone in his eyes whenever he beheld the Parson. Lee Fong had never forgiven.

A man half rose from a booth far in the rear and beckoned. The Parson strolled toward him with that light, sidling gait of his. When he reached the booth, he said, " 'Lo, Jake," in an offhand deep voice and hung his hat on a hook.

Jake Mund was nervous and inwardly excited. He lighted a cigarette, holding the match with trembling fingers. He was a compact, lithe, handsome man with crisp blond hair. His thin, well formed wrists slapped leanly against his starched white cuffs; his strong fingers, ivoried by nicotine, were eloquent in motion.

The Parson had known him back in New York when Mund had driven an armor-plated, bullet-proof-glass Rolls for Carl

Dorn. It was a hard mob that Dorn ran but somehow they couldn't knock the innate honesty and decency out of young Jake Mund. He merely drove the car and the dirt around him did not even touch his trouser cuffs.

The Parson, in those days, had been running the gaming tables for the Vince Guard-Poggi syndicate. The Parson's nickname had come with him from New York. He had acquired it by his precise and almost gentle manner. It had nothing to do with the incredible speed of his draw.

There had always been something about Mund that had attracted the Parson. Once Mund had tried to break out of the rackets and the Parson had half-heartedly tried to help him with a stake but Carl Dorn had cracked down and forced

Mund back into line. That was the last the Parson had seen of him in many years until he had turned up in Cariba with a wife. The Parson was in Cariba because he had crossed his gang and both they and the police were interested in him.

Mund sat across from the Parson, his lips moving without opening, the corners twitching. Presently he said, "You'll have to lend me ten grand. I've got to get out of town with Nina in a hurry. Dorn's gang have found me here and they've put the finger on me."

"Hm," said the Parson. "Tell me about it. Does Nina know?"

There was a bottle of brandy on the table and two glasses. The Parson poured drinks. He downed his but Mund merely toyed with his glass, turning it round and round.

"You're the only person in this town I can turn to," he said. "I ain't scared for myself—it's Nina. She knows nothing yet." His voice hardened. "Lee Fong's on to something. He's had us shadowed for a week."

The Parson was surprised. "What's Fong got to do with it?"

"Hell, how should I know? They shouldn't have a connection with him but somehow they have. The whole thing's driving me nuts. How about it? Can you let me have the money?"

"The dough's O.K.," the Parson said crisply. "But why so much?"

"I got to get far so no one will ever find us again. That's why! I haven't a cent to my name!" His fists clenched. "Me, I'm a sweet man. I live off what Nina makes singing here. Isn't that funny? Me, livin' off a girl!"

"Nina don't mind," the Parson interrupted. "Forget it. Who of Dorn's crowd traced you?"

Jake Mund's voice cracked with bitterness. "Dorn himself

and Alex Morton and a wren named Eva. She's plain poison."

"Don't know her. Morton's name is familiar, though."

"He's Carl's pulse man. Eva is Carl's woman."

"Oh. Well, look, liquor's no good in a glass."

Mund laughed. "I ain't scared, see, just rattled. Liquor won't help; I tried it. It just feels hot and hard inside. Gosh, it's ten o'clock. I come here every night and wait for ten o'clock."

"Why?"

"To throw curses at myself. Y'see, Nina goes on in five minutes. That's when I begin cursing. God, I'm a heel! Making her sing in a cabaret owned by a Chink, exposing her to danger. You don't know the kind of girl Nina is. She's different, see? She ain't used to a life in a cabaret. Why, she used to have twenty servants waiting hand and foot...."

"Button your fool mouth!"

There was such savagery in the Parson's voice that Mund subsided, limp against the back of the bench. He rubbed a hand over his forehead, smiled weakly. "For about a second I thought I was going to blow my top."

"I'll help all I can," the Parson said.

But inwardly he was revolving the whole thing in his head. A boy and girl get into trouble and there he is ready to step in and play godfather. And a lot of guys thought he was tough! He had thought so himself. His shoulder twitched with irritability.

Then another thought crowded out the first. Carl Dorn was no kill-crazy mobster but a business man. He wouldn't be down in Cariba merely for his health. Something more was involved, something big. What? The Parson mulled over possibilities. Well, anyway it would be something involving a lot of money; that was a safe bet. A lot of money....

The Parson's eyes narrowed speculatively; he fingered a cigarette. A lot of money.... Why not cut in? Jake Mund, wittingly or unwittingly, was offering him the chance. His eyes glittered and a mocking half-smile touched his lips: perhaps he'd jockey himself into a position where he'd be able to outsmart Carl Dorn. The idea appealed to him, a crook outmaneuvering a crook. Yeah, he told himself, why not help Jake Mund, especially when he could help himself at the same time!

"Parson," said Jake, cutting in on his thoughts, "you're swell!"

"Huh? I can get along without the soft soap." He leaned forward. "Listen, once. I ain't got the dough on me but I can get it, say midnight."

Jake nodded eagerly. "Then bring it to the cottage."

"What about your getaway?"

"That's all arranged."

"How?"

"A motor launch will be waiting at the fruit pier. The guy who owns it said we'd make Port of Spain by morning. From there we get a liner."

The Parson sat silent a moment. Then he said, "Look, when you broke from Carl Dorn, you broke clean, didn't you?"

"Yeah. Yeah, sure I did." But Jake's voice lacked conviction.

"I mean there was no reason for a kickback, was there?"

"Of course not. Gosh, Parson, I know you got reason to be suspicious but you'll have to trust me, see? I can't—"

"Why did Dorn follow you down here?"

Jake's face was working. He leaned wearily across the table. "Parson, listen to me. I can't tell you. I—well, I can't, is all. If that means you won't help me," his lips came together in a firm line, "that's my hard luck. I'll see it through alone somehow."

Sitting there, white-faced, a desperate shimmer came into his eyes, his fists clenched and his jaw muscles knotted.

The Parson's chin was sunk to his chest. "O.K., boy. I was only trying to make conversation. Forget it. I'm with you. But," his voice was low, hushed, "what are you going to tell Nina?"

Jake Mund groaned. "I'll tell her something; I haven't thought it out yet." He broke off speaking suddenly; his gaze whipped across the room. "She's coming out for her first number."

She was fragile and pale with luminous black eyes beneath a coronet of braided black hair. She drifted across the floor almost shyly, her hands limply clasped before her.

All at once the noisy cabaret became hushed as a cathedral. Her face was nun-like in its reserve; she looked about her with a combined wonder, exultancy and sadness. Then she began to sing.

Her voice was not strong; it was even meager; but it had a touching almost child like inflection of purity that chained her listeners. No matter how tawdry her surroundings, she brought with her the armor of simplicity and innocence. Her fresh treble recreated the smoke-filled Montecita into a cottage or a flowery lakeside retreat. Her wide-spaced haunting eyes were open with the magic of her voice as if she could follow with them the waves of music, dissolving and recurring with the whisper of the orchestra.

Suddenly there was a commotion at one of the packed tables. A man stood up as though with his action he were breaking a spell. The Parson had a glimpse of him—a tall, white-haired man of about sixty-five, the rigid bar of his white mustache trembling with the tremble of his lips. Instantly, a shorter, much younger man, with sandy hair, who looked vaguely familiar to the Parson, stood up beside him and said something. The older mustached man shook his head violently and strode forward.

The girl stopped singing. Her face lost color; she took small retreating steps. Jake Mund leaped to his feet, dived toward the rear of the cabaret. The Parson saw his hand snake up toward the master switch.

The place was plunged into darkness. People became frightened. Feet pounded. As the Parson moved out from his table, he was caught in a milling throng. Minutes later, the lights went on. Lee Fong himself had clicked the switch. His arms were upraised and he was bawling like a banshee, "Evlybolly him happy! No mo' tlubbul! Evlybolly him dance!"

He signaled the orchestra to play. People quieted down. The Parson looked about. Jake Mund and Nina were not to be seen. He remembered that there was a back door to the cabaret. The sandy-haired man was gone, too. Then, with curiosity, he watched the tall, white-haired man speak to Lee Fong. Lee Fong was smiling, he bowed profusely but he looked troubled. At length, he took the arm of the old man and piloted him to his tiny private office. The door closed.

The Parson squinted at the door, wondering who the tall man with the white military mustache might be. He shrugged and strode out.

A TRIANGULAR SHAFT of moonlight broke through the leaves, slashing the Parson's body from shoulder to hip. It left his chiseled features in semi-darkness but showed up his black suit and black tie in striking relief against the brightness of his scrupulous white shirt. His shadow was firmly stenciled on the powdery white coral dust of the roadway as with black ink.

It was ten minutes past midnight. The town of Cariba was asleep. Here and there through the close-woven roof formed by intertwining mango and guava trees, a sudden shaft of moonlight struck down. Under the leafy tunnel nothing moved. The branches themselves were never quite at rest. The warm breeze traversed them by slow vibrations, breaking into ripples through the leaves.

There was just the one house at the end of the straggly street. Two hundred yards beyond it were the phosphorescent waters of the Caribbean, endlessly slapping against the sunken piles of the tarred-wood docks. The house was a one-story bungalow built on stilts which were concealed by rotting latticework.

Thick, rope-like vines reached from the ground to the roof; flowers, fragile and white, crowned their highest point like very delicately wrought diadems.

The Parson knew the house well. On a number of occasions he had accepted the hospitality of Nina and Jake Mund. It had been for him a sort of oasis for his loneliness, a refuge in his exile. The two young kids had made him welcome, had granted him a niche in their lives.

Shades were drawn to the sills of the three front windows, cutting off the light from within, but themselves glowing orange. The Parson had a fleeting impression, not of catastrophe, but of ominous danger. He could not explain the feeling but he did not try to shrug it off. He felt the ten thousand dollars he was going to loan Jake Mund. Then he reached under his coat and transferred his Luger from the shoulder holster to his pocket. From another pocket he took a handkerchief and studiously wiped his fingers dry. It was a meaningless gesture but characteristic of him. He liked a dry finger on the trigger of his gun.

Then he walked down the brick walk toward the front steps. On either side of the walk was a patch of lawn. Directly below the porch grew a stunted banana plant. Its broad, shirred leaves, mottled with reflected traceries of leafage, were bright under the silver-white glare of the tropical full moon, which sometimes is almost as luminous as sun. All else surrounding the plant was in darkness. The effect was that of an intense spotlight.

The Parson stepped up on the tiny front porch and the harsh murmur of a voice reached him. Then another voice cut in. The Parson rapped sharply on the door.

The murmur of voices was louder now, but nobody came to the door. The Parson turned the knob, flung the door wide and went in.

He nearly collided with a red-haired handsome woman in a suit of white flannel who apparently was coming to answer his knock. The Parson had never seen her before. She had a .45 pocket automatic in her hand. Her hand was small and white and the gun looked enormous in it.

She stepped back, pointing the gun at him. Her eyes were wide but not frightened. Her eyes were bright green with strange gold flecks in the pupils. Indecision and a sort of puzzlement was written in the lines of her creased forehead. She was waiting for his move.

The Parson said sharply, "Put that gat away!"

The tawny flecks in her eyes glinted, but she lowered the gun to her side. The Parson moved quickly, grabbed her wrist. She offered no resistance; the gun clattered to the floor.

"That's better, sweetheart. If I should call the cops in, you wouldn't want them to catch you with a gun." He stopped picked it up. It had a comfortable, balanced feel.

Wrinkles appeared and disappeared on her smooth forehead. "Oh, then you're not the cops?"

"Did you think I was?"

"Nothing less. That's why I didn't shoot. Who are you, mister?"

"Are the Munds at home?"

"I think they're out for the evening," she said. Then she smiled, showing white, even teeth. "Yeah, they're *out* for the evening. I asked who you were, runt."

"I heard voices a little while ago—men's voices, not a woman. Where did the Munds go? And don't call me runt."

"You go to hell, runt."

His hand struck out like a rapier flash. It didn't look like a hard blow but all his fingers were traced in red on her cheek. She went back, brought up against the side wall. He went past her and looked in the open door on the right. She was gasping for breath, muttering behind him, but he paid no attention.

A man lay face down on the rug. He was a fat man, broad-beamed and short. A couple of chairs near him were over-turned. The rug under him was twisted. The dark flooring was marred by scratches.

The top of his head was a mass of blood. Some blood had dripped on the rug, directly beneath his head. One arm was pillowed under his head and the other was outflung at right angles to his body. A carved mahogany stick, such as the natives sold in Cariba's water front markets, lay close to him. Short black hairs stuck to the end of it. The hair was plastered with blood.

The Parson walked into the room, knelt and turned the body over. It was Lee Fong, the owner of the Montecita. Lee Fong was dead.

Something creaked. It was a door opening. The Parson turned his head sidewise without moving his body. A thick-set, broad-shouldered man in a white linen suit came in. The suit was dark with sweat under the armpits, though the rest of it looked freshly laundered. The man was smiling, jovial.

"Parson," he chortled. "Parson, of all people! Remember me?"

"You're Carl Dorn. I remember you."

"A small world, eh? A small world."

Another man came through the door. It was the white-haired old man the Parson had seen at the Montecita. He was followed by a thin, eagle-nosed individual with a gun in his hand. The white-haired man's shoulders drooped wearily. He looked like a thoroughly cowed and beaten old man. His was the whitest face the Parson had ever seen. The thin, eagle-nosed man standing beside him wriggled his gun but he did not point it at anything or anyone in the room. He did not look at the Parson.

Eagle Nose growled, "Who's the clerical looking gent?"

Carl Dorn laughed coarsely. "Hah! You took the words right outa my mouth. He sure looks like a peaceable parson, don't he? Well, that's what they call him—the Parson. Hey, Parson, meet one of my boys, Alex Morton."

The white-haired old man looked as if he were about to say something. Alex Morton took a step closer to him. The old man looked at him, did not speak.

The red-haired woman swaggered in, pointed a finger at the Parson, bawled, "That son-of-a —— whammed me one!"

Carl Dorn scowled sharply. Beady eyes regarded the Parson. Then the smile of joviality returned to his face. He said, "Don't count that one, Eva. The Parson's really a gentleman. He was one of the boys in New York."

When she began to curse, Dorn put fingers in his ears. "Such language!" And when she stopped for breath, "That's about enough, you!"

She looked at him with her green, gold-flecked eyes but subsided.

The Parson said, "Excuse me for pointing but there's a dead guy on the floor."

Dorn laughed again. "Hah! So there is. So there is."

"How come?"

Dorn said, "Well, I guess it was self-defense. The fool Chink came at you and you gave him a couple of hard ones on the beano. With a little rehearsing Alex, Eva and me can tell the story that way."

The Parson's eyes merely widened a trifle. "Don't you think I'd need the old gent here as a witness, too?"

Dorn made a gesture with his hand. "Why, I imagine that could be arranged."

"Why not ask him?"

"He can't talk so good."

"Hm. Who is he?"

"Just a pal."

The Parson let the .45 he had taken from the woman slap against his trouser leg. "Correct me if I am wrong, but I am under the impression that this house is occupied by a guy named Jake Mund and his wife, Nina."

"You call the turn every time," said Dorn.

"You wouldn't happen to know why they're not here, would you?"

"That's where you got me, pal. Yessir! I'd sure like to know where Jake Mund and his wife are, myself."

The Parson shot him a quick look. "Why did you follow Jake Mund down here?" He added quickly, "I'm just asking for my own sake. If he ain't strictly on the up and up, to hell with him."

"Why, Jake's fine," Dorn said soothingly. "We just dropped in for a kinda social visit. Jake's fine."

The Parson shot him a sharp, biting glance and abruptly changed his line of attack. "Where does Lee Fong tie in?"

Dorn looked blank. "Who?"

The Parson pointed impatiently to the dead man.

"Oh, him. The Chink. Well, look my friend, I don't know." He looked genuinely puzzled. "I'm just damned if I know."

The white-haired old man took a deep breath, said quickly, "The poor Chinaman was simply slaughtered. When I came in and found him murdered—ugh! Only about an hour and a half ago, I was talking to him in his office in that cabaret. I promised him five hundred dollars if he would give me the address of this place. He wanted ten thousand to guarantee that no harm would come to Nina. I said I'd give him five thousand. But I didn't know that he'd be killed."

"Who killed him?" the Parson snapped.

The old man glanced at Dorn meaningfully. "When I came in, he was already dead.

"Go on."

"These two men were in the house. Upstairs."

"Alex," said Dorn quietly.

Alex said, "Yeah," and turned cold eyes on the old man. "How many times we gotta tell yuh we had nothin' to do with the Chink. Shoot off your mouth again and I'll plant my knucks on your kisser."

The eyes of the white-haired man flamed but he said no more, as though in fear. But not fear of physical punishment. The Parson sensed that somehow without knowing why.

The Parson said, quite dispassionately, "You lousy punks!"

"Now, now, Parson," Dorn said placatingly.

"Tough guys, aren't you? Yeah, with an old man. And you know what he's aimin' to say—that you murdered the Chink."

"Don't say that, pal!" Dorn protested. "We had nothing to do with it. We come in and there he was—cold meat. Just like I'm telling you."

"The British cops won't see that as an answer."

Dorn laughed nastily and Alex Morton said, "This guy needs a lot of slammin' around."

"As a matter of fact," Dorn told him, "he don't slam so good. He's tough like rubber. He bounces back at you."

"Oh yeah? One bounce'll be all he'll get!"

"Ah, forget it. We're friends! We're goin' to help the Parson, not pick a fight. Ain't that right, Parson?"

"I'll toss a coin to see if I can believe you or not."

"Kidding won't help." Dorn made a sucking sound with his lips as if in commiseration; a frozen-fish smile appeared on his face. His eyes, though, were hooded, glittering, and he said levelly, "You're in a jam, Parson."

"Nice of you to remind me. But I can't seem to remember—what kind of a jam?"

Dorn spread his hands in a gesture of acceptance. "Well, you killed the Chink. Just one of those things, I suppose. Too bad, too."

"What's too bad?"

"Too bad you whacked the poor departed Chink with that mahogany walking stick. The trouble with you, old pal, you don't know your own strength. Now most times you hit a guy, he goes down and that's all. He's down maybe ten minutes, maybe even half an hour. But he gets up. He may have a head-ache or something but that's all."

The Parson gave a harsh, dry laugh. "You must be soft in the head."

Dorn was purring, "Self-defense, though, will put you in the clear."

"Talk sense!"

The frozen-fish smile was full of cunning, of malice, of evil. Dorn nodded his head solemnly. "Self-defense. That's our story. Yeah. We'll stick by you. These limey cops can't be too bright."

"Listen, you damned ghoul! You can't hang such a crude frame on me."

Dorn spread his hands indulgently. "Self-defense. You wait and see."

"You mean I'll see *if* I wait," the Parson banged out in a grim, menacing voice. "To hell with you. You think I'll be standing still while you pin the kill on me? Not while I'm conscious."

"We," said Dorn, "will attend to that part of it."

The woman had been sidling close along the wall toward the Parson. She was only a foot or so behind him. All the time Dorn had been talking, she had been moving by inches. Whipping his head about, the Parson saw the leather thong twisted about her hand. With his sudden motion, the thong leaped like a live thing from her hand. At the end of it was a weighted leather sap. The woman handled it with the elan of a virtuoso.

Mid-air, it changed direction as the Parson dodged. He didn't dodge enough. A blow on the crown of his head seemed to split it wide open. The .45 in his hand boomed unexpectedly in response to the convulsive jerk of his whole body. But since by that time he was traveling in the general direction of the floor, the slug went wide.

He heard the woman's voice as from far off. "That's for the slap, runt."

Alex, the eagle-nosed, leaped on him from behind and tore the gun from his grasp. They didn't seem to think he had another gun on him. He lay on the floor, nostrils wide, pumping breath, waiting to summon enough strength to get at his gun.

Dorn said complacently, "Nice going, Eva."

"Yeah. These big gun boys, they're always suckers for a sap."

Dorn came over, prodded the Parson with his foot. He was laughing as at a huge joke known only to himself. But it wasn't a pleasant laugh.

The Parson looked up at him as if the effort hurt. He said, "The laugh's on my side."

"Yeah?"

"Yeah. Look at the window behind you."

Eva yelled. Eagle-nose Alex looked white. Dorn jerked his head about. His yell was louder than Eva's.

The middle porch window had been raised and the drawn shade lifted aside. The Parson had been looking straight at it past the others. A slant-eyed Chinaman stood in the window with a gun in his fist. The Parson recognized Soo Gee; he had seen him at the Montecita before, Lee Fong's bodyguard.

The shade whirred up with a hoarse rattle. Soo Gee didn't say anything. He didn't have to; the gun in his fist, the implacable expression in his face were both eloquent.

Alex jerked up the .45 he had snatched from the Parson. A shot boomed. Glass tinkled musically, showered to the floor. The Parson dug his right hand into his coat pocket and fired through the cloth. Soo Gee's gun cut loose.

Alex shivered, dug his left hand into his groin. Two more shots burst forth as he started to crumple to the floor. The Parson jerked his gun out, free of the pocket. Something hit him a terrific blow in the shoulder, paralyzing the arm. It was Eva's efficient little sap. The gun spun out of his hand, hit the baseboard of the wall, skidded across the floor.

Dorn was behind a chair, a gun in his hand, snapping shots at the window. Soo Gee suddenly went down; there was not a sound out of him.

Powder smoke made the air thick, gaseous. In the sudden stunned silence, the Parson thought he could hear the insects outside in the still tropic night.

He lay perfectly still, feigning death. Carl Dorn was top dog-now. Soon the Parson heard footsteps, then Eva's voice, "The damn Chink's dead. You got him clean in the forehead, Carl."

Dorn said, "The yellow punk was layin' for us. He thought we'd killed this Lee Fong. Bet he was workin' for this Fong guy."

"Yeah. Watch the major, Carl. He's got the fidgets."

"Oke," came Dorn's voice. "You scram, major.' Forget what you saw. Forget everything. We'll get in touch with you."

There was a muffled sound of assent. Then Dorn's voice again, "And don't forget the price, two hundred grand. Cash on the line."

"You will get your money, sir."

"Oke. Now flit. A word to the cops and you know what'll happen."

"I will not breathe a syllable."

A door opened and shut close to the Parson. Footsteps hurried out in the hall. The street door opened and shut.

The Parson heard Eva say harshly, "Alex stopped a cupla fast ones. He's croaked." But her tone of voice was merely informational. "Hey, the Parson looks dead, too!" She poked him with her foot.

"Yeah," said Dorn carelessly. "He musta stopped one of my bullets."

The Parson lay quiet, breathing imperceptibly.

Dorn went on: "We got the major buffaloed anyway."

Eva said, "Say, I wonder who did croak this Lee Fong. Maybe it was Jake Mund. He was here sometime tonight, all right, he and that doll-face wife of his. The bedroom upstairs is topsy-turvy, clothes and things lyin' about, like he and the wife packed a bag in a hurry."

There was a shrill whistle somewhere. Then another, answering it.

"Cops!" said Dorn. "Let's blow, Eva. Jeeze, I wish we knew where Jake Mund and Nina are. Boy, I'd sure like to put my hands on them!"

Eva smirked archly. "The major thinks we got 'em."

"Yeah, that's almost as good as havin' 'em, if he'll kick through with the dough. Jeez, what a mess! First, we gotta find this Lee

Fong dead, then Jake and Nina gone and on top of that, the Parson barges in!"

"You afraid of him?" Eva asked scornfully.

"Hell, not when he's dead I ain't. Too bad about Alex, though."

"Yeah? What's bad about a two-way split, 'stead of three?"

Dorn gasped, then laughed shortly. "I'm damned if you don't beat all for brains and guts, kiddo! Two-way split, huh?" His voice sounded troubled again. "But what about the tipster? You know...."

"Him?" Eva spat. "What in hell's he done?"

"Yeah. We'll handle him. Well, let's get going."

The Parson heard footsteps running out of the hall. A door slammed. For about a second he lay as still as before. Then an eye slyly opened. He saw he was alone. His gun lay across the room from him. He stepped over the still form of Alex, retrieved it, then got his hat and clapped it on his head. The shrill whistle got louder. Footsteps were pounding in the street. He went through a back door and stumbled through a dark kitchen. He was surprised to find a back door there unlocked.

Voices were shouting at the front of the house as he plunged through a tiny square of garden. He stepped over a low picket fence and reeled dunkenly down an unpaved back alley. Silver-white moonbeams chased him. He slipped fast into the gloom of the shadows.

THE FRUIT PIER was at the other end of town. But the Parson did not use a cab; he walked. Twice he had the feeling that he was being tailed but when he stopped short and turned about, there was no one to be seen. He moved warily. The pain was not yet out of his head.

Only one boat was tied to the pier. It bobbed gently against the swell, straining against the ropes. There was a pleasant odor of tar. Lights hung fore and aft. It wasn't a big boat but it looked as if it could sleep six or eight persons. Its bow lines were sharp, betokening speed. A man was pacing the foredeck, smoking a pipe.

The Parson leaped nimbly aboard, forged past empty boxes piled along the rail. The man looked at him placidly. He was a mulatto, more white than black. His face was large, ruddy in the cheeks, deeply tanned and wrinkled at the corner of either eye. His broad mouth uncurled slowly in a smile as he took the pipe from his mouth.

The Parson said, "Hello. I'm lookin' for the skipper who was to have taken a young couple to Port of Spain." The man's expression did not change. "Brother, you're lookin' straight full and at him now." His voice was a rumbling, dreamy baritone.

"Swell. My name's Ormond. I'm a friend of the young couple."

The tanned face beamed. "Glad to know you. Maybe you can tell me when they is comin' 'board. They's overdue maybe an hour, maybe more.

"Oh, so they didn't show up."

"That's correct, mister. I been waitin' on 'em."

"Maybe they decided not to go," said the Parson.

"Mebbe you're right."

"Well, if they do come, will you tell 'em to get in touch with me at the Victoria? That's my hotel."

"Glad to, mister."

"Thanks, Cap'n—"

"Deerman is the name."

"Cap'n Deerman. How do you make a livin' out of your boat?"

"Little fishin'. Take out parties."

"And dope runnin, huh?"

"Fishin's nice out beyond the headlands. You come around some time, mister, and I'll show you where the tarpon run."

A cabin door opened and a flood of yellow light flitted across the deck surface. A handsome, full-bosomed young negress stood in the doorway, applying powder industriously to her cheeks from a flat silver compact. As she came toward them, the Parson was aware that her dress reeked of gardenia perfume.

Captain Deerman said, "Tha's my woman. Narcissa, go 'long in and fetch out the rum bottle. You like a drink, Mr. Ormond?"

"Sure."

The woman sauntered out, swinging shapely hips. She returned in a few minutes with a plaited straw demijohn and a couple of glasses. The man held the glasses while she poured the liquor. He handed one to the Parson. They drank. Deerman grinned dreamily, sucked at the rim of his glass.

"You in trouble, mister?"

"Hell, no!" the Parson snapped.

"Well, you look like you been banged around some." He looked out over the broad expanse of water. "That young couple now, *they* ain't in trouble, is they?"

The Parson lifted his chin, his mouth hardened, his brows drew together. "What makes you ask that?"

"Why, nothin' but idle curiosity." Deerman was undisturbed. "They seemed like nice kids, kinda devoted to each other, like me and Narcissa. I wouldn't see harm come to them for a thousand *pesos!* And I'm a poor man."

The Parson looked at him for a long moment, then drew forth a fat wad of bills and counted off five of them.

"There's a hundred bucks," he said grimly. "Not *pesos,* American money. If you run into them kids, look after 'em."

Deerman beamed, palmed the money. "Shu' will, mister."

"And tell 'em if you see 'em to get in touch with me at my hotel."

"The Victoria, you said. I'll do that." The shadow left the Parson's face. His thin, chiseled features cracked into a tight, lopsided grin. He swung on his heel, caught hold of the pier and hoisted himself up.

" 'Night, mister," came Deerman's voice.

"Good-night," said the Parson.

He turned briefly, saw the handsome young negress stick a shiny, nickel-plated gun back into the bosom of her dress. She had drawn it when she had gone in to fetch the demijohn, held it half-concealed under her armpit when she had poured the drinks. The heady odor of the perfume which saturated her clothing wafted to him briefly, was replaced by the fetid odor of rotted fruit as he paced down the pier toward the street.

Shadows moved away from the dark warehouse, moved with him. The Parson's hand dropped into his coat pocket, closed on the butt of his Luger. A man moved toward him with a bleak sort of smile, casually stopped about ten feet from him.

The Parson stopped, got set, muscles tense and waiting. The man said, "Take your hand off the gun, pal. I'm a friend."

He came into the light of the moon, a tall, thin man, dressed in tan gabardine. He held his hands in front of him, palms upward.

The Parson relaxed. It was the man he had seen in the company of the military looking white-haired old gent in the Montecita.

The man said, "I followed you all the way from Jake Mund's cottage. Carl Dorn and Eva think you're dead but I'm glad you're not. It's a swell night. Mind if I walk with you?"

They walked to the cobbled street, turned in the direction of the flickering lights.

The Parson said, "I didn't catch your name."

"Joel Knight. Maybe you've heard of me."

The Parson turned his head sidewise but kept on walking. After a while he said, "Yeah, I've heard of you. You were a lawyer back in New York last I heard of you."

"Truth is, I still am. This is something of a vacation for me. I'm down here representing Major Hugh Amberly Rowe. He owns a couple of railroads, a lake steamship line and three or four continental bus companies. He pays income tax in six figures."

"That," said the Parson thoughtfully, "would be the old gent with the handlebar mustaches."

"Check. I've wanted to talk to you for some time, Parson."

"So you know my name, too."

Knight grinned indulgently. "Who hasn't heard of the Parson?" He made a sound with his lips. "Umm. Nothing doing on the little boat, huh?"

"What'd you mean?"

"They didn't go aboard the boat, did they?"

The Parson looked at him sidewise without checking stride. "If we're talking of the same people, they didn't."

"We are. Did you like Carl Dorn and li'l' Eva? I thought it was nice that Alex Morton got clipped... the rat. I don't think Carl Dorn is so tough. But Eva, my! She's the guts of the outfit."

"So you were peeking, huh?"

Knight laughed. "Uh-huh. Right through a crack in the drawn shade. I was about to take a hand myself or call copper but that damned Chinese chopper cut loose."

"That," said the Parson grimly, "was Soo Gee, Lee Fong's bodyguard. But don't blame it all on the Yellow Peril. After all, they murdered Lee first."

"Who did?"

The Parson shrugged. "Search me. Maybe Carl Dorn, maybe Eva. And maybe Jake Mund. I'm not good at guessing games. Are you?"

"Lousy."

"Still, I distinctly heard Dorn say that he wondered who had knocked off the Chink, indicating that he hadn't. What about the major?"

"No. Oh, no. Not the major. I was stationed outside the window when he entered the house. Lee Fong was already dead on the floor."

"That leaves Jake Mund," said the Parson.

"And us out in the cold."

"Us?" said the Parson.

"Sure. I'm cutting you into the deal. We can't find Jake Mund and Nina, either of us. We might as well not find them together."

"I could tell more about that if I knew what this was all about."

Knight stopped short, looked keenly at the Parson. "You mean to say you don't know?"

"I'm a friend of Jake's, that's all. But he told me nothing."

"Whew!" Knight blew out his cheeks.

"Surprised?"

"You could bend me in two with a breath of air. And I was blithely cutting you into the deal."

"There's dough in it, huh?"

"Interested? Hell, of course, you are! You got a rep for keeping your eye on the main chance. Always a money player. I suppose I can bank on that. What say? Can you spare a dime's worth of time?"

The Parson said, "What can I get out of it?"

"Maybe about fifty, sixty grand. Maybe more. It'll be a two-way cut."

"I've heard *that* some place before. Shoot!"

"First, you got to promise you're in it with me."

"If I'm in, I'm in."

"Good. I know you don't go back on your word. And I need help. Who do you think Nina Mund is?" And when the Parson remained silent, "Major Hugh Amberly Rowe's only daughter!"

The Parson looked at him.

"Yessir! Nina Rowe's her maiden name. You know who Jake Mund is, you know his connections."

"Yeah. He was with Dorn but the kid's a leveler."

"Maybe so. But that doesn't change the fact that he was planted at Major Rowe's home as a chauffeur by Carl Dorn to kidnap Nina."

Knight looked at the Parson with triumph, the sweat of excitement beading his forehead. The Parson looked at him wide-eyed, too dumbfounded to say anything. But his mind clicked into reverse, went swiftly over the ground. Yes, that explained a great deal. Things slipped into place, were firmly grooved. After a while Knight went on:

"But he didn't kidnap her. The plant went sour on him. He couldn't bring himself to follow out Dorn's orders. He fell in love with the girl. And the girl," he stopped, held the Parson's arm, "went nuts over him! Do you get it? Of all the crazy things to happen, that happened. They went into a love clinch. The day Jake was supposed to have brought her to the hide-out Dorn had prepared, he upped and eloped with her!"

"Where'd you promote all that?" the Parson asked gloomily.

"The whole set-up came out through Carl Dorn. He wasn't in touch with the hide-out, but he took it for granted his orders had been carried out. He demanded five hundred grand from the old major for the safe return of his daughter. That same night the major got a wire from Nina. She and Jake Mund had taken a plane for Mexico, they were married and would Papa forgive. Papa wouldn't. His daughter, heiress to millions, convent-bred, married to a common criminal! He damn near hit the ceiling. When Dorn found out what had happened, he exploded. Both he and the old man were left holding the bag. One lost his daughter and the other the biggest cash haul of his life."

The faintest shadow of a smile wreathed the Parson's lips. "Those kids really had guts," he said. He looked very pleased.

"Puppy love," said Knight scornfully.

"You," said the Parson with finality, "wouldn't know about that. Why didn't the major go to the cops?"

"Because of Dorn. Dorn made him promise to keep it all a

dark secret. Otherwise he threatened to put a man on Nina's trail and have her killed. So the major kept his mouth shut."

"He was a fool."

"Maybe. But he thought a lot of his daughter. He wasn't going to take a chance. Just the same, he moved heaven and earth to find her."

"How'd he finally trace them down here?"

"That's my work," said Knight proudly. "Major Rowe used about six private detective agencies. They all picked up the trail—Vera Cruz, Havana, Montevideo, Buenos Aires, and lost it again. Then I came down here on a vacation cruise. I saw Nina singing at the Montecita. I cabled the major and he hired me, sight unseen."

The Parson frowned. "Then how did Dorn get here?"

Knight shrugged. "Don't know. Maybe he trailed the major."

"I still don't see where there's any dough in this for me."

Knight grinned very slowly, as if reluctantly. He stood still under a Spanish elm. The Parson stopped. Knight whispered:

"You heard Dorn and Eva talking when they thought you'd been killed. Dorn has talked the major into thinking that he's got Nina. You see, Nina and Jake were gone when the major arrived. He doesn't know where they are. And when Dorn said he had them both salted away, the major had to believe him. And two hundred grand—Dorn's price—is pin money to the major. He'd pay a million to get his daughter back safe and sound. So he'll pay Dorn. He won't get his daughter back but he'll pay."

The Parson leaned his face closer. "And what do we do, produce the daughter, my friend, and shake the major down a second time?"

The sense of menace implicit in the Parson's voice got to Knight. His hand shook. "No," he said thickly. "You're too fast. We don't know where the girl is, do we? How could we produce her?"

"Yeah. That's so."

"Of course," said Knight heartily. "Hell, let's stop kidding each other, pal. You know what I mean."

"If there's any kidding, it's not from my side. Suppose you deal me another card."

"Hell, I thought you were quick on the uptake. Here's the layout. Dorn hasn't got the girl but I'm pretty sure he's going to be paid."

"How can you be so sure?"

"Well, I'm not the major's personal adviser for nothing."

"Oh."

"The instant the money changes hands you relieve Dorn of the burden of counting it. Do you get it now?"

"Check. It boils down to a simple hijack." The Parson was silent a moment, thinking. "But why cut me in?"

"Well, I couldn't handle it alone. I've got a clean reputation to uphold. Besides some fancy gun-work will be needed. You've got a rep for work with a gun. Without you I wouldn't get a nickel. With you I can split and still have mine. I'm no hog. What do you say? Are you in?"

The Parson drawled, "I'd be a dope to turn it down."

"Boy, that's talkin'. How about a cab?"

They had reached a main artery. Knight hailed a cab and they climbed in. Knight said, "Drive to Ching's bar." In the cab they talked plans.

But when they reached the bar, the Parson said, "I don't

believe I'm drinking." Under his breath he added, "With you." Aloud he went on, "My face—I can't show such a damaged mugg in a public bar. I'll trot along to my hotel. I'll wait for your call."

Knight nodded. "Boy, we sure make some team—my brains and your gun. That's what I call a combination. We can't lose. Now remember, there'll be a key waiting for you at the desk. You go right up and slip into the closet. I'll leave it to you when to crack out."

"Yeah," said the Parson, "you just leave it to me."

THE PARSON HAD his breakfast sent up to his room at ten the next morning. The one English daily printed in Cariba informed him that two dead Chinamen, Lee Fong and Soo Gee, had been found, one by and one in the cottage occupied by a Jake Mund and his wife, Nina, who was a singer at Lee Fong's Montecita. A third corpse had been discovered, that of an unidentified white man believed to be an American. Soo Gee and the white man had been shot; Lee Fong had been clubbed to death. No motive for the triple killing had been unearthed as yet. But police had sent out an alarm for Mund and his wife who were mysteriously missing.

The Parson spent the day in his room, hovering close to the telephone. He killed a couple of hours cleaning and oiling his gun. He played about fifty games of solitaire. Then he sat at the window, staring out. It was getting dusk. Lights in the street came on. Lights festooned the piers and appeared on the mast-heads of ships riding at anchor in the curved sweep of the harbor.

At last his phone rang. Nervous before, he was instantly calm when he heard Joel Knight's voice.

Knight said, "All set, boy. The payoff is for seven-thirty. Carl Dorn is smart at that. The Pan-American plane leaves for Curacao at eight-ten. He'll be figuring to be aboard that and away before the major tumbles to the fact he's been taken in. You see, Dorn's promised to produce Nina by nine. But of course he can't. The key will be waiting at the desk. I've arranged for the whole transaction to take place in my room. You use the clothes closet near the window."

The phone clicked. The Parson cradled the receiver, thoughtfully stuck a cigarette in his face, lighted it. Then he took a last look at his gun, clapped a hat on his head and went out.

The taxi took him to Knight's hotel, the Royal Palms. At the desk he stopped, said to the clerk:

"Mr. Knight left a key for me."

The clerk bowed. "He said you were to go right up to his suite."

"Thanks."

The suite consisted of a sitting room, bedroom and connecting bath. There was only one closet, though, near a window. There was no one there. The Parson took mental note of the whole layout, paced restlessly up and back. His watch said seven-fifteen.

At seven-eighteen he was electrified by carpet-muffled footfalls outside the corridor door. Frowning, he stood listening while they came closer. There was something vaguely disquieting about them. The door did not immediately open. No key was inserted in the lock. He sensed that whoever was outside was listening first with an ear pressed against the panel. Swiftly, he opened the closet door, slipped into the stuffy darkness and noiselessly drew the door shut. He estimated a thirty-second wait. Then he heard the corridor door open and close.

He pressed his ear against a crack. Hurried, yet stealthy footsteps sounded within the apartment. There were at least two men who had come in, perhaps three. No, two; he could tell by the way the footsteps sounded. But there was no conversation between the men. The sound of their movement ceased suddenly.

Minutes dragged by. The Parson wondered where the two men had gone. They had not gone out. Then he remembered the bedroom. They had gone in there. Yet strain as he would he could hear nothing. These newcomers could not be Knight and Major Rowe; they would have stayed in the living-room. Certainly, they would have talked. And they couldn't be Carl Dorn and Eva. There had been something heavy in the tread—they were the footfalls of two men. What could it mean?

In the wait ahead of him, the Parson speculated on the identity and purpose of the newcomers. Then his thoughts were interrupted by the corridor door opening a second time. This time the show was on. He recognized Knight's voice and afterward Major Rowe's.

Rowe said, "Take a chair, miss," with old-fashioned courtesy.

Eva's voice came to the Parson, saying, "Thanks, sport."

He pictured red-haired Eva with the green eyes and gold-flecked pupils. Instantly, a fourth voice, a man's, said, "Oke, major, let's get this over right away."

That was Carl Dorn's voice. He was across the room somewhere, farther from the closet than the girl was. The Parson had slipped his blunt-nosed Luger from the underarm holster, had soundlessly squatted on his haunches so as to bring his eyes level with the large old-fashioned keyhole. He saw the four of them. The lawyer, Knight, stood to one side but near the chair in which Eva sat, trim silken legs crossed, both hands closed over a handbag. Carl Dorn was near the hall door; a few feet from him stood the white-haired major. The major, however, moved out of the Parson's line of vision, as he said:

"Yes. You must give me some guarantee of my daughter's safety when I pay over the money you demand."

"Have you got the dough on you?" Dorn asked.

"Yes."

"Let's see the color of it."

The major moved back within range of the keyhole. The Parson saw him reach into the breast pocket of his coat and take out a flat manila envelope. He laid it down on the table, stepped back.

Carl Dorn leaped at it like a dog after liver. The Parson was tense, muscles bunched, lines of worry creasing the space between his eyes. He saw Knight casting anxious glances at the closet door as though inviting him to crack out. But the Parson held back. There was still unexplained in his mind the two men who had come in just after him. If they were a couple of hijackers, perhaps he had best move fast. But if not....

Dorn had torn off the flap of the envelope and had drawn out a packet of bills. But suddenly view of him was blocked by the intervening body of Major Rowe. The old man stood there with a gun in his fist!

The Parson couldn't see Dorn but he distinctly heard his gulp of sheer astonishment. He could just barely see the girl. She had not moved but a cruel and wolfish grin suddenly appeared on her sensuous face. The most surprised person in the room was Joel Knight. He stood with mouth agape, eyes fairly popping, Adam's apple working up and down like an agitated pulley-weight of his emotions.

The major straightened his shoulders. His jaw stood out like a chunk of granite. He said slowly and distinctly:

"Kidnapers, are you? You'll return my daughter safe and sound? Did you think you could really get away with a bluff like that?"

Carl Dorn purpled, started to speak, spread his thick tongue over his lips instead. The gun steadied on him.

"You're a couple of fools," Major Rowe went on with quiet dignity. "You didn't fool me any. I know where Nina is. You haven't got her. You never had her."

Dorn jerked out, "It's a d-double-cross."

Eva moved her legs. She was still smiling but she said nothing.

"You'll think about that when the police have you behind bars," the major said softly. His voice raised a bit. "All right, officers; you can come in now."

There was movement at the other side of the room and then two men came into the Parson's narrow gauge of vision. They were thick-fingered, burly men. Police detective written all over them. They held guns.

The foremost of them said, "The pair of you are under arrest. I advise you that anything you may say will be used against you. Put the handcuffs on them, Tom."

Carl Dorn got white. His knees quaked. He took a backward step, brought up against a table. They were watching him. The Parson wanted to yell a warning. But he kept his mouth shut. Eva had opened her bag. She stood up with a black automatic in her hand. It coughed, ejected flame and sound. She was laughing, white teeth showing. She fired again.

The second shot struck Major Rowe. He staggered like a tree about to topple. His gun boomed. Wood splintered. Something shot past in the darkness above the Parson's head and behind him plaster detached itself from the wall. The slug had gone through the closet door.

Major Rowe bumped to the floor on his knees with the shock of the bullet in his chest. Then he gently keeled over.

Carl Dorn snatched a gun from his pocket. It cleared the cloth and flamed simultaneously. One of the detectives spun about like a top. When he stopped spinning, he slammed down. The other detective fired. Joel Knight dragged forth a gun, too. But he ducked, went down and stayed down and didn't use his gun.

Dorn, Eva and the second detective were all firing at once. Powder smoke reeked. The detective snapped a swift shot from behind the shelter of a chair. Carl Dorn turned as if he were going to walk out of the door; he crashed resoundingly to the floor. The Parson could just barely see his head. The head did not move.

The detective's gun clicked as he leveled it at Eva. She streaked for the door, got it open. Knight fired at her. The bullet split the glass knob, shattered it. She was through safely and running down the hall. The detective snatched the gun from his partner's hand and raced after her. Shots boomed distantly.

The Parson flung the closest door open and faced Joel Knight. His lips were blue, knees shaking. For a split second the two of them stood motionless. Then the Parson sidled over to the table where the money still lay.

His grin was sour, mocking. "Well, all I gotta do is take it."

Knight gulped like a stunned carp. "N-no. We can't dare touch it now. Listen! Get out! Before someone comes in. There's a back staircase… door… other room."

The Parson fingered the money lovingly, then let it fall back to the table. He looked down at Carl Dorn. He lay on his side, eyes open and sightless. Dead as a taxidermist's window display. Major Rowe was groaning, stirring. The detective was dead.

"Somebody crossed somebody," the Parson snarled softly. "Then somebody else crossed somebody else." He looked at Knight. "What do you make of it?"

Knight was still dazed. He rubbed a hand over his eyes, over his sweating forehead. "I'm still in the dark."

The Parson's sour grin came back fleetingly. He said, "The old major was smarter than we figured, is all. Two dicks planted in the next room. Not bad, not bad at all."

"God, what a shock!" Knight breathed like a spent runner, haggard lines lengthening his face.

The Parson said over his shoulder, "Don't let it get you down, guy. We gotta learn to expect our share of surprises." He knelt briefly by the major's side. "Hm. Slug went through the top of the chest. Not much blood, either. He'll be O.K."

Footsteps were pounding far down the corridor. Voices were shouting.

Knight said, "You'd better get out before you're seen."

The Parson rose leisurely. "Yeah. But I sure hate to leave all this dough behind."

There was silence and then Knight, his face convulsed, whispered violently, "No! I can't allow— That detective, he'll remember I was the last person left behind. If the money's gone, they'll blame me. To touch it now would be suicide."

"Not for me," said the Parson tranquilly. "Anyway, it wouldn't be suicide just to touch it."

"No, no! Don't—I'll—"

"Don't run a fever. Funny thing. I broke into this shebang for the dough was in it. Now I don't care so much about the money. All I'm thinkin' of is them two kids. Funny, huh? With the dough starin' me in the face."

"Listen! They're at the door. Get out!"

"Yeah. Well, s'long. Our combination was a bust, huh? Your brains didn't work and my gun didn't shoot. Maybe we'll get together again some time. Look me up."

He slipped through to the bedroom. There was a bolt on the back door. He eased it open, stepped out into the corridor. No one saw him. The stairs were dark and odors of food wafted up from the restaurant kitchen below. He passed the kitchen. It was deserted. He walked out into the night. He crossed a wide expanse of lawn, the garage driveway and went through a gate. He walked up the street to the corner and faced the hotel's front entrance.

The street was choked with humanity; white, black and yellow men jabbering away in three tongues. It was very lively; people spoke excitedly. There were a dozen versions of what had happened. All of them cockeyed.

After a while, the Parson saw the detective who had raced out of Knight's room after Eva, returning doggedly to the hotel. Uniformed policemen were with him. But not Eva. Bicycle cops pedaled up with stolid urbanity. Pretty soon they formed a knot of about a dozen in front of the hotel. They talked to each other in calm British voices and shifted from foot to foot, not knowing what to do. Then it occurred to them that the crowd needed dispersing. The night boat for Curacao let forth a mournful, deep-toned blast. Her lights formed a twinkling pattern on the dark blue water.

The Parson moved away from the press of the crowd, circled the street and slouched into a broad avenue lined with restless, nodding palms.

For a long time he walked aimlessly, as if merely for the sake of walking. Then he looked up and found himself in front of Ching's, the biggest bar in Cariba. He went in, perched on a high stool and ordered rum. He sipped thoughtfully, face expressionless and rigid. His glass was refilled and he repeated the sipping process. The bright lights, the clink of glasses and bottles, the bustle and hum of conversation passed over, beyond and through him. He spent nearly three-quarters of an hour that way. Finally, he paid up and walked back into the street. A line of cabs was parked at the curb. He crooked a finger at one, climbed in. "Fruit pier," he said.

THERE WERE THREE small boats moored to the pier. The boat the Parson sought had been moved but not far. It bobbed gently against the oily swell. In the quiet, ropes creaked and sea water slapped against the pier, sucking out and slapping in with endless rhythm. Aboard the boat, nothing moved.

The Parson leaped nimbly aboard but made no effort to muffle the sound of his movements. He strode across the tiny deck. A cabin door opened and Captain Deerman's broad bulk was outlined against the streaming panel of light. The Parson stepped into the light.

"Oh, it's you, Mr. Ormond," Captain Deerman said softly, recognizing him. "Come in. Come in."

He stood aside and the Parson went into the closet-size cabin. Deerman's colored woman was seated in a rocker. Her white teeth shone in a smile of welcome. She didn't get up. The air was heady with the gardenia perfume that came from her clothes. The Parson sat down on a bench. Deerman closed the door and sat down opposite him. On the table before him was a stock of wood, a big clasp-knife and a pile of shavings. Deerman was whittling a sailing ship model. He took up the knife and the stock of wood and trimmed the edge with deft, graceful movements of the blade.

His dreamy voice crooned. "I got about a dozen of 'em, all types. Makin' 'em keep your hands out of trouble. This one don't look like much now but it'll be the *Cutty Sark* when I'm finished. You like sailin' ships?"

The Parson leaned his elbows on the table. Deerman's woman rocked and the smile played about her handsome chocolate features. The Parson reached over with one hand and began playing with the neat pile of shavings.

"Heard what happened to Major Rowe about an hour or so ago?"

"Friend, I been aboard this here boat since evenin' fell." But both Deerman's eyes were wide open and fixed on the Parson's lips; he had stopped whittling. And he said nothing about not knowing the major.

"He stopped a piece of lead," the Parson said.

"Daid?"

"No, just hurt."

Deerman laid down the wood and then the knife. His eyes regarded the Parson for a long moment. "Who done it?"

"A feller named Carl Dorn and his woman, Eva. She's a snake; she wriggled clear. Dorn got himself killed…."

Deerman's face was blank. He removed his gaze from the Parson and glanced over at his wife. She was no longer smiling. Both shook their heads.

"Remember them?" questioned the Parson.

"Friend, I never heard of 'em. Besides there was no woman."

"But there was someone who came to see you, huh?" the Parson prodded.

Deerman shrugged. "Ain't they always someone?" Without turning his head, he added, "Narcissa, put up that fool gun. This gentleman's friendly."

The Parson turned and saw the gun in her hand. She was not in the least embarrassed. The same piquant smile returned to her lips. She laid the gun in her lap.

Deerman chuckled, said, "Narcissa can hit a flyin' fish mid-air at a hundred yards. And pick her spot. Crease his spine, nip his head or clip his tail. She is sure fond o' guns."

"And perfume."

Deerman looked quizzically at the Parson and shook his head, smiling.

"Gardenia perfume," said the Parson.

"Um. Call your play, friend. Narcissa can have some target practice or pour us a coupla swallows of rum. What you mean by that last remark?"

"Make it rum."

"So?"

The Parson leaned forward suddenly, said into Deerman's face, "Nina Mund used gardenia perfume. Also a silver compact with her initials. Narcissa was dolling up with the compact yesterday." He sniffed. "And gardenia—it's all over the room now."

Deerman's deep, soothing voice said, "That ain't why you gave me a hundred dollars last night."

"No. That hundred was a deposit on Nina and Jake's lives. As soon as I saw the compact and smelled that perfume, I was sure they'd been aboard. But since you acted like you were waitin' on 'em, I figured right off that Jake Mund had given you something to button your mouth. That hundred of mine was to button it tighter. Not knowin' what the game was all about at the time, I thought it was safer for 'em to be undercover, I figured that when the time came for me to find out where they were, I'd find out."

Deerman had listened impassively. "Not all of that's correct."

The Parson nodded solemnly. "As soon as the major got shot, I knew I'd figured somethin' out wrong. That's why I'm here."

"Narcissa," said Deerman, "get out the rum 'john."

Narcissa did not move. Light, delicate footsteps sounded outside on the deck above the sighing of the night wind through the rigging. The footsteps approached to the door. The knob rattled and the door flung back. Joel Knight came into the cabin; a small .32 was in his hand.

"Never mind the rum," said Deerman softly.

Knight stood in the door with his eyes only on the Parson. He had been drinking. He looked at the Parson and seemed uncertain whether to show welcome or embarrassment. It was evident, though, that the presence of the Parson had thrown him off stride.

The Parson said, "Go right ahead with what you intended doing. Don't mind me."

"No. There's nothing. I was just— That is, I meant—" He gulped, took a noisy breath. "There's evidently some misunderstanding.

"All on your part, pal," the Parson said. "Listen to me! You've been the key double-crosser in this mess since it began. What kind of a sap did you take me for? Your deal with me to hijack the ransom money was about the fourth double-cross you'd attempted. By that time you were tied up in knots."

"Please, please!" implored Knight. "What are you talking about?"

"This, fathead! You murdered Lee Fong. You'd made a deal with him to keep Nina Mund watched night and day so she couldn't slip away before her father or Carl Dorn arrived. Not that you told Lee what it was all about. Oh, no! You were too smart. But Lee smelled money. He got a promise of five thousand from Major Rowe if he could keep Nina from harm. That's why he hot-footed it to the kid's cottage. But you were there first. You couldn't have him horn in on your game. So you socked him two, three times. When the kids came in, you slipped out the back door.

"They were scared witless to find a dead man in their house. They packed a bag quick, flung things into it and scooted. They lit out to the boat—this boat. You followed them. It wasn't hard to figure their plans—a quick getaway. You had a confidential talk with Cap'n Deerman, gave him some money. Obligingly, he tied them up for you."

Deerman chuckled. "He gave me five hundred."

"Yeah," said the Parson. "His game was to cash in but with no partners. Oh, he wanted partners for the dirty work but not for the pay-off. Y'see, Jake Mund used to be in Carl Dorn's gang. He was supposed to have kidnaped Nina so Dorn could collect a five hundred grand ransom. Instead he fell in love with the girl and she with him. They skipped, got married; her father spent a small fortune trying to find her and take her back home."

"So that's how it was."

"Yeah. Our pal, Knight, decided he'd collect two or three times. Instead of handing them over to Dorn, he was going to hold them for himself, then fleece the major when the right time rolled around. But before that he had to let Carl Dorn and Eva get theirs from the major. He'd overheard them speaking; he knew they hadn't much use for him and that they'd freeze him out if they could. So he took me on as a temporary partner to get the shake-down dough from them but principally to see that they got wiped out. After that, he figured it as clear sailing to squeeze some real money out of the major for the return of Nina.

"The major himself spoiled the party by planting a couple of dicks in the next room. The ground was cut from under Knight's feet. He put two and two together. That's why he's here, Deerman. To kill you so you can't spill what you know."

Deerman smiled. He looked over at Narcissa. She smiled.

"I don't think he will do that," said Deerman dreamily.

No one moved. It was very quiet in the cabin. Then Knight, his face gone gray, said:

"He's raving mad! I brought Jake and Nina Mund here myself to—to protect them from Dorn." His voice gained shrillness. "That's it—to protect them!" He caught at the phrase as though it automatically cleared him.

"Did you?" said the Parson gently. "Then why did you bring

Dorn and his killers to Cariba in the first place? At the same time that you informed Major Rowe, you tipped off Dorn. Yeah. When I first ran into you on the dock, you asked me if I remembered you. I remembered. I remembered that about twelve years ago when Dorn was dealing in beer you were counsellor for his gang. Not many people knew that. You always had a cover of respectability. When he planned to snatch Nina, you were probably still his attorney, That's how come you knew all the ins and outs."

"You got it wrong!" Knight mopped his face and turned to Deerman, said, "If only you'd listen. Don't believe his insinuations. It...."

His voice trailed to silence. He turned a tortured face toward the open door, haunted eyes groveling in his head. Footsteps clop-clopped over the deck in slow, measured tread. A head appeared suddenly in the oblong of yellow light.

Major Rowe stood in the doorway. He wore no hat. He carried his shoulder stiffly.

Knight backed up out of his way and brought up against the wall. The major stared hard at him, as if not quite understanding his presence. Deerman slipped past the major and out the door before anyone could stop him.

The Parson said, "Just in time. Knight and I've been talking. Sort of threshing things over. He's the baby responsible for the whole mess."

Major Rowe jerked a glance at the Parson without comprehending what he meant. He came into the room. The slight bullet wound had weakened him obviously. He put one hand on the table to support himself.

"I have come for my daughter," he said.

"Sure," said the Parson. "And the guy who planted her here—Joel Knight."

Again the major looked at the Parson. Then he looked at Knight.

Knight's lips were quivering. "D-don't believe a word he says. Let me explain. He's got it all wrong."

"He's got it right," said a voice from the doorway.

The Parson's head pivoted about.

The red-haired woman, Eva, stood there holding a gun in her hand and looking very menacing with drooping lids over her green-gold eyes.

The Parson laughed. He made it a hearty, diverting laugh to cover the slight movement of Narcissa's hand toward the gun in her lap.

"Li'l' Eva," he said warmly. "And just in time."

She looked at him not without surprise. "The runt, eh? I thought you'd been plugged. I'll get around to you in a moment. I'll kill the rat first, then you, then the old man. He got Carl killed. I'll kill him!"

The word seemed to intoxicate her. Her nostrils were dilated.

"Hoist the mitts," she said. "All of you. You too, chocolate. I said hoist!"

Nobody moved. Her wild face said plainly that she would shoot at the slightest movement, even to obey her commands. Knight swayed slightly as if he would faint. Her glittering orbs flicked to him.

"You were bright, huh? You tipped the major to the bluff; you told him we didn't have his damn daughter."

Knight tried to shake his head. He tried to smile reassuringly. But he couldn't move a muscle.

"I slipped back to the hotel," she went on, "to watch for you. I didn't care any more about being caught; I just wanted to burn a bullet through your heart. I saw you come out and I followed you. Then just as I was about to come aboard, the old gent showed. I slipped behind a barrel and let him go first. I wanted him, too. But I wanted you most."

Knight made a bleating sound with his lips but no words came forth. Suddenly there was a diversion. Eva stiffened, crouched. An inner door to the right of Narcissa opened. Jake Mund stood there with Nina beside him. Deerman was behind them.

Eva looked at them and her teeth showed. "Jake! This is swell, swell! Now we're all here. Come in, come in!"

"Dad!" It was Nina. She ran across the room, flung her arms about the quivering old man. "Dad, you're hurt! Is anything—"

"Let go of him!" Eva snapped. "Just step aside. Yeah. Now watch me cut him down. Just like—"

The Parson realized that there was no time to go for his gun. Something quicker was needed. He saw Eva's gun move until it was on a line with Major Rowe's heart, saw her finger whiten under pressure on the trigger. Nina screamed. The Parson was about to fling himself out of his chair.

Jake, from the doorway, moved faster. He hurtled across the room under Eva's gun. Her trigger finger twitched. The gun blasted and a slug burned Jake's ribs. Almost perceptibly it seemed to halt him. He shivered but came on doggedly. He hit her sidewise and she flung into a corner.

Narcissa got her gun up and shot her twice in the chest. Eva's shoulders hit hard into the V of the corner; she was grinning.

Knight was throwing himself toward the open doorway that

led to the deck. It was that which brought forth the grin.

Eva shot him in the back.

The gun action jolted her away from the corner. Her feet tangled but with her left hand she caught the table and stopped her fall. She bumped against the major, held herself erect. Knight was falling through the door. She shot him again.

The Parson had jerked his Luger out. His mouth was pulled down grimly. Before he could fire, Eva moved her head slowly toward him; the grin was still on her face. Then her knees buckled, struck the floor. She pitched forward on her face.

It was deafeningly still in the cabin. Gun smoke swirled to the overhead light. Water lapped gently against the boat's side. Jake Mund got to his feet slowly, his handsome young face grave and haggard.

Nina fluttered to him. "Jake, are you hurt?" She began to cry.

He sank into a chair, smiled wanly, put his hands on her cheeks. "Don't cry, sugar. I'm all right. Everything's all right. You've got your Dad now and we got the Parson. He'll make it all right. The Parson's our friend."

The Parson moved out to the deck. Deerman followed him. A crowd was gathering on the pier. Deerman looked out over the water. The Parson said, "You tipped off Major Rowe, didn't you?"

Deerman nodded. "I got to thinkin' after I tied up that boy and girl. I listened in at the cabin door while they was talkin'. It was mostly about her father Major Rowe and how she was scared he'd come to take her home. So I just went aroun' to all the hotels in Cariba until I found a man answerin' to the name, Major Rowe. That boy and girl was in trouble and I figured her father ought to know about it."

"But weren't you afraid he'd go to the cops?"

"Ah, he was a gentleman. He promised to tell the cops nothin' until the whole thing was cleared. He was to have come aboard and gotten them himself and the police'd never know I was mixed up in it. When he came aboard a little while ago, why I just went back and untied them an' brought them in here. Glad I did, too. That young feller handled that red-head woman good."

"Yeah," said the Parson thoughtfully. "I guess he's got guts at that." He looked pleased. "But why did you mix in the mess at all?"

"Well, the fishin' this time of year is poor and that feller Knight's five hundred looked big."

"Hm. But how come you went to the major at all after Knight had paid you five hundred to be on *his* side?"

Deerman cocked his head to one side as if that were something to puzzle over. "I'm damned if I know, 'cept I got to thinkin', I guess, an' I don't mind makin' a dollar by winkin' at the law but when you got a chance to make a little honest money and help out a couple of kids just married besides, well I guess that's all there's to it."

"Yeah," said the Parson, "I know just how you feel."

Jake Mund appeared beside him and said, "Parson, I don't know how I'm going to thank you."

"Phht! Listen, once. The cops will be here in a jiffy. Here's your story. You weren't tied, see? Deerman's a friend who gave you shelter because you were afraid of Carl Dorn and Eva and Joel Knight. That's the mugg Eva shot. Got it straight?"

Mund's face darkened. "You're wrong. Deerman crossed us."

"You listen to me," the Parson said savagely. "Deerman's your friend. You'll find out why soon enough. You'll do as I say. Is that clear?"

Mund looked at him. "All right," he said.

"How's your side?" asked the Parson with unexpected gentleness.

"All right, I guess."

"Hurt much?"

"No."

"Then why in hell ain't you in there with your wife?"

"No," said Mund. "I guess they caught up with us. She'll be going back with her father."

"Listen," said the Parson. "I blew fifty grand getting you clear of Carl Dorn. I could've had the dough. All I had to do was take it. I'll be damned if I don't have to get you out of this, too."

"What are you talking about?"

The Parson gripped his arm. "Come on." He pushed into the cabin, dragging Mund behind him. "Listen!" his voice crackled. Major Rowe and Nina looked up. "This kid's gone through hell with your daughter. If you think you're going to snatch her back home and leave him behind, you got another think coming. These two belong together. Why, he even saved your life a few minutes ago."

"Don't yell," said the major. "Nina's been telling me about him. Jake, I'm proud of you! Will you shake hands?" The Parson turned to go. "Wait a moment. Nina's explained about you, too. Jake told her. I don't know if I can repay you for all you've done but if money will help…."

"Money? Money!" said the Parson. "Mister, I could fall over with surprise at that crack."

He stalked out on deck. The crowd had parted and two big

policemen in white drill jackets and blue trousers were pounding toward the boat with beefy determination.

The Parson moved forward to meet them at the rail.

A Deal in Coconuts

Revenge bites the Parson

THE CAB STUTTERED down Prince Edward Street, motor gasping. It expired with a flutter before the Royal Victoria Hotel, and the Parson stepped out of the tonneau. Life was slow-paced in Cariba, "the little Paris of the Caribbean," and the city's cabs, battered old wrecks, were in complete harmony with their tropical surroundings.

It was a beautiful night, star-studded, fragrant with the lazy warm breeze from east-lying Ventura Island. The Parson, heading for the hotel entrance, skirted a thick palm trunk.

A hand reached out of the darkness, closed over his arm. A dim figure stood in the dense shadows, holding a gun.

The Parson blinked, dainty as a doll in his suit of midnight black.

"O.K.," he said disgustedly. "Now I'm taken for fair." He did not try to make for his holstered Luger. He had too much respect for an unsheathed gun.

The figure suddenly let go of his arm, said, "Hello, Parson. I'm Jim the Greek. Remember me?"

The Parson peered through the dark at him. "Hell, yes. Jim Kardis!"

Kardis smiled a bit ruefully. "Long time since we met, huh, Parson? It's a long way to New York. I saved your life once. Remember? A drunken gambler pulled a gat on you. I winged him before it could go off."

The Parson's beady eyes gleamed. "I remember," he said. He was aware that Kardis was shivering, despite the warmth

of the night. He stared up and down the street. It was a little after midnight.

"I got here on the *Buccaneer*," Kardis said. "She docked at five o'clock."

"Did you come on a vacation cruise?"

Kardis laughed. The relief of that laugh was sensed by the Parson. It let out all the tension in Kardis' tight nerves.

"I came here because I had an accident," he said. "I took a shot at a guy back in New York—and missed. I had to run."

"Tell me about it. Who was the guy?"

"Nick Pagany."

The Parson fixed a hard, dark stare on him. He remembered Nick Pagany. He remembered that Jim Kardis had been Pagany's chief gun. Back in the days when the Parson had run a string of gambling houses for the Guard-Poggi syndicate, Pagany had had some business dealings with Guard.

In those times, Pagany had been the power behind a lot of money-making propositions—a dope ring, organized prostitution, gambling, money lending. The newspapers had played him up into somewhat of a national figure: the Crime Colossus. He had always possessed a flair for color, a genius for organization, a knack for doing the unexpected.

"Pagany is in Cariba," said Jim Kardis. "He flew here with his boys. I need your help, Parson."

"Help in what?"

"In keeping alive." Kardis giggled. "I shouldn't have missed when I shot at Pagany. That was my mistake. Now Pagany knows everything."

"Everything? I got a room in this dump. Let's sit this out."

"Sure. I'll stay the night with you. In the morning I'll get a boat somewhere."

"Oh, you can get a room to yourself."

"No! listen." Kardis clamped a hand over Parson's arm again. "Don't leave me alone, guy. Don't let me alone! I'll give you anything! I got dough. I wanted to talk to you soon as I hit this hole. That's why I waited outside your hotel."

"Pull yourself together," the Parson's voice was sharp. "How'd you know my hotel?"

"Wang Hoo Shan told me over the telephone."

They were moving toward the garden entrance, through which ran a walk to the hotel patio. The Parson moved with his smooth, flowing gait which had something deceptively pious and clerical about it. It was this odd mannerism, added to his habitual sober garb of black, which had combined to tag him with his nickname.

"Wang Hoo Shan?" he repeated. "Where does that Chink come in?"

"He's in it deep, up to his neck—him and Donald Segrave, who runs the Segrave Lines. Segrave's been here a week. Him and his wife. She's the brains. And a looker."

The Parson stopped short. Kardis stopped and the Parson faced him. "You sound like you were hopped."

"No, honest. Hell, I wish I did have a card. But I'm giving you the straight of it. Pagany can't kill Wang and Segrave. He

160 / James Duncan

needs 'em. He's got something special up his sleeve for Wang, though. Something for a kid, named Harry Kane. I don't know what. But it's good. Anything Pagany does is good,"

"The hell you say," said Parson. "Why did you shoot at Pagany?"

"So I'd be the kingpin."

"Um," mused the Parson. "You've been seeing too many movies. And Pagany can't kill Wang and this guy Segrave."

"No. But he can kill me."

"You mentioned that before." The Parson stared at him.

"Uh-huh. I'm plain scared. I could use something to warm me up inside. Here it is the tropics and I'm cold. Isn't that something?"

"What about this kid, Harry Kane? Who is he?"

"Don't know. I'm putting you in a hole, Parson, hanging around you. You might get shot at by Pagany's cannons."

The garden they were walking through was strewn with hibiscus petals. The thick stamens had been trampled underfoot and oozed a kind of yellow blood. Three arbor houses dotted the English lawn. Frogs shrilled in the lily pool. A covey of wild parakeets grrawked in a dark, earth-bending tree. Ahead of them were the lights of the patio. The Parson kept pace with Jim Kardis.

Kardis suddenly stood still, neck distended, peering down the flower-fringed path. "Someone is hiding behind that slanted palm, near the door. He's got a tommy gun. I can't see it. But I know it's there. Run, Parson. You're a pretty swell sort o' guy. You can still keep out of this."

"If it's just one guy, we can take him," the Parson said. "But there's no one there. Your eyes are playing tricks."

"Not my eyes. I can see in the dark like a cat. There's more'n one of 'em. They're all over the place. Ain't it funny? I ain't cold any more."

"Come on," said the Parson impatiently. "Let's get inside and get you a big drink."

"Maybe some other time. Geez, I'm sorry I dragged you into this. I should've known it was too late."

"Good grief!" snapped the Parson suddenly. "Hey, where in hell you going?"

Kardis had wheeled abruptly and was now running across the grass. His crouching body was weaving in and out among the waist-high rose bushes, dislodging the full-blown flowers, scattering them in the wake of his flight.

Someone appeared at the brass-studded patio door and light came down the garden path. It was the night clerk of the hotel. He yelled as he saw an armed figure behind the slanted palm six feet from him. A man jumped from behind the palm, a chopper cuddled in his arms. The light fell on the drum.

Someone whistled near-by. It was a call to action. A second figure detached itself from the trunk of another tree. The outstretched hand gripped an automatic.

Kardis was headed for a six-foot, white-washed wall. The Parson muttered something under his breath; his hand snaked upwards and drew forth his Luger. The man with the chopper ran beyond the pale light and crouched against the dense shadow of an arbor house surrounded by many bushes.

All this happened in less than half a second and seemed to float before the Parson's eyes like a series of separate, jerky pictures in slow motion.

Then the shots followed.

The Parson had been hoping Kardis would scale the wall. Kardis actually got his hands up to vault over it when the automatic coughed in one swift burst. Eight or nine shots. Kardis' hands were still stretched up above his head as he spun about.

The Parson fired at the chopper. Simultaneously, the automatic of the second man was turned on him. The Parson fell flat to the ground. The submachine gun riveted away in his direction. The Parson stayed down. The firing ceased.

It was very still in the night now. Quite suddenly a car racketed to life. Then it was quiet again, as it sped away. The Parson got to his feet, straightened.

The hotel was on a slight eminence. The Parson looked toward the east where there was no wall. From the palm and bamboo groves plumes of mist were rising, distilled from the fetid marshes, coiling and uncoiling like steam from a witch's cauldron. Beyond was narrow Boca Passage, leading past the headlands to the open Caribbean, its ribbon length sparkling like burnished sapphire.

The hotel clerk was squealing. He came running toward the Parson, did a neat pirouette when he saw the Luger. The Parson pocketed it.

"What happened?" said the Parson, innocently.

The clerk fooled with his trouser legs as if they were skirts. He was a malzito—the island name for mixed breed. White, black and even a trace of Chinese blood flowed in his veins. His white blood spoke.

"A man was shot," he said. "We'll have to get a doctor and the police."

He was backing away as he spoke. That was the breed in him.

Three men came running from the street. The Parson crossed the lawn to the wall, and looked down at Kardis.

Jim Kardis lay perfectly still on his face. The bullets had struck him in the upper back, the neck and the base of his skull. Blood trailed across his neck where the hair-line began.

The three men came over and bent over him. People poured out of the hotel.

Minutes later two policemen on bicycles came up and fussily took charge. One of them straightened up and said, "Anybody here know him?" The hotel clerk looked at the Parson out of the corner of his eyes but he didn't speak. "Anybody see it happen?"

The hotel clerk told his story. He pointed diffidently at the Parson, but made no mention of the Luger. He felt the Parson's eyes full on him.

"Well," said the officer, "what do you know?"

"I live in the hotel," said the Parson. "I was going in when the shots were suddenly fired. I didn't see who fired them or who was hit. It was dark."

The policeman drew out a notebook and a pencil and the clerk and the Parson repeated their stories, while he wrote them down.

The Parson was permitted to leave. He went up to his room, kicked off his shoes and stood on the cool tile floor in his stockinged feet. He felt tired. After a while he poured a tall drink of rum from a bottle on the dresser. From a drawer he took out a box of cartridges. He got out his gun and replaced the one cartridge he had fired with a fresh one.

Then he got out his handkerchief and thoughtfully wiped his sweaty fingers. He liked a dry finger on the trigger.

THE VERMOUTH HOUR in Cariba is always a gay close to the monotony of the tropical day. It brings together in the early evening the island's three dominant races in a district called the *Barrio Catedral*—a sort of neutral territory, a common meeting ground and a combined business and pleasure district. It is also the oldest and in its architectural lines the most Spanish-looking section of the island city.

The Parson strolled among the sidewalk cafés toward dusk of the following day. Hatless, his jet-black hair was crisp, flat against his scalp. He was surprisingly small of stature and pinch-shouldered, and his delicately modeled face was tight and swarthy, with a sort of underlying pallor.

The tables were well filled at this hour and the Parson's quick eye took in everyone.

He stopped before the silver and glitter of the Café Martinique. His black eyes, expressionless as buttons, coursed over the tables and then settled on the one before which sat plump, rubicund Wang Hoo Shan. He strode over.

"*Buenas,*" greeted Wang with a good-humored grin. "Sit down, please."

"Why not?" The Parson smiled, shrugged his immaculate shoulders.

"I am pleased to see you," Wang said.

The Parson knew Wang pretty well, knew that he was reputed to be rich. He was something of a legendary figure in the tropical islands. He had a white wife. But his wealth could not be judged from his clothes. He wore a cheap, shapeless South China suit of cream-white drill, buttoned up to the neck, and a battered Panama, yellowish with age. He was about forty, perhaps a few years older. Numerous fillings made of his grin a thing of golden effulgence; he was proud of the amount of gold in his teeth.

His business was antiques, tropical fruit, coffee and a host of other sidelines in which he acted as a broker. That afternoon the Parson had phoned him and Wang had selected the Martinique as a meeting place.

Wang was drinking wine. He would have preferred tea but he had learned long ago to adapt himself to other customs, just as he had learned to speak English with almost no accent. His speech was racily and colloquially American.

He was offhand, genial. "You phoned me, my friend."

"Yeah. Jim Kardis came to see me last night."

Wang twisted the stem of his glass between his fingers. He spoke to the glass, very thoughtfully.

"I'm sorry about Jim."

"Then you know he was killed?"

"I know everything that happens in Cariba."

"Jim was murdered by Nick Pagany or Pagany's men."

"Did you see them?"

"No. It was too dark. Why couldn't you save Jim?"

Wang made a grimace. "Well, I'm not very good with a gun. Jim messed up his big chance. Even if he could've gotten away from Cariba, Pagany'd get him some time or other, So I sent him to you. I thought if anyone could help, it would be you. How much did Jim tell you?"

The Parson grinned. "You're worried. You know Jim talked to me but you don't know how much he spilled."

"He had orders from me to tell you a little."

The Parson stiffened, but kept his voice calm. "So you're pulling all the strings, are you?"

"Don't get angry, my friend. I had hoped you could help Jim. From that, I thought we could work further, sort of step by step."

The Parson gave him an odd, sidelong glance.

"Ever since you came to Cariba I have watched you," Wang went on. "You are a strange man. You have the reputation for being a lightning-fast gunman. You would cheerfully outwit a crook but just as cheerfully risk your life for your loyalties, for a friend. Once you were a power in New York. Now as an exile in Cariba, you are fast becoming a power here. I can use you."

The Parson brooded. Two tables away sat a man and a woman. Both had been hawkishly watching the table at which he and Wang sat. They were too far away to hear any of the conversation but their fixed attention indicated that it was of vast importance to them. He knew who they were—Mr. and Mrs. Donald Segrave; their pictures had adorned the pages of the local paper on their arrival a week before.

Segrave ran a line of freighters from Cariba and Port-au-Prince to Boston. The local reporter had made much of the fact that Segrave had inherited the line some three years before in a bankrupt condition and had forthwith proceeded to put new life into it and make himself a mint of money.

He looked to be about thirty-five, handsome and distinguished. He and his wife made a striking looking couple. She had blindingly blond hair, great masses of it hanging almost to her shoulders, curled up like a page boy's to frame her face in a luminous halo. Her features were perfectly wrought but perfection had not made them cold. She made an instant subtle feminine appeal. The Parson found himself watching her. Something that was almost a reminiscent smile touched his lips.

He looked up. "That woman there, the blond menace, d'you know her?"

Wang gave an elaborate stare. "Of course! She's Mrs. Segrave. Everyone knows Penelope Segrave. That man is her husband."

"Um. Where does she fit with you, with Jim Kardis, with Pagany?"

Wang's thick body stirred. "What do you mean?"

"Jim told me about her. And I got a funny feeling I used to know her some place. She wasn't married to Segrave then."

The Chinaman glanced at him slyly. "She is an unusual woman," he said, and smiled.

The Parson tapped a cigarette on the table, and smiled back. He found he was beginning to enjoy Wang's company.

He said, "A blue-blood like Segrave, his unusual wife, Pagany, Kardis and you. The combination adds up to something big." He lit his cigarette, leaned back. "Only Harry Kane is missing from the picture. Know him?"

He was startled when Wang leaned over suddenly and clamped thick fingers over his arm. The Chinaman's eyelids descended like shutters. His soft womanish lips whispered, "What do you know about Harry Kane?"

"Take your damn hand off," growled the Parson. "I only know what Jim Kardis told me. He said Pagany had something up his sleeve for you, something in relation to Harry Kane."

"Oh." Wang's face became solemn, reflective. He removed his hand.

"Jim didn't know what it was," the Parson added.

Wang said, "Harry Kane is a sort of protege of mine. I used to know his father, who was my friend. I want to make something clear. Harry Kane is a fine kid. He's like my own. So I don't want anything to happen to him."

The Parson didn't speak.

"I got ten grand for the man who can keep Harry Kane out of trouble," Wang said softly.

The Parson stared at him. "You think I'll bid into a blind set-up?" he said.

A young man crossed the sidewalk at that moment. Wang caught sight of him and his solemnity dropped away. His golden grin worked up to the proportions of a sunset. Yet there was a troubled look in his eye as he glanced briefly at the Parson.

He stood up as the young man came straight to their table. "Hello, Harry," he greeted. "Glad to see you, my boy. When did you make port?"

Harry Kane looked at the Parson. "A couple of hours ago," he said. "I left Port of Spain at dawn. Mabel said I'd find you here."

Wang pushed him affectionately. "Sit down, my boy. Say, I want you to meet the Parson. Funny name for a man, but he looks like one, doesn't he? Parson, I want you to meet the captain of my fleet, Harry Kane. He runs one of my motor launches. Does a good job too."

"I've heard Wang talk about you," the Parson said to Kane.

"Yeah? What did the old heathen say?" Harry Kane leaned toward Wang and gave him a friendly thump on the back.

"How was your trip?" Wang interrupted.

"Good enough." Kane launched into an account of bolts of cloth, rum, fruit and other articles of inter-island trade.

The Parson listened, studying him—the graceful slimness of him as he lazed in his chair, the clear profile, dark eyebrows and lashes, the sudden contrast of a shock of corn-colored hair above bronzed skin.

He looked to be no more than 19 or 20, yet he carried himself with a certain air of maturity. The Parson found himself trying to line the suave Chinaman with the youth, and could not. Harry Kane came from another world.

You would expect to see him on a polo field, in flannels at an exclusive tennis club. But running a trading boat for Wang Hoo Shan? Never!

The Parson said, "How do you like living in Cariba, Kane?"

"Oh, Harry likes it well enough," Wang put in. "It's a long way from New York. You see," he was smiling gently, "Harry came here to get away from it all."

The Parson glanced over to see how the boy was taking this good-natured ribbing but young Kane was not listening. He was staring past Wang with an intensity that was arresting.

Surprise, shock, pleasure—all three showed in his stare. His head was held high, like a listening creature of the wild. The corners of his mouth were quivering. Then the Parson saw that he was staring at Penelope Segrave. At that second she looked up and saw him.

Harry Kane slumped suddenly against the back of his chair, a bitter twist to his lips; his jaw muscles rigid, bunched. Wang was regarding him uneasily.

The Chinaman looked more surprised than anyone. He started to say something but Harry rose abruptly and strode stiff-legged to the curb where a line of taxis was waiting. It was as if he were running away. He got into one and a second later the cab trickled into the flowing stream of traffic.

Then Donald and Penelope Segrave rose from their table.

As they walked away, Segrave was talking very earnestly to his wife.

Wang's mouth was open so wide the Parson could leisurely count each of the gold fillings in his teeth. He shut his mouth with a sudden click.

"So she's Harry's woman," he whispered.

The Parson chuckled ironically. "And you thought you were pulling all the strings," he said. "Sometimes they get tangled up into a knot."

Wang turned his eyes on the Parson. "That offer of ten grand still goes."

"To look after the boy? What in hell could I do?"

"Get him out of Cariba! I don't care if you have to bop him over the head and drag him out. But get him out. You can both go on my launch."

The Parson folded his arms. "I don't need jack that bad. Not," he added, "not that I couldn't be a sucker for the truth."

"What do you mean?"

"Give me the whole set-up. Why did Jim Kardis try to kill Pagany? Where do you fit and the Segraves and Harry Kane?"

Wang's smile was slow and a little tired. "First of all, Harry Kane is not any part of this."

"Sure," said the Parson, without conviction.

Wang was speaking just above a whisper. "But why should I talk if you won't come in with me?"

"All right, I'm in if I can get the whole story."

They regarded each other for a few seconds. Wang's face was owlish, solemn. Presently the Parson grinned.

"I said I'm in, if I like your story, China boy."

Wang nodded. "You're O.K., Parson." He hitched up his

chair closer. "Well, this is it. You know my business—antiques, fruit, a lot of trash like that. But that isn't where the big money is. To make a real pile you got to deal in a money-maker."

"Ice," said the Parson.

Wang pursed his lips. "Ice is all right, but there's something even better. Cocaine—French crystal cocaine."

The Parson leaned forward suddenly.

Wang clasped his hands across his chest, smiled benignly. "It begins to get clearer, eh?" he said. "It works like this. I got the European connections. The stuff comes from three, four European countries and is landed at about a dozen of the West Indies islands. My little trading boats shuttle back and forth among them, take on cargos of fruit—melons, mangos, tamarinds, papayas. A legitimate trade. The coke is planted inside the fruit in little doses. I collect it here. That way it's practically impossible to trace."

The Parson leaned back. "It's a clever layout. And the shuttling among the islands in a trading boat is done by Harry Kane, of course."

Menace gleamed from Wang's eyes. "I told you Harry Kane has nothing to do with the set-up."

"That's right, you did say that. But you've shown me only part of the hand. What's the rest?"

"The rest," said Wang, "is distribution. Cariba isn't big enough to absorb that much junk. So it goes up North. And that's where Pagany comes in. He gives it protected landing and distributes it among his own organized dealers."

The Parson grinned. "And it goes up in Segrave ships, eh?"

Wang's gold fillings gleamed. "You catch on quick. Mrs. Segrave put the deal across with her husband. He was just the man we needed. An old respectable name, a famous old line—above suspicion. Besides, he was about to go bankrupt and scrap his ships. Carrying our kind of cargo made him a lot of money. He's doing all right."

"Uh-huh. What's your cut?"

"Fifteen per cent."

"And Segrave?"

"Ten."

"Umm. That leaves the lion's share for Pagany. I begin to see angles."

Wang clenched his fists. "Pagany wants to swallow it all for himself. Yet he can't get rid of Segrave or me. We can't be replaced. So all he can do is intimidate us."

"And Kardis?"

"Kardis was a fool! Segrave and I cooked up the plan. That is, Mrs. Segrave and I did. Kardis was Pagany's right hand gunman. He was supposed to get Pagany, take over the organization and run it with us on a three-way, share-for-share split."

"And Kardis missed."

"Yeah, but Pagany didn't. Kardis tried to square himself by tipping Pagany to our lay. Pagany took the information but he got Kardis just the same. I've made a first delivery to Segrave already." Wang picked up his glass. "On the new basis. Without Pagany, that is. It's worth two hundred grand at New York retail prices. Maybe more. Anyone who'd distribute it would rate a clear third."

"It's a good proposition. I'll think about it."

"And that's only a beginning."

"Uh-huh."

"Now what about Harry? Will you take that job?"

"Well, your story is O.K. China boy."

"Swell! Harry must be down on his boat. He lives on her. She's moored at Pescado Pier. You can't miss her—the *Cormorant*."

"Yeah," the Parson said.

Wang rose, beckoned the waiter, paid. He moved beside the Parson as they made their way to the street. Dusk was stealing over the city. Street lamps were coming on one by one. The Parson went toward a cab, stopped, came back.

"I was thinking," he said. "How was that delivery made to Segrave, the one on the new basis, I mean? How is—"

"Like always. Concealed in something. This time it was coconuts."

"Coconuts!" said the Parson. "That's nutty."

He went on to the waiting cab.

DISMISSING HIS CAB about a block from Pescado Pier, the Parson walked the rest of the way. Although it was still early, this part of Cariba was somnolent. The dock was silent, deserted. Dark and creaking fruit boats huddled wearily together. Smaller, faster motor launches were moored apart. He stepped out onto the pier.

There was a prison-like warehouse building to the right, a black blot in the blue darkness. A sagging white-washed fence formed a stockade around it. From far off came throaty Negro laughter and the sudden snarl of distant car horns mingled with the sound of a soft guitar and the faint ghost of singing voices over the water.

The Parson found the *Cormorant*. She was a trim, thirty-foot craft, a composition of mahogany, steel, glistening brass and a razor-sharp prow. No lights showed aboard her. He clambered on her. The forward hatch was locked.

He crossed the tiny deck, then wheeled in a half-crouch as he heard the faint creak of a footstep; his hand moved up to grasp his Luger. Slowly, his frame relaxed and his hand lowered to his side.

The figure of a woman appeared from behind the tiny wheel-house. She emerged slowly, came toward him. The Parson took a step in her direction. He was so close to her he could smell the elusive perfume of her hair. He smiled.

"Hello, Penny."

Penelope Segrave drew in a deep breath. "Wh-who are you?"

"They call me the Parson. Last time we met, you were Nick Pagany's woman. You saw me a little while ago at the Marti-nique with Wang Hoo Shan. Didn't you remember me then, Penny?"

"Yes."

"What are you doing here?"

Her head turned slightly toward the dock. "I came to see the man who runs this boat—Harry Kane."

The Parson smiled. "He's nuts about you. He's just a kid burned up over his first love affair. He doesn't know the kind of woman you are. But I know. You're no good," the Parson went on relentlessly. "Pagany threw you over because he couldn't trust you. All you want out of a man is money—big money. You're tied to this Donald Segrave because through him you can swing big deals. But that's his affair. He's old enough to wipe his own chin. Harry Kane isn't. You let him alone. Don't drag him into this."

He spoke evenly, with no particular emphasis. All of it was

seemingly casual and coldly matter-of-fact, but a cold thread of fear ran through her.

"You're crazy or—I don't know what!"

"No," said the Parson. "I'm hep to the whole lay. I know why you're here and why your husband is here. I know why Pagany is here. But that doesn't concern me. I've just got a job to keep the boy out of trouble."

She shivered. There was infinite menace and cruelty suddenly in every movement the Parson made and in every word he uttered, although he said everything and did everything behind that eternal deceptive air of softness, of piety that cloaked him. He was two people, one visible and quite harmless, the other subtly ruthless and retributive.

As if he had dismissed her with a wave of the hand, she moved away from him and climbed over the rail to the dock. His eyes followed her. She was walking very swiftly toward the warehouse. Suddenly a figure appeared from behind the white-washed fence.

She veered toward it. In the faint light the Parson could make out that it was a man. Penny came up to him and a moment later they were hurrying toward the steep, cobblestone street. The man was Donald Segrave.

The Parson heard the growl of a car a short distance away, and knew that they had driven off.

He moved about the deck slowly. Evidently Harry Kane had not come aboard as Wang had reasoned. The Parson stood at the stern, looking out over the water. Presently, his eyes strayed downward and his glance fixed on the shimmering water slapping against an anchor chain. His glance momentarily strayed but came back to the anchor chain again.

The chain was not steady. It swayed with the movement of the water.

AT ABOUT EIGHT-THIRTY, the Parson descended into the narrow streets of the Chinese Quarter. Lanterns swung before the tea houses, played dim light over yellow faces absorbed in fan-tan. There were a few women, too, huddled in dark doorways, seductive, lacquer-faced maidens, almond eyes gleaming, furtively plucking at the sleeves of passers-by.

The Parson turned into the principal thoroughfare, and stopped before a small shop window on which was lettered: *W.H. Shan, Antiques.*

He pulled a bell, heard its faint tinkle within. A minute passed. Impatiently, he pulled it again. A door in the rear of the shop was opened and a panel of light invaded the dark. Presently a bolt was shot back and the street door swung inward.

The Parson gazed at a woman wearing a loose Chinese dressing gown of black silk. She was Wang's white wife.

"Hello, Mabel," he said. "China boy home?"

"Yes."

He walked in past her and she closed the door. Then she floated after him to the inner door. It opened onto a modest little room, hung with drapes. Like a sleep-walker, she pointed listlessly to a door beyond, said, "In there."

The Parson regarded her with curiosity. This was not the first time he had ever seen her. Yet her personality somehow eluded him.

Her eyes were a liquid gray-green, deep and fathomless. At the moment, she looked half-asleep, detached from her surroundings. Her lips began to form words, then relaxed loosely. She put a hand out as if to center his attention, then let it drop limply to her side.

He smiled, said, "Nose full o' junk, Mabel?"

She looked at him in her about-to-float-into-space way but did not answer. Her face, which must have been handsome once, had remained intelligent.

"Wang is in there," she said in a strained, peculiar voice. Her hand moved slightly in a warning gesture.

A premonition of impending disaster swept over the Parson, held him rigid, A drapery stirred to the left of him.

He merely flicked a glance in that direction. His left hand moved for the knob. His right crossed without undue haste for his shoulder-holster. But it never reached there. Mabel clawed at his wrist.

The drapery swept aside and a gaunt, bony man stepped into view. He had a shiny Colt .45 in his fist. It was pointed at the Parson.

"This gun's a lulu, 'bo," he said. "She spits dum-dums. Wanta start something?"

The Parson looked at Mabel, at the man, at the gun. "No," he said.

"Then go on in."

The Parson turned the knob and pushed the door wide.

Wang Hoo Shan sat in a throne-like chair made of teakwood and inlaid with mother-of-pearl. His arms were strapped to the chair arms; his feet were tied. Blood showed on his face. One eye was badly discolored. A few welts stood out in thick ugly bands on his cheek. The Parson knew a fist could not have inflicted that much punishment. Wang had been gun-whipped.

The gaunt man with the gun pushed the Parson in, shoved

Mabel to one side. She stumbled to her knees, blank-eyed. Two men separated themselves from the walls at either side of the room, converged on the teakwood chair. They stared wide-eyed at the Parson.

He said, "Hello, Lonny. Hello, Frog."

They did not speak. A man, hidden behind Wang's chair, stepped into view suddenly, straightened. Nick Pagany's face was pointed, firm-fleshed. His eyes were a curious colorless blue, set wide apart under dark eyebrows. His nose was thin, sensitive, his mouth finely cut, thin and cruel.

"Hello, Nick," said the Parson.

Nick Pagany coolly measured him from head to foot. "So it's you," he said deliberately. "You couldn't keep your nose out."

The Parson shrugged. There were four of them arrayed against him. He looked each one over separately. He said, "I remember your gun boys, Lonny Crone and Frog Gorla. But who's the baby with the dum-dum toy? He's all business."

"That's one of my new boys, best in the organization. Toby Smith."

"Was it his chopper that cut down Jim Kardis?"

"Yeah."

"Nice shooting," said the Parson. He pointed to Wang. "What is all this about?"

"This," said Pagany, "is a dose for a double-crosser. Want some?"

"I don't even know what you're talking about."

"You don't huh? Only Kardis runs to you soon as his feet touch this damn island. The Chink here has a conference with you the very next day. Naw, you don't know nothing."

"What's the pay-off?" the Parson asked in a steady tone.

"I tell you I haven't the least idea of the set-up. Jim came to me, sure. But he didn't tell me why. All I got out of him was Wang's name. So I tried to get Wang to tell me the angles. He clammed up, wouldn't talk. I'm still in the dark."

Pagany's eyes narrowed. Toby Smith said, "Nuts, boss. Lemme take this guy."

"Hell!" snarled the Parson, pretending anger. "Just what kind of a dumb play is this anyway?"

Pagany looked unimpressed. He said casually, "The Chink and Kardis and another guy, who's got a wife who thinks she's got a brain, tried to throw me over. I fixed Kardis. A little while ago I had a talk with the guy and his wife. Seems like the Chink here has made a delivery to them that's worth at least two hundred grand. Get it? Cuttin' me out. The stuff's in coconuts—no less!"

While he spoke Pagany was watching the Parson narrowly. But the Parson listened with a blank face as if he understood not a word.

"The guy to whom delivery was made is named Segrave," Pagany went on. "He got wind of what happened to Kardis and got scared and shed the nuts. So when I asked him where, he told me. On a little boat named the *Cormorant*. Only we looked all over the damn boat and the stuff ain't where *we* could find it. So we been workin' the Chink. He says he knows nothing."

The Parson shrugged. "Maybe this Segrave guy was lying, then."

Pagany smiled thinly. "He started to. But when we worked his wife over down at the warehouse, near where the boat was docked, he came across with the coconut story. He knows he couldn't get away with it if he lied. I'd get him and get him good. His wife, too. The Chink must know just where on the boat the stuff is."

"Boss—" began Toby. He stopped speaking suddenly, eyes turned to the closed door.

Every eye in the room turned in the same direction. The street door could be heard opening and closing. Footsteps approached. Pagany gestured his men back. The Parson stared at the door for a second, then bent his gaze on Toby Smith and Pagany. The door opened.

Harry Kane strode in.

His frank young eyes bounced in his head. He saw Wang's battered face, and his fists clenched. But Toby held the shiny .45 trained on the boy's chest.

"O.K., handsome," Pagany said quietly. "You walked right into our parlor."

PAGANY'S MAN, LONNY, slid around Kane and shut the door. Frog and Toby Smith, like scissors, closed in on him from either side. Harry Kane's eyes moved from the Parson to Wang to Mabel in utter bewilderment.

"What's this mean?" he got out at last.

Pagany said, "Your girl friend talked. What we want now is the coconuts."

Harry Kane knit his brows. "Huh? What coconuts?"

"Drop the dumb act," Pagany roared. "Give, handsome. Penny told us the whole lay. The stuff's supposed to be aboard your boat. Where is it? Tonight you and she were going to make a break for it together. You two have it!"

Red leaped to Harry Kane's cheeks. He said jerkily, "I—I didn't know she—I haven't seen her." But his eyes were shining suddenly. His shoulders were thrown back. "Penny said she was going to go away with me in my boat?" He spoke deliberately, carefully, anxious there should be no mistake.

Pagany grinned. "That's what she said. But don't make a poem about it. You're gonna tell us where she planted the stuff. We looked all over your damn tub but couldn't find it."

Kane shook his head, and his voice was steady when he spoke. "I don't know anything about any stuff. I haven't been to the boat since I docked this afternoon. I've been walking the streets...."

"Listen!" Pagany's voice was vaguely threatening. "I got another way to make you talk. Wang knows how. So does Mabel."

Wang's mouth twitched. Mabel swayed slightly, closed her eyes momentarily. She whispered, "No, no. Please!" Anguish twisted her face. When her eyes opened, they were flaming. "We'll get the stuff for you. We'll do anything. Only let us alone!"

"Yeah? We got the boy here, we got you and Wang. If you want me to tell him...."

"You're not half as tough as you talk!" Harry Kane said suddenly. His jaw was earnestly set, his lean muscular frame tensed.

The faintest shadow of a smile touched the Parson's lips. He looked immensely pleased. Courage, guts—one of the few traits he admired in others.

Pagany stared at Harry. The lines at the corners of his thin mouth creased deeper.

"Not tough, eh? What do you think those cannons are— water pistols?"

"That's all you got, just the guns. I don't know what this is about. But you've been talking to Penny, you say, and she told you some crazy story. So you've been putting the screws on poor Wang. Without your guns, you're nothing. Even with your guns, I could take you."

Pagany stared at him, actually rattled. People he knew were frightened before guns. A new light of interest sprang into the Parson's eyes. This was not just bravado on the boy's part.

Harry Kane was not a stunter. He was cool-headed, a leader in the making; and it would be easy making for him. Despite his absurd youth he gave the impression of possessing untapped reservoirs of strength.

Perhaps, then, it had been strength, not weakness, which had driven him from Penelope Segrave, brought him to Cariba. Just as now this quality slapped the lien into the teeth of the gunmen who threatened him.

His fists doubled; his right fist lashed out and hit Pagany cleanly on the jaw. It was as sudden as that.

Mabel was poised on her toes, screaming.

Pagany went back two steps, stunned. Mabel was upon him, tearing at his face with her fingernails in cold fury.

The Parson snapped his Luger from his holster, aimed at Pagany and fired as he dropped to one knee. His movement spoiled his aim.

Harry Kane shoved at Toby and simultaneously stuck his foot between Frog's legs. Toby hit against the wall, bounced off. Harry and Frog went down in a swirl of legs. Lonny Crone was dancing over them, hopping first on one foot then the other, unable to make up his mind what to do.

Harry Kane caught Frog's gun hand, tore the weapon away.

Frog and Lonny started backward under the muzzle. Kane lunged at Toby.

The Parson ran smack into Toby, just as Harry Kane charged in from the other side. The Parson hit Toby first, went down with him. Toby had hold of his gun arm, was holding it at bay.

"Get him off me!" Toby yelled. "Kill him!"

Frog and Lonny were grabbing at the Parson's coat. He brought up his bent knee against Toby's groin, tore his arm free. Toby screamed. The Parson pressed the muzzle of his Luger against Toby's side and when he was clouted in the back of the neck, his teeth rattled and his finger twitched on the trigger. The blast of the gun was muffled. The slug knocked Toby backward.

The Parson had time to mutter, "The guy you kissed with a chatter gun last night kind of saved my life once. That was a revenge slug."

Then something hit him on the crown of the head with crushing force and he went out like a candle in a cyclone.

WATER WAS COLD on the Parson's face. He opened his eyes and the movement exploded firecrackers inside his skull. Someone was squatting beside him on the floor, saying, "How do you feel?" It was Wang.

The Parson raised to a sitting posture. "Lousy. How's by you?" He saw a figure a few feet away hugging the floor. It was the dead gunman, Toby Smith.

Wang said, "All right, except my face feels like railroad tracks were built across it."

"What happened?"

"Almost everything." Wang helped the Parson to his feet,

piloted him to a chair and took one opposite. "After you shot Toby, one of Pagany's gorillas bent a gun over your head. Mabel grabbed Toby's gun and started in shooting. Pagany and his two toughies beat it fast."

"They weren't so tough," the Parson said.

Wang's eyes gleamed. "That boy, Harry, he's all right."

"Yeah," said the Parson. "Where is he?"

Wang spread his plump hands. "He's still crazy in love with that Segrave woman. Pagany's telling him that she had said she was going to run away with him on his boat, set him afire. He's that kind of boy."

"You shouldn't have let him go out alone. Pagany maybe was waiting outside to pounce on him."

"Mabel went after Harry. She'll watch to keep him out of danger."

"How long have I been out?"

"About an hour. That was a tremendous wallop you took."

"Why didn't you go out with Harry?"

Wang spoke with a shade of embarrassment. "I couldn't leave you alone. I thought you might need help. You were hurt bad."

The Parson was startled. No one had ever been that considerate of him before. A sudden black reaction closed like a shutter over his mind. He moved always alone, an exile who lived by the power of his wits and his gun. For a brief moment it seemed that a fatigue, welling up out of a sense of the futility of his life, would rob him of his customary concentrated flippancy, of his usual brittle shield against men and their affairs.

However, he looked at Wang and put forth his hand, said roughly, "Here, shake it, pal, before I bust out crying."

A curious dignity came to Wang's demeanor. Solemnly, he shook hands.

The Parson said, "Let's percolate outa here."

Wang's shrewd eyes stabbed him with a searching look, "Where to?"

The Parson sounded non-committal. "Well, you must know where Mr. and Mrs. Donald Segrave are putting up. It might be a good idea for you and me to buzz around there and have a talk with them."

Wang was on his feet. "The India House. Wait a minute."

He skittered into another room, was gone about fifteen minutes. He had cleaned up his face, changed his clothes to his South China suit and donned his Panama. In these clothes and with his innocent looking round face, he looked like a kindly Chinese uncle. But his eyes were troubled and restless.

"If we're going," he said, "I'd like to go fast."

They went out to the street and walked two blocks before they caught a cab. The ride took twenty minutes; India House was on the other side of the island in the very center of the fashionable *Punta Guaira* residential area of the whites where *Avenida de Muralla* skirts the beach and the thatched *cabañas*.

"Hey, slow down," the Parson told the cabbie suddenly.

The front of the hotel was mobbed by people. A police motor lorry was drawn up at the curb. Someone was shouting, "They're bringing him down!"

"Weave in closer," the Parson told the cabbie.

Someone leaped on the running-board and a red face was thrust at the Parson as the cab tried to get closer. Above the face was a white helmet with a silver shield on it. The cop grabbed hold of the Parson.

"*Cariba Post,*" the Parson said quickly. "I'm a newsman."

The jagged murmur that was rising from the crowd changed to a sudden rumbling growl. The Parson's eyes snapped quickly to the hotel entrance.

Three white-helmeted cops appeared there, shepherding a slow-moving man among them.

The Parson jerked at Wang: "It's Harry Kane!"

The Chinaman's face seemed to fall apart. A strangled sound issued from his throat but no words; only his eyes spoke.

The Parson put his head out of the cab. The cop was still on the running-board. "What happened?" the Parson said.

The cop stared toward the hotel entrance. "He filled 'is sweetheart full of lead. A crime of passion, as you might say. And she a respectable married woman! He just stood there cool as you please and gave her what-for with a bloody 'orse pistol. The weapon was on 'im when we broke into the room. Gor! And she was beautiful! Married to a Mr. Donald Segrave. Shippin' man."

"When did it happen?"

"About three-quarter of an hour ago we got a ring at the precinct that she was dead," the cop said. "And when we got here, there was this young chappie with the weapon in his fist, large as life. He was dazed-like and put up no fight. Just kept saying he didn't do it. Kept pointing to the doors leading to the balcony and saying the shot came from there. But we searched the balcony and no one was there at all."

Wang grabbed the Parson's arm, pointed to a car that had drawn up beside the police motor lorry. Two men slammed out. "It's Pagany's men—Lonny Crone and Gorla!" he said fiercely.

The Parson stiffened. It was Crone and Gorla, all right, and the man behind the wheel of the car was Nick Pagany.

Crone and Gorla jerked guns into plain sight. British colonial police, like their counterparts, London bobbies, are armed with nothing more deadly than night-sticks. Pagany thrust the snout of a sub-machine gun across the open window and said something, but the Parson and Wang were too far away to hear. Apparently, it was an order to the policemen. Slowly, the cops surrounding Kane fell back.

Harry Kane did not stir until Crone grabbed his arm and Frog Gorla pressed up close against him. Even then he looked utterly lost, bewildered.

The Parson's voice was calm, detached—the voice of one professional critically examining the work of another. "It's a snatch. They're moving him to the car."

"Do something!" Wang said in a fierce whisper. "Shoot!"

"No," said the Parson. "At the first sign of trouble they'd plug Harry. Look!"

Just before entering the car, Harry whirled, elbows and fists pummeling, as if he had just awakened to what was happening to him. Crone clouted him behind the ear and carried him bodily the rest of the way. The car hummed into high.

The bobby had leaped off the cab's running-board and was shouting to his startled fellows. The Parson leaned forward, tapped his wide-eyed driver. "Follow that car," he ordered.

But the crowd was thick before the cab. The driver toed the machine to life, leaned on his horn. The crowd parted. The cab was starting forward cautiously when two explosions blasted above the roar of human voices in the street.

The shots dug into the metal of Pagany's receding car, jolting it. It slewed over perilously for a split second, threatening to overturn, then righted itself just in time and sped on.

The shots came from somewhere off to the left, quite close at hand, but the Parson could not see who had fired them.

The crowd began yelling in sheer panic, but the Parson and Wang sat in their cab, tense and motionless. The police were hopping about and telling each other how their prisoner had been snatched from them. More police came. The crowd grew and grew. And the night surf boomed on the near-by beach.

A bitter smile came to the Parson's lips. He said almost tenderly, "Ain't this the nuts?" He began getting out of the cab. "Wait here a minute."

Wang stared after him as the Parson cork-screwed through the crowd. Suddenly the Parson stopped beside a man. It was Donald Segrave. The Parson was speaking to him in a low voice right into his ear. Segrave looked frightened. He kept glancing at the policemen who were but a few yards from him.

Then slowly he turned and walked in front of the Parson to the cab. His mouth opened like a cod at the sight of Wang. The Parson prodded him and Segrave got in beside Wang. The Parson climbed in, said:

"I spotted our friend in the crowd. If Pagany could pull off a snatch job, I figured I could, too." He turned on Segrave. "Your wife is dead. She was murdered, shot."

Segrave shivered. "I—I just heard."

"You killed her."

"N-no! For God's sake, what are you saying? I killed her? Oh, my God, no!"

"Yes. Then you fired those shots after Pagany's car."

Segrave gagged. He started to get up. The Parson pulled him down. He became limp. "I didn't fire at anyone," he whimpered, lips quivering. "I don't know what happened."

"Have you got a gun?"

"N-no."

The Parson made a rapid search of his clothing. "O.K.," he said. "Now, listen, mush. Earlier this evening Pagany took you and your wife to a warehouse by the *Cormorant*. Why there?"

Segrave looked startled, but he answered: "Pagany picked that place so he could keep a watch in case Harry Kane tried to make a quick getaway. An office on the lower floor—"

"Driver!" the Parson barked. "Pescado Pier and step on it."

"But it's insane!" Wang muttered. "The woman murdered, Harry accused of the crime, kidnaped by Pagany!"

"And long life, sons to worship you after you are dead," the Parson said mockingly. "You Chinese!"

"Yes," said Wang. "But who fired those two shots?"

The Parson leaned back on the cushions, eyes inscrutable. "You got something there, China boy."

SHARP PAIN BROUGHT him to but it was seconds before Harry Kane could localize it; he seemed to be a lump of aches. His brain peeled off layer after layer of fog. He recalled the street outside the India House, the guns at his side, the two men, the waiting car, his futile attempt to get away, the clout behind the ear. He had passed out then. They must have beaten him while he had been unconscious: his body ached so. Then all the pain seemed to draw downward and he realized it was in his leg. No, not his leg—his foot, the sole of his foot. He jerked it up and his eyes opened.

"Like I told you," said a husky, triumphant voice. "Foot-toastin' 'd bring a dead man to. I know, boy."

"Pipe down, Frog."

Kane raised his head slowly, looked into a pair of wolfish, colorless eyes of the man who had just spoken—Nick Pagany. The other two men stood to one side. One of them was Crone. The other, Gorla, had a book of matches in his hand.

Kane's foot was bare. There were half a dozen burnt matches on the floor beneath his foot. The air was heavy with an acrid odor of burnt flesh. He was sitting in a straight-backed chair and his arms were lashed to it. A hand grabbed his chin, jerked his head up. Pagany's face was thrust close to his own.

"So you don't think we're tough," Pagany said slowly. "Well, we're down to cases now. Where is it?"

"Where is what?"

"Now there's a fast one for you!" croaked Lonny Crone in deep disgust.

"I don't know what you want," said Kane distinctly.

"Jeeze, Nick, lemme at him. This match stuff is too mild. A dum-dum through his hand'd do wonders for his memory."

"I'm handling this, Lonny." Pagany turned to Kane again, his voice vibrant with menace. "Listen, feller. Segrave and Penny wouldn't dare fool me. They were frightened green, see? I know when a dame's ribbing me and when she ain't. The same goes for Segrave. His guts were hanging out when he told me the stuff's planted on your tub. So I'm starting from there. It's on your boat; see? We searched it from end to end and we didn't find it. We went back to check with Segrave and we found that Penny had been shot—"

"You killed her!"

Crone grinned. "This guy's her everything, boss."

"Naw!" grunted Gorla. "It's the other way around."

Pagany went on: "We lamped you being dragged off by the

cops. I couldn't let the cops sweat you. Hell, they might hang you before I could get a chance to find out what I want. So, wise up. Get it over with."

"I keep telling you I don't know what you want. What kind of stuff are you talking about? And why should Penny hide it on my boat?"

"Bozo, when you work for a smoothie like Wang and you're hooked in with a stink like Segrave and a girl like Penny, you ought to have the answers," Pagany said. "Hell, I knew Penny when— You can't tell me a thing about that dame. She was my girl until I threw her out."

"That's a damnable lie!"

Pagany put hands on his hips. "B'jeepers, I think Mealy-Mouth believes that!"

"Little Boy Blue won't hear his sweetie's reputation knocked down."

The good humor vanished from Pagany's face. "Hell, I'm sick of this. Give, feller, give, and make it fast!"

Kane sighed. "How can I when I don't know the first thing about it? Maybe Segrave was stalling you about it all, whatever *it* is."

"*He* was stalling, huh? What in hell you think you're doing?"

The chair teetered crazily as Pagany's fist crashed on Kane's temple. There was a signet ring on Pagany's hand; it raked skin and drew blood. Another blow struck Kane on the jaw roundly. His head began to droop slowly and his eyes closed.

Pagany snarled, "He needs a treatment, Frog."

Frog Gorla knelt down with alacrity, struck a match. "This is better than water in the face," he said cheerfully. "Ha! Water clears their heads but this shocks 'em awake." He was holding the match steady. "Boy, can he take it! Oops! Looka his foot jerk away."

The fierce pain snapped Kane back to consciousness. His eyes opened but it was some seconds before they registered vision. Pagany was bending over him, speaking in a low, intimate voice:

"Wang must've used your tub, like he uses the others. So there's more to it than meets the eye. Somewhere aboard is a secret room or a secret panel, and you're the baby to lead us to it."

Kane wearily shook his drooping head. "If there's anything like that aboard, I don't know about it."

"So what, Nick?"

"So nuts!"

"How's for trying my dum-dum idea?"

Pagany roared in a savage voice: "Take it away." He wheeled about, pointed. "Last chance, smart guy."

Kane again shook his head. "I told you the truth. I can't help you."

Crone said, "Stand back, Nick, so the blood won't smear you."

He jammed the muzzle of his gun down on Kane's lashed right hand, held it there.

The boy looked full at him, unflinchingly. "Well," he said, "what are you waiting for? Why the theatrics?"

But Crone was not just pausing for effect. His head was turned toward the door. A slight whispering of footsteps sounded from behind it.

Pagany gestured Crone back so that he would be hidden by the door when it opened, thus effecting a neat trap. Frog Gorla swiftly uncovered a big Smith and Wesson. The knob turned suddenly and then as suddenly the door flung back.

The Parson stood on the threshold behind a Luger. Pagany and Gorla started back in horror as if utterly cowed. The Parson took a single step into this room in the old warehouse. Only the thin panel of the door separated him from Crone. Crone held his breath, finger trembling on the trigger.

Suddenly glass smashed, fell in jagged shreds at the feet of Pagany and Gorla. Heads jerked upward to the shattered window, away from the Parson.

Wang thrust in a fat forearm, fat fingers curled around a .32. He said good-naturedly, "Up with you hands, boys. You behind the door! Ah, that's better!"

His wide, clear grin filled the room with golden effulgence.

The Parson moved swiftly into the room so that he could cover Crone. Crone's hands were raised, the gun limp in his fingers. Pagany and Gorla stood quiet. The Parson said, "O.K., Wang. You can come in like regular folks. I'll hold 'em."

Wang's fat arm slowly withdrew and his gun disappeared. His footsteps could he heard pattering outside.

The Parson shifted his weight to the balls of his feet. "Drop the artillery, boys," he said, "all the way to the floor." He said it casually as though he were well aware that his order would not be obeyed.

There were too many guns out; something had to happen. Pagany and his men wouldn't have to ease out with an apology.

Wang, still smiling, appeared in the door. As he came in, his elbow gently pushed the door back, momentarily obscuring Crone.

The Parson instantly dropped to one knee. Crone's gun exploded as he snapped a shot at him, but the Parson was under the slug.

"Wang, look out!" he yelled.

Crone shot dum-dums twice through the door. Chunks of wood ripped out of the panel, large as silver dollars. Wang jerked around and, groaning, slammed abruptly to the floor. He clapped a hand to his side in utter wonderment. A patch of red appeared under it, spread between his splayed fingers.

The Parson sent three shots hurtling through the door panel. Then he scrambled behind a battered desk with the speed of an agile monkey. Lead bit furrows into the top of the desk, sent splinters flying to the ceiling. Two or three of the bullets ricocheted, dug into the pale plaster of the wall. The shots were coming from Gorla.

"Lonny!" screamed Pagany, demanding action. But Lonny did not answer.

"Guess they got him, boss," Gorla yammered.

Pagany was crouched over, sheltered by a chair, eyes fixed feverishly on the desk. He had no gun. He turned his head suddenly, panic-stricken.

Harry Kane, lashed to the chair though he was, was not sitting idly by, letting others fight his battles. He had braced his feet against the floor and shoved hard, throwing his weight to the left. He and his chair went over side-wise on top of Pagany.

Pagany screamed, arms and legs writhing madly. Gorla was shooting doggedly at the desk top, holding the Parson at bay. Pagany got one arm loose, one leg, but he was still pinned.

The Parson, watching warily, muttered, "Good boy, Harry!"

In his panic Pagany did not realize that he was wriggling clear on the wrong side of the overturned chair straight into the range of fire. But the Parson knew and waited until Pagany was on hands and knees. Then he fired. Pagany slammed down, dazed. The Parson's Luger boomed again. Pagany coughed, blood and spittle bubbled at his mouth. Slowly his head began to droop until his cheek pressed against the floor.

Gorla stood stock-still for the space of a watch-tick, then in a kind of wild desperation, whipped in toward the desk, shooting as he came. A foot away from the desk, his gun clicked hollowly. His teeth bared in terror. He flung the emptied weapon at the Parson's head. The Parson ducked. The gun sailed over his head, smacked into the wall.

Gorla sidled toward the door, his face a mask of fear. The Parson rose deliberately, stepped into the middle of the room, said: "My inning."

Gorla's arm was raised to protect himself. "For Gawd's sake, Parson," he whined. "Gimme a break. Jeez, don't cut me down. Oh, don't...."

"Lay down on the floor, snake. Smack on your belly."

Gorla started down slowly. He got to his knees. Suddenly he threw himself forward. His hand shot out, caught the Parson's ankle, yanked. The Parson sailed into the air and came down with his gun beneath him.

Gorla flung himself on top of the Parson but the Parson rolled, swept him off. Gorla drove his heavy shoe to the Parson's head.

The Parson sagged down again under the crushing blow, muscles twitching. Gorla stood aside a second, panting. Then he got both hands on the Parson's wrist and twisted. The Luger clattered to the floor.

Gorla snatched it up. "This is where you take it, Parson. Right where you live."

Then the roar of a gun sounded once with final authority. Gorla went backward two steps. His head and knees started coming together, joint by joint, like a jack-knife slowly closing. His eyes, jiggling stupidly in his head, looked down uncomprehendingly at the Parson, at the Parson's empty hands. His slow salaam ended at the floor. He pitched forward on his chest, landing heavily.

Face twisted and ugly, the Parson looked up blinking. Mabel stood in the doorway, head inclined downward, eyes burning madly in her head, an automatic in her hand.

IT WAS VERY quiet in the little office for a long second. Smoke coiled toward the single overhead light bulb. The endless slap-slap of the water could be plainly heard outside. Then a faint chuckle came to the Parson's ears. He tore his gaze from Mabel, looked down.

It was Wang. His grin was so wide, his gold teeth were threatening to leap from his mouth. Mabel looked down at him, as if she saw him now for the first time. Then she stepped over him and strode over to where Harry Kane lay.

Her voice was timorous. "Are you all right?"

"Yes. Untie me."

The Parson dragged himself over to Wang. The Chinaman was still chuckling. The Parson got to his own feet, then helped Wang up. He led him across to a chair and eased him down. "How do you feel?" the Parson asked.

"Fine," said Wang. "A little puncture in the side. A lot of blood, yes. But dangerous, no."

"Your wife don't seem to give a damn." Even as he spoke, the Parson wondered why he had said that.

"Mabel's all right. Don't say anything against Mabel. She saved your life. She just thinks more of Harry than of me."

Harry Kane, young face drawn and haggard, was trying to walk. His injured sole gave him a sharp twinge. He hobbled to a chair.

"Harry!" the woman cried. She followed him to the chair, hands clasped, nails biting into her palms. "Harry, did they hurt you? Is anything—"

He smiled wanly, patted her shoulder. "They toasted my foot a little but I think I can walk. Get me that shoe and sock."

When he had them on, he walked gingerly to Wang. "You've got to tell me what this is all about," he said gravely. "I've got to know."

The Chinaman looked uncomfortable, worried; the grin slithered off his face.

"I'll tell you," the Parson said suddenly. "It's like this. Pagany is a gang leader. He sells dope. Segrave and his wife were shipping it to him from here to New York on the Segrave freighters. Segrave tried to double-cross Pagany. He tried to involve Wang in order to save himself. He mentioned your name to Pagany, too. So did Penelope. They—"

"That's a damn lie!" Harry Kane interrupted. "Penelope had nothing to do—"

"You don't have to believe me," the Parson cut in blandly. "Just listen, is all. You were arrested for her murder, weren't you? Did you kill her?"

"No! Kill her? I loved her!"

"Then how'd it happen?"

Kane did not answer at once. It seemed as though Wang and Mabel had ceased breathing, waiting.

Words came slowly then from Kane's lips, each cutting into his heart as he recalled what had happened. "I came up to her rooms. I told her what Pagany had told me—that she had hid something aboard my boat and that she was planning to run away with me. I asked her if that were true. She acted nervous, afraid. She said, 'Harry, will you save my life? Then I'll go with you."

"Just as she was talking, there was a shot. It came from the balcony. I could almost swear I saw a hand and a gun appear; the door was partly open. Penelope fell to the floor. I was too dazed to think clearly. I rushed to her. Then I got my gun out, the one I'd taken from the killer at Wang's shop and ran to the balcony. No one was there. Then the police came."

A whistling sound came from the floor. It was Pagany, moving slightly, lips flat against his teeth. Instantly, the Parson knelt down beside Pagany, shook him slightly. "Nick!" he called. "Nick!"

Pagany slowly opened his eyes.

"You're dying, Nick. Come clean. You had Penny shot. You had her killed. Tell us!"

Like a mechanical toy, slowly unwinding, Pagany shook his head.

"Be regular, Nick. This is the first time in your life you got a chance to do a decent thing. The kid didn't plug her. He's in a spot. Tell us. You killed her or had her killed."

The lips formed the word, "No," but did not utter it.

The Parson stood up, said crisply, "Get a pen, Kane. Write out a confession. Pagany's admitted everything. Well, don't stand there staring. This guy ain't gonna live forever! And you don't want to swing. Start it something like this: 'I want to clear the slate before I die. I hereby solemnly confess to the murder of Penelope Segrave.' Then tell how it occurred. Hiding on the balcony and all that and end up: 'This confession is my dying statement in order to clear the name of any persons wrongfully accused, particularly Harry Kane,' and so on. Go on. Break into it!"

Minutes later the Parson was pressing a pen into Pagany's hand. "O.K., guy. Just scrawl your name on this. This way." He started to guide Pagany's hand and arm. The half-opened eyes stared unseeing. Automatically, by a reflex action, Pagany completed the signature. Then suddenly, his neck went loose and his head lolled back on the floor.

A spot of blood had dropped on the paper. The Parson flourished the document in the air. "Here, boy, it's signed and sealed; it's up to you to deliver. This is your story for the cops. Penny was once Pagany's woman. Hey, don't look at me like that! It's true—back in New York he paid her bills. She came to Cariba because she was afraid of Pagany who wanted her to go back to him. She wanted you to help her. Pagany was jealous of her attentions to you, so that after he had killed her, he kidnaped you in order to kill you, too. But Wang and I stepped in. You know the rest. Except one thing, leave out the dope angle."

Kane's voice leaped abruptly. "You want me to smear Penny's name in the mud in order to clear myself. I won't do it!"

"So you still think she was an angel, huh?" The Parson's voice was gentle. "Wait a second."

He went out, was gone about two minutes and came back with Donald Segrave in tow. Segrave was white-faced, his eyes tortured, restless. He recoiled at sight of the inert bodies on the floor but the Parson shoved him in.

"I've had him outside in the cab," the Parson explained, "in the custody of the driver. I'm going to make him tell you things.

Maybe they're gonna hurt, but you asked for it. O.K., Segrave, spill it. Was your wife ever Pagany's woman? Were you and she shipping joy powder north to Pagany? Did you try to double-cross Pagany? Speak before I knock it out of you!"

Segrave's voice was a frantic whisper. "Yes, it's true. But Penny dragged me into the mess. It was all her idea. I never wanted any part of it. She was crazy for money. All she wanted was money. Because she had been Pagany's woman, she could put the deal across with him. She dragged me down with her!"

The shattered thing in front of him disgusted the Parson. He shoved Segrave toward the door, made a motion with his hands as if washing them after touching something unclean. "Get out!" he growled. "And get out of Cariba by tomorrow morning. If you don't...."

"I'll go!" Segrave shrieked. "I'll go." He ran out into the night.

"Penny.... She couldn't. She wasn't that kind...." Harry Kane's voice was weak, puzzled.

"That's the whole of it, kid," the Parson said softly. "I know this hits you hard, but it's best to know the truth. Penny didn't care buttons for you. She just wanted to use you when she got into a mess. You'd better get down to the police with that statement. And remember, you got witnesses."

Kane nodded. He drew himself slowly erect, his shoulders squared. He strode out of the door, misery stiffening his shoulders.

The Parson watched him go and there was a light of admiration in his dark eyes. "Nice kid," he said curtly as if dismissing the subject forever from his mind. "Pagany thought the kid really knew where the junk was hidden by Penny. That's why he used the hot-foot cure."

"You could have asked Segrave," Wang reminded him.

The Parson looked off into space. "Yeah, I could've at that. Segrave and Penny didn't lie to Nick. They really hid the stuff."

"Where?" Wang shouted.

"Like they said, on the *Cormorant*. Pagany searched and didn't find it. You'd search and not find it either. How much would you pay if I found it?"

"Ten thousand above what I promised you to keep Harry out of danger."

The Parson started toward the door. "My chips are in," he said quietly.

SALT-LADEN BREEZE BLEW in gently off Boca Passage. The Parson stood for a moment looking out at the empty street that straggled away from the pier. Nobody seemed to have heard the shots. He strode across the pier to where the *Cormorant* was moored. The boat swayed as his weight hit it. He moved to the forward hatch. The lock on it had been smashed; a staple had been wrenched loose. Pagany's work. But the Parson did not go below, He went to the stern of the craft and stood looking down at the water.

There was a windlass bolted to the deck. He took hold of the crank and slowly began drawing up the stern anchor chain. It was very heavy. All his strength went into revolving the crank. There was a sucking splash as the anchor came clear of the water.

The windlass wound tight, and it was not an anchor that came swinging up above the aft rail. It was a big slatted box.

"Hey, Mabel," yelled the Parson. "Come here."

Mabel supported the box on the rail while the Parson undid

the slip-knot which attached the box to the anchor chain. Together they eased the box to the deck. The Parson ripped off a few water-soaked slats.

There were stones on top but the rest of the space was filled by coconuts.

The Parson removed one, examined it minutely but it appeared to be untampered with. Mabel took it from him. "This is the trick," she said.

She ran her thumb-nail across the top, dislodged a black-brown seam of paraffin and disclosed an opening that looked like the slot of a penny bank. She shook the nut and through the slot appeared a small manila envelope. Another followed it, and another.

"Hm," said the Parson appreciatively. "Decks and decks of happy powder. Stuffed nuts."

He straightened, clambered up on the pier and sauntered back to the warehouse office.

As he came in, Wang's bright eyes flicked a challenge at him. Something that could be a smile or a look of derision wrinkled the corners of the Parson's mouth.

"Well, I got it," he said, at last. "It was in a box tied to the stern anchor chain. I got the idea from seeing that chain in the water. It didn't have a right to be lowered. Anchor's aren't dropped on small boats when they've been tied fore and aft to the dock. And even if they are, at least the anchor chain is steady. This one was swaying with the movement of the water, which meant that whatever was at the end of it was not fast in the bottom but floating above it."

Wang's eyes were wide with surprise. "That was good reasoning, my friend."

The Parson was silent a moment, thinking. "By the way, that was Mabel who fired those two shots at Pagany's car, wasn't it?"

Wang nodded. "She saw Pagany grabbing Harry, just as we did. When she saw us get hold of Segrave and start away, she followed us."

"Funny her turning up there." The Parson mused. "Y'know, Pagany didn't kill Penelope Segrave despite what the cops are going to think."

Wang smiled gently. "No."

"I know who did. Mabel killed her."

Wang did not look perturbed. "You're right, my friend. Segrave and Penny planted the stuff on the boat to get Harry in trouble. Mabel wouldn't stand for a double-cross as dirty as that. When Segrave and his woman told Pagany where they'd hidden the stuff, they intended to save their own necks by directing Pagany's fire against Harry. Then when Mrs. Segrave tried to get Harry to run away with her on his boat, she wanted to save the hidden dope and get away even at the risk of having Harry murdered. I'm not sorry she's dead. I'm only sorry I didn't kill her."

"You and Mabel think a lot of Harry Kane."

Wang nodded.

"Enough to murder for his sake?"

"Yes!" Wang's voice was vibrant and earnest. "Harry, you see, is Mabel's son."

The Parson looked up, his eyes widening.

"It's nearly twenty years that I met Mabel," Wang said. "She was married to a doctor then. Harry was only an infant, a few months old. Her husband, Dr. Kane, was my most valued friend. He had practiced in China. During a cholera epidemic he saved the lives of many people. One of them was my father.

"When I came to America, I sought him out and he made me welcome. I opened a fan-tan parlor in New York's China-town and Mabel and Dr. Kane dropped in often. Then I began to notice that there was trouble between them. She was using narcotics heavily. She'd acquired the habit years before on the stage. Her stay in China only confirmed it. She found she couldn't break it, not even for the sake of her husband or her baby son. Dr. Kane was about fed up.

"He threw her out, divorced her, and told their child she'd died. I left New York, came here to Cariba. One day Mabel turned up. We were old friends; I understood her need of drugs. It was easy to get along with me. We married.

"Then we heard that Dr. Kane had died penniless. I made a trip up to New York and looked up Harry. He was a boy of about ten then. I told him I had been a great friend of his father, that his father had once saved the life of mine and that I was under eternal obligation to his family.

"We sent him to school, Mabel and I, then to college. We were proud of him. Then one day out of a clear sky he came to Cariba. He couldn't stay in the States because he loved that Segrave woman. Only then I didn't know it was Penelope Segrave. He never told me her name."

The Parson's chin was sunk to his chest. "He doesn't know his mother is living?"

"No. And he never will."

"Why don't you tell him?"

"For what? So that he can find her, after all the years he's built up a shrine of her in his memory, married to an old, dope-deal-ing Chinaman? No. Mabel doesn't want that. She doesn't want him to see her as she is now."

The Parson stood up. "And Pagany knew the story?"

"Yes. He kept me in line by threatening to tell Harry the truth. Then other things came up, but that money and dope part wasn't so important."

"Well, what about now?" said the Parson. "If you're crazy about that boy as you say you are, why don't you keep your paws out of coke?"

Wang sighed. "With Pagany and Segrave smashed, I may be forced to get out of the game. It was a good one, too." He sounded wistful.

"Well, my dough still goes!"

Wang nodded. "You have more than earned it. Call at the shop tomorrow."

The Parson went out the door. Slowly he crossed the pier to the *Cormorant*. Mabel was standing at the rail, her eyes fixed on the restless water.

"Mabel, Wang just told—" The Parson stopped. He knew he could not find words that would be comforting to a woman who had murdered because another scheming woman had endangered the life of her son—a son who thought of her as dead.

"Well, good-night," he said again.

She looked up at him keenly for a long second, and found the reassurance she sought. Calm returned to her pale, haunted face. "Good-night," she said.

The Parson turned toward the beckoning lights of Cariba.

Murder for Pennies

It's "policy" with the Parson to clean up
on—and with—the numbers game

THE BEACON AT the seaplane base was seven miles away, on the other side of the island, but because the moon was full with a blazing tropical fullness, the Parson could see it plainly from where he stood before the door of the little white cottage on San Pedro Road. He gave a last searching look up and down the street, an under-sized man with dark moody eyes and sharp chiseled features. Then with a shrug of his shoulders, he rang a bell next to the door.

It was hot. Cariba, a dot of marl and coral in the Caribbean, was always hot; panting, like a tiger lying in watchful repose. Even with the breeze, it was hot. But because it was outwardly a civilized, pleasurable, tight little island, under British rule, a queer melting pot of races and breeds from the four corners of the earth, Cariba was called "the little Paris of the Caribbean."

Actually, the indolent breeze, pungent and heavy with the incense of papaya, ripening bananas, wild orange trees, humid with the smell of writhing gourd vines, somehow suggested how close to the surface was the sudden blind violence of the hot countries; the sheathed claws of the waiting watchful tiger.

There came the sound of footsteps in response to the Parson's ring and then the door was opened. A tall man with a stubborn mouth stood looking down at the Parson. He had thin red hair and the sort of complexion, fair skin and freckles, that goes with hair of that color. He looked about, under and around the Parson without actually looking directly into his eyes.

"What d'you want?" the man said, mumbling as though he were shy.

One hand was loosely hidden behind his back. It held a gun.

"I want to talk to you, Tex," the Parson said. His own face was expressionless, mild. It was this deceptive mild manner, his soft way of speaking and his delicate pious air which had earned him his curious nickname. But his outward appearance gave no warning of his skill in handling a 7.65 Luger; no hint to the amazing fact that mere mention of the Parson in certain quarters was enough to reduce both criminals and detectives to gibbering incoherence; for, in his time, the Parson had outwitted crooks and police alike.

Without invitation, the Parson went past the man he had called Tex, past his gun into a small room furnished sparsely with a tropical regard for airiness. Tex closed the door, then followed the Parson in. His gun was now in plain view. He held it carelessly, lightly, like a man accustomed to guns.

"So you know my name," he said quietly, "and you want to talk to me."

The Parson said, "Yeah. I know your name, Tex Kent. I know all about you. You were Cig Wolfe's triggerman. Sort of private executioner. That was three years ago. Cig Wolfe had New York sewed up. It was all his. Including the policy numbers racket. Remember the take on those numbers? Fifteen million a year. Oh, you paid off six hundred to one to winners. But didn't the suckers pay, the non-winners! It was too good, if you get what I mean. The protection was O.K. Cig paid out heavy sugar to the right people. But there was competition. And Cig was rubbed out. Cig Wolfe, the biggest racketeer since Capone, kissed lead."

Tex Kent was remembering aloud. "That chopper was good. When he got through, there was nothing left of Cig's face. Nothing you could recognize. Twenty dum-dums tore holes in it big as silver dollars."

"A swell guy, Cig," the Parson said softly, reminiscently.

"You think so?"

"Every day in the week and twice on Sundays."

Tex Kent put his gun out of sight into a pocket. His shy, diffident manner had not altered. He said very thoughtfully: "If it's talk and not gunplay, how's for wettin' our whistles?"

The Parson nodded, watched him get a quart bottle out and two glasses. They drank. The Parson said, "You're a nice reasonable guy, Tex."

"Uh-huh. And you're the guy they call the Parson. I remember you now. You used to run gamin' tables back in N'York for a guy named Vince Guard, though I don't believe we ever met. You carry quite a rep."

"Thanks. Shall I continue my little story? I got a chance to throw a little business your way."

"Business?" For the first time Tex fixed his strange smeary blue eyes directly on the Parson. They were the kind of blue eyes redheads often have. "I like business. What kind of business?"

"We'll come to that in a moment. Cig Wolfe had a woman—they called her the Dutchess. It was more than a nickname. She was bright as a whip. She'd built him up. She carried on when they planted him. But the going got too hot. Not competition, this time. The law. It seems they got themselves a new D.A. with guts and no price. He just didn't know the color of money. So he sailed in and banged things around. First thing he gunned for was the protection. Not the racket. You know. The papers are still full of it."

Tex said nothing. The Parson went on:

"*The* protection was a bird named North—Judge Edwin North. He was never really a judge. That was just complimentary. But he could fix judges, get Cig's boys out of trouble when the law got curious about the numbers game. But no sooner does the Grand Jury get ready to hand up an indictment on old Judge North than he swallows runout powders. The new D.A.—Linton's his name—is stumped. Without North, he's got nothing. He needs North. So where is North?"

Tex sat still, waiting.

The Parson took a deep breath. "North is here. Here in Cariba. But he's hiding out. Am I boring you?"

"Yeah. Bore me some more."

"Linton, the Boy Scout D.A., isn't asleep, though. He sent his ace investigator, his most trusted man down here to ferret out

North and bring him back home. That guy—Jerry Lord—got in touch with me. Do you know Jerry?"

Tex said, "Sure. Everyone knows Jerry Lord. Why did he get in touch with you?"

"It seems that there's no extradition treaty between our country and Cariba. See? Even if Lord locates Judge North, he can't get him out unless…."

Tex drawled, "Unless what?"

"Unless, he's arrested outside of Cariba, say three miles out, in international waters. Or better yet, on an American ship. Then he's legally Lord's prisoner."

"Is that the job? Put North where Jerry Lord can put cuffs on him?"

The Parson grinned. "You catch on quick. Tex. It isn't like you'd be selling out on North. Hell, he'd turn you in himself if he had half a chance to get his own skirts clear. With me, it's just a professional job. Lord offers twenty grand. Ten will go to me and ten to you. How're you fixed for dough?"

"I'm broke." Tex said quickly. "I had to come away fast."

"Ten will come in handy then. How do you like it?"

"Lousy. I'm through with trouble."

"This won't be trouble. Not when you and I are handling it."

"Hell, you take it for granted I know where Judge North is hidden."

The Parson grinned again, nursed his cheek. "You got here a day after North arrived. Funny you should both pick on Cariba to hole up in."

"When do we do it?"

"Tonight. No better make it tomorrow. North will keep, and we don't have to lose sleep over it."

Tex Kent lit a cigarette. "How about another jolt?" He stood up, smiled a little and said. "Oh, well, what the hell? I don't owe North anything. I guess I like a little double-cross myself. Ten grand, huh? Couldn't Jerry Lord be upped a little on the ante?"

"Maybe," the Parson said. "He's strictly a business man. There's just one thing. Lord has to keep his name out of this. If it ever got out that North was forced aboard a boat under a gun on Lord's orders, his case would be blown sky-high. You can't do things like that when you're the law. That's the system and I'm working with Lord on that understanding. He never appears in the case."

"Yeah, I know the system."

"Then it's a deal?" The Parson held out his hand.

Tex put his hand briefly into the Parson's. "Right," he said softly. "Here's your drink."

"Thanks." The Parson looked into its amber depths for a brief moment. "Say, whatever did happen to the Dutchess? I was always curious about her."

Kent put down his drink in one piece. "Didn't you hear? She lit out for Havana after Cig died and when the pieces started falling around her head. The pieces of the numbers business, I mean. I haven't seen her since, but I was told she's married again to a bird named Blue. Carl Blue. A race-track man or a broker or somethin' like that."

"Quite a gal, the Dutchess," the Parson said.

Tex grinned appreciatively. "Yeah, quite a gal."

The Parson chatted for a few more minutes. When he rose to go, he told Tex Kent where he could get in touch with him. They arranged to meet at ten o'clock the following morning.

As the Parson went out into the night again, his dark eyes

lazily probed the reach of the moon-plated sky, the length of the moon-drenched road. The door closed softly behind him.

Two streets down was an open-air cantina. The Parson hurried to it, went inside to a telephone booth, called a number. When a grave, sing-song voice answered, he said:

"Hello, Ching. I want the master." He tapped his foot, crowded the transmitter with his lips. "Jerry Lord? This is the Parson. So it's on the up and up. He bit. Well, yeah. He heard me out. But I don't think I fooled him. He's one palooka I couldn't fool in a million years. I'll hang around but don't expect me to be a Dracula the rest of the night. I can't be everywhere. O.K., Jerry. Hey, you got a cold? Your voice sounds funny.... Uh-huh. Oh yeah, you'll hear from me. S'long."

He walked around the corner to where he had parked a trim little British-made Austin, got in behind the wheel. He moved it close enough so that he could command a good view of Tex Kent's house, but he was still a block away.

He switched off the lights and waited. He waited about three-quarters of an hour. Then a tall shadowy figure emerged from the house. The figure moved rapidly to the corner, away from the Parson. When it turned the corner, the Parson trailed after.

He rounded the corner in time to see the tall figure climb into a waiting car, lugging a small suitcase in after him.

The Parson scowled moodily through the windshield. The suitcase puzzled him. He had not counted on Tex Kent's carrying a suitcase.

He trailed the car.

PUERTO DE LAS DAMAS is at the extreme eastern tip

of Cariba, a little city all by itself, separated from the rest of Cariba by tradition, blood and unchallenged crime.

Its narrow streets, roughly paved with cobblestones, ended at a high cliff which frowned down on a narrow beach where lashing combers broke high through a tangle of reefs. The docks were to the left; but, long-abandoned, they had rotted and sagged until now they joined, edge to edge with almost perfect closeness, the limitless tropical sea of silver. Fishing stakes, upthrust like gnarled old fingers, were plunged into the sea; a mysterious crazy system of half-submerged bamboo fences, marking a channel passage that was no longer used.

In the days of caravels bearing the proud standard of Spain, Puerto de las Damas had brimmed with life and commerce, but three centuries of English rule had moved Cariba's center of gravity to the other side of the island within easier hail of Trinidad, and then Puerto had been abandoned to sun and history.

Its ancient houses with courtyards and doors barred with iron gratings were today inhabited by a fierce and savage mixture of Lascars, Chinese and tall, proud blacks, who paid no rent and answered to no authority except that enforced by their own keen knives. This rule existed despite regular, scheduled raids and arrests by Cariba's efficient police force, carried out mostly for effect, not results. For the most part, the dreary, vice-ridden Puerto was permitted to go its own way so long as its activities did not extend beyond its ancient walled confines.

Hands planted deep in his pockets, the Parson stood in the lee of an ancient rusty cannon, jutting out of the pockmarked face of an old stone ruin in the very heart of Puerto de las Damas. Around the base of the cannon, grass sprouted. This ruin of three-foot thick masonry had been a dungeon and fortress in the days of Spanish rule of the West Indies. Now only scorpions and bats lived within its damp, musty interior.

The Parson kept his eyes fixed on a rambling house of rubble and crumbling stucco, flat-roofed and squat, some two hundred yards away on the other side of the road. Tex Kent had stopped his car in front of that house fifteen minutes before. Because of the angle from which he kept vigil, the Parson could not be sure that Kent had climbed out of the car. He could not even see the car from where he stood. He decided he had waited long enough.

He moved lightly down the street, blending with shadows. He was nearly opposite the car when he heard the soft-toned whimpering of a little child.

The sound lingered in his ears for just an instant and was gone. The surprise of its coming from the house, the impossibility of its belonging there, shocked him to an immobility as controlled and rigid as a pointer's.

On the street nothing moved. Threads of light stole secretively from lower-story windows in the house before which the car was standing. There was no other sign of life save that elusive wail of a child, either hurt, lost or frightened, that was instantly swallowed up and absorbed in the dead silence of the night.

His eyes were boring into the blackness that enveloped the car before him; his ears were alert to the slightest sound. But the child's whimpering cry was not repeated. For a long moment the Parson stood there, wondering if he could have mistaken the plaintive call of some night bird for the voice of a child. He moved silently across the cobblestones to the car, and as he moved, his hand reached into his coat pocket and brought out his flat, hefty Luger.

He could see a figure now, seated in the driver's seat of the car. The figure was utterly silent, watching him without movement. The Parson did not stop short nor did he call out. He kept on coming toward the grim, waiting figure as if he were being drawn to it by a magnetic force outside himself, stronger than his own will. The figure did not move. The Parson reached the car, touched its sides until he moved around to the steering wheel.

Seated before it was Tex Kent. A knife had been plunged into his heart. The haft still protruded. A lot of blood had dripped down, and instead of being absorbed by his shirt front, had formed a little pool on the leather of the seat in the V of his thighs. His head was slightly bowed toward his chest so that he appeared to be gazing into the pool.

For a silent minute the Parson stared at the inert figure of Kent. His own lips were twisted, bitter; his face sallow. He could not explain to himself why the death of Kent should touch his sympathies, but he felt strangely moved. Kent had been struck down suddenly without a chance to defend himself.

The Parson peered into the interior of the car. The suitcase was gone.

A shot crashed inside the house, echoed like distant thunder, and before its flat echoes had died, it was followed by another.

The Parson blinked. His Luger jerked up in his hand. He started toward the house, moving past trailing hibiscus ghostly and redolent in the moonlight, past sail-like banana leaves that grew in the courtyard. Before he reached the house a woman's angry scream, not terror-stricken but angry, sliced the deafening silence.

The Parson ran swiftly toward the front door of the house, which stood slightly ajar. He pushed it wider and slid in. It was a sort of hall. A staircase angled upward at the further side and doors from it led into other rooms. From up above he heard gasping sobs. The Parson waited, he had heard footsteps coming down the stairs.

In the dim light a woman appeared, carrying a child of four or five in her arms. A little girl. It was she who was sobbing. The woman held a big automatic pistol in her right hand.

When she saw Parson, she stopped her descent and pointed the pistol at him. He said disgustedly, "Ah, I wouldn't shoot when you got a kid in your arms."

"That's manners anyway," the woman said. She came the rest of the way down the stairs, put the child down. Enormous solemn eyes with grave childlike dignity peeped at the Parson: then the child clung to the woman's skirts, hiding her head from the Parson, but still sobbing softly.

The Parson looked at the woman, shook his head with a faint smile. A point by point description of her would leave out everything essential. It was the intangibles about her that counted. The lift of the brow; the intelligent, expressive light in her eyes. The Parson could catalog to himself a strikingly tragic, beautiful face, triangular in shape, of an unusual creamy pallor. But that would leave out too much. The fierce glint in the hazel, swimming depths of her eyes, for example; the auburn-haired head, bravely, proudly carried; the tip-tilted nose; the wide, almost barbaric flare of her nostrils.

But even these details were not really significant. What was significant and definite was her personality, her passionate awareness. A vivid, daring quality; an aliveness, a keen zest. A woman not afraid of chances, who would stake everything on the turn of a wheel.

"The Dutchess!" the Parson said softly.

She had been appraising him from head to foot. She said matter-of-factly: "I know you, too. You're the man they call the Parson. You were a gambler in New York."

"Cig Wolfe's widow. Here! That's a laugh!" said the Parson. "Who's the little girl?"

The woman did not answer. The Parson saw that her eyes went beyond him. He turned and saw a man in an open door, holding a gun.

The Parson had never seen him before. He had brown, wavy hair, brown eyes that were steady and deadly serious. His chin was neatly cleft and his nose was perfectly modeled. Altogether a handsome face but surprisingly cold, somehow devoid of emotion and human feeling. Only the eyes seemed alive in that face.

"Who's the boy friend?" the Parson asked.

The woman said. "My husband. Carl Blue."

"Oh."

Blue wagged his gun impatiently. "Hey, you! Drop your gat!" he said.

The Parson did not move. Blue crossed the hall to the little girl, who was still crying. He dropped on one knee and began to pat her hair and talk soothingly to her. The Parson blinked, then got the idea. There was to be no shooting in front of the little girl. Carl Blue had not been afraid for himself. It was strange to see Carl Blue comforting her, without showing a trace of expression or emotion on his own face. It was eery, too.

There were still tears in the child's eyes. But almost the instant Carl Blue bent down to her, she was stretching out her little arms and laughing with a sob as little children do.

The Parson crossed the hall to the door through which Carl Blue had appeared, and looked in. On the floor in the middle of the room lay a suitcase. It looked like Tex Kent's bag. The lid was open.

The Parson moved over to it. His nape bristled, his eyes narrowed and he threw a hard angry stare back of him at the open door. This was Tex Kent's suitcase all right. His initials were burned into the leather. Floor boards creaked under the Parson's feet as he knelt down and peered more closely into the bag.

It was crammed full of currency in little packages, spilling over with thousands—hundreds of thousands of dollars.

He heard a furtive footstep behind him. He whirled, caught a glimpse of a short-statured gorilla-like man, arm out-flung toward him. The man was strangely silent, furtive, red-eyed like a harbor rat. The arm had flung a sap, attached to a leather cord. The Parson ducked but not enough.

He sprawled, legs and arms outflung, but he never knew when he hit the floor. All he knew was that he was hurtling through space with blackness cascading down upon him. He heard a scream—it was the Dutchess: "They're back! Oh God, they're back!" Revolver shots thundered. And then there wasn't anything.

Coming to, the Parson lay motionless for a moment or two, conscious of severe pain in his head. Then he sat up. There were voices in the next room. Stiff British voices. "After all that shooting, there should be at least something besides a man stabbed to death." Cops! The Parson got to his feet. He remembered the bag suddenly and stared.

The bag was no longer there.

The Dutchess, Carl Blue, that little child, the man with the sap—all had pulled a fade-away.

He heard the cops moving about in the next room. He sped silently for the door. He would have to get out. Cordite fumes still hung acridly in the air. The door led to another room in which there was an open window. The Parson slid through it into the night.

CARIBA'S FINEST HOTEL was the Queenshaven. It was laid out like a park with golf courses, tennis courts and private swimming pool under nodding palms, and a host of little white stucco and red tile cottages. The Parson occupied one of these cottages, number six, but he did not go to it. Instead he went to one marked number two. It was only an hour since he had quitted the twisting streets of the Puerto and his head still ached.

He came in with a cigarette between his lips, however, and a droll half-smile hovering on his mouth.

"Well. I'm back. Linny," he said.

The man he called Linny stood up from a wicker easy chair, surveyed him with alert gray eyes, his heavy leonine head held almost to one side. Presently he too began to smile, slyly, jovially.

"Same old Parson. Is that a bump on your head or are you parting your hair in a new way?"

"Both. It's a bump and I've got to part my hair around it." He dropped into a chair facing the other man, blew smoke toward the ceiling. "Want to hear about it?"

The man called Linny was a striking, distinguished figure of a man with aggressive features, graying hair. He sat down again, nodded. "Let's have it all."

The Parson rapidly sketched what had happened at the house in the Puerto. "That's what we got to go on," he finished complacently. "Riddles."

"It's a mess. I can't understand the Dutchess. Far as I can see we're not closer but further from our object."

"And don't forget that bagful of money!" the Parson said warmly.

"Yes, that certainly complicates matters. So does the presence of the child. I'm going to a lot of trouble to sew this case up. It would be too bad if the thing got out of hand."

"Things moved fast," the Parson agreed.

Linny shook his head impatiently. "You see, we're moving forward on a hunch. There are strings attached to this we have absolutely no control over."

The Parson shrugged. "Want to chuck it?"

"How can I—now?" The older man's eyes narrowed shrewdly. "You can, though, any time."

"You know I wouldn't do that."

"Thanks, Parson."

A tall man with smooth dark hair and dark eyes idled into the room, hands in his pockets. Almost imperceptibly the Parson tensed. Force of habit as well as the urge of precaution made his hand creep toward his gun.

The movement was not lost on Linny. He laughed. "Parson, this is Ed Clancy. He just arrived from New York. I had him come down in case you might need help. Ed, this is the Parson."

The men nodded to each other. "I don't need help," the Parson muttered. "I work alone."

"I know, boy. But in a case like this you never can tell. Anyway. Clancy will be here any time you need him. Are you going?"

"Uh-huh. It's home and bed for me." When the door had closed on him, Clancy said: "Chief, I don't altogether approve of this. The Parson's a notorious gunman and a crook. How can you trust him in such a delicate case?"

"You don't understand. The Parson's a peculiar sort of crook."

JERRY LORD, SPECIAL investigator for New York's D.A., swung in his chair, pushed back his emptied plate and drained his morning coffee.

This was another day, cheerful and serene, with blue sky and golden sun benevolently bright overhead. Ford was a square-built, stocky man with bright whimsical eyes, a frank broad face, an easy engaging grin. He watched his Chinese boy place food deftly before the Parson, said:

"Ching, if I want you again I'll ring."

"Very good, master." The boy padded out, closed the door.

Lord said, "Don't let that bump on the head spoil your breakfast, Parson." The Parson pushed the food away from him. "I'm not hungry. Besides, it's not the bump; it's knowing all those people were there and all that money."

"You did your best. And anyway think of my position. I send you to get the cuffs on Judge North, and he's not even there."

"I didn't see him," the Parson corrected. "He may have been there. Anyway, somebody else was there. The Dutchess."

Lord grunted. He lit a cigarette, took three quick drags, spoke through the smoke. "What kind of a guy is her new husband, this Carl Blue you told me about?"

The Parson shrugged. "Just another guy, I guess. Cold, though, like a fish. You can feel it just looking a him. Good looking. Perfect features. Maybe too perfect."

Lord got up, went to the window and peered out. After a minute he came back to the table solid-heeled and sat down, eyes clouded and bemused. He looked up at the Parson.

"Boy, I can't make this out. Not yet. You're likely right when you say you frightened Tex Kent into running to the Judge's hideout with a bagful of money, if the Judge was really there. But what the hell is the Dutchess doing here? She bailed out of the rackets two years ago, a few months after Cig Wolfe was killed." His hands balled into fists and he repeated forcefully: "Why should the Dutchess be in Cariba?"

The Parson said, "And that kid. Somehow I think that kid is the whole story. You say you heard about that kid?"

Lord waved his cigarette. "Well, there were rumors that she and Cig had a little baby girl they were keeping under wraps, away from the seamy side of life. But I never saw it and I never met anyone who had. It was all very vague."

"Tell me more about the numbers racket," the Parson said. "When Cig was torpedoed, somebody else took over the trade, didn't they?"

"Well, yes. The Frankie Moore mob from Jersey City stepped up to the big time. But by then, Linton, my boss, had his sleeves rolled up and was breaking things up fast. So Frankie Moore never got to earn the big important dough that Cig Wolfe had rolled in. In fact, before he got started, Frankie Moore was out."

"Was it Frankie Moore who gunned Cig?"

"Huh?" Jerry Lord looked sharply at the Parson. "It was never cleared up who killed Cig. It was just one of those things.

But it was never believed that Frankie was responsible for the rubout."

"How come? If he stepped into Cig's shoes, isn't it more than likely that he knocked off Cig to get there?"

Lord shook his head. "I see where you're heading. But you're making a lot of mistakes. In the first place, Frankie Moore got his start under Cig as a racket man, and secondly he was Cig's friend; he owed a lot to Cig who had practically made him a gift of the Jersey City territory."

The Parson dug in. "That was always the Wolfe's way. Not kill off but buy off the competition. Divide and rule."

Lord was silent, intently watching the Parson. He snapped a finger against his cigarette, flicked the ash into his cup, said: "Well, what do you think?"

"This: Something went blooie last night. I don't say I know why Tex Kent was killed, though that bagful of dough could be motive enough. I don't even say I know who put a knife in him. But I do say motives don't start here in Cariba, they stretch away back to New York. Judge North didn't show last night. It's even possible he butchered Kent. I don't know. I'm sure he was there somewhere.

"The Dutchess and her fancy new husband, Carl Blue, are thick in it. And that little girl…. I don't think that suitcase of money was intended for Judge North. I think it was being delivered to the Dutchess. And above all I think there was opposition present that neither the Dutchess, Tex Kent, nor Judge North had counted on. Keep this in mind. Just as I was passing out I heard her yell: 'They're back! Oh God, they're back!' It was a general mix-up, a scramble, a root-ta-tootin' lead party."

"You're lucky," Lord sighed, "one of those bullets didn't wing your way. The whole thing sounds like a bad dream."

"Sure. But things happened faster than in dreams. That yell of the Dutchess' now: 'They're back!' Who was 'they?' The opposition. And the opposition almost spoiled the plant."

"Plant?" Lord's head bobbed up. "What do you mean?"

"Just what I say. Plant. Something fixed beforehand." The Parson was relaxed, eyes somnolent. "Everything that happened last night was planned, figured out before it happened. But the opposition was the unpredictable event that spoils the best of plants... and murders."

"You mean there was some gang present, some gunmen who were after the Dutchess?"

The Parson nodded. "Somebody who took a licking from her and Cig Wolfe sometime back, probably in connection with the numbers racket."

Lord shrugged. "You may be right. As far as you go. But remember, my job is to bring Judge North back home. I could take the Dutchess, too. That would help. But I don't give a damn about the dough or Tex Kent or that little girl or what you so quaintly call the opposition. That's incidental."

"Yeah. But sometimes it's the incidentals that count most."

Lord smiled ruefully. "You're telling me. Listen, boy. No racket's been bloodier than numbers. It's pennies, just pennies. A business in pennies. But millions upon millions upon millions of pennies. And each one is red with blood. Soaked in it. Dozens of people have been murdered for control of those pennies."

"What are you driving at?"

"There's a whole lot involved here. It's not your quarrel. If you want to, you can slide out."

The Parson frowned. This was the second time he had an offer to quit. He stuck a cigarette between his lips, lit it, sent up a white balloon of smoke. "Hell, I'm in it this far, I might as well stick."

Lord reached over the table and put friendly pressure on the Parson's arm. "Boy, you're tops. In New York they used to say you were one of the best shots and one of the smartest heads in the rackets. I can well believe that. You got what it takes."

The Parson shrugged. "I look out for number one. I had an eyeful of that bag of money last night. I'd just like to put my hands on it. That's why I'm sticking with it. And then this is the first time I'm working with the law—even if only from the outside."

"You like working with the law?" Lord asked.

"It's a new experience. It gives me a kick to watch a respectable law like you at work."

Lord looked quizzical. "I don't know if you're kidding or not. Anyway, I still think this is not your quarrel, and that you ought to quit. I'll pay you whatever you think you ought to get for your work last night and you can drop it right as is. I mean if it's money...."

"It's not money," said the Parson.

Lord grinned. "Oke. I'm glad to have you, boy. I'm glad you're so set on sticking. Tell me," he added curiously, "what makes you and Linton such pals? When I left New York, Linton said, 'Get hold of the Parson. He'll help you.' You didn't know me when I arrived here, yet soon as I showed you Linton's letter, you were ready to pitch in. He's New York's crusading D.A. and you're supposed to be a red-hot. Where's the connection?"

The Parson nodded reflectively. "I can see where you'd be puzzled. You know the old Five Corners district, backwash of the docks in New York? Linton and I played there together as kids, we went to school together. When he was admitted to the bar, I was his first case. He got me out—"

The Chinese boy looked in the door. "The milk is here, master."

"The milk? Oh, yes. Yes. Very well, Ching. I will take it later, chilled."

"Chilled, master?" The boy's head ducked. "Very good, master."

"Milk?" said the Parson. "Do you drink stuff like that? Say, that bottle of Demerara looks good. Break it out, will you? I could inhale a slug. Breakfast doesn't seem to be what I need."

THE TROPICAL MORNING air was fresh and the bright-plumed birds poured song abandonedly from throbbing throats.

The Parson entered his cottage at eleven, whistling soundlessly to himself. He liked living at the Queenshaven with its spacious country club air, cottage-plan and privacy. There were rooms to be had at the main building, but these were mostly for tourists. The cottages were for more permanent guests.

He peeled off his dark jacket, lit a cigarette and dropped into an easy chair. He unstrapped his holster, laid gun and holster on a tabouret beside him.

When the bathroom door across the room began to open toward him, he did not stir nor did he snatch at his gun. He sat and watched it.

The door took a long time in opening. Then a gun peeped

through, held in a white hand. Behind the hand came a man. His face was ruddy, well packed; his hair white. His clothes were good but wrinkled as though they had been slept in. His gun was a Police Positive .38, but he did not seem to be sure of it or of himself.

He moved hesitantly to the door leading to the bedroom and peered in. He came back to the middle of the room and with an apologetic smile, said:

"I just wanted to be sure we're alone."

The Parson accepted this as the natural order of things, nodded sagely.

"I've been waiting almost an hour for you," the man went on. "I'm Judge North. Edwin North."

"You don't look much like the pictures the New York papers printed."

"Those were old pictures, taken ten years ago. I've changed, I guess. Listen." His words dragged to a stop. The room was quiet. The Parson could hear the man's soft breathing.

"Listen," he said again slowly. "We're ready to make a deal. We'll lay the dough on the line. We're through fighting."

The Parson stared at him unblinkingly. The lines at the corners of his mouth drew down skeptically. He waved his cigarette, said: "Call off the artillery and take a chair."

North nodded. He pocketed his gun gingerly, sat down. He looked tired.

"O.K.," said the Parson. "You said 'we.'"

"The Dutchess and I. Listen. She knows when she's licked. That's why she sent me to you. You're working for Jerry Lord. I saw you last night in Puerto de las Damas. I know what's wanted. We'll kick in."

The Parson said, "Tex Kent was kicked—out. He was murdered."

North lifted his head. "I know that. It was tough. We liked Tex. He was good oats. But we won't try to make it tougher by going at things the hard way. I mean with guns. We're licked, see? And we know it. That's why I'm here. We want to make a deal with Jerry Lord."

"Oh, a deal with Jerry Lord?"

"Yes."

"When do you want to see him?"

"Right away. Now."

The Parson rose to his feet. "Then why wait?" He strapped on his holster, sheathed himself in his tight-fitting black coat. "Does Carl Blue know about this deal?"

North fidgeted, shot a sidelong glance at the window. "Oh, of course."

"And it's oke with him?"

"It's oke."

"Hm." The Parson was silent a second. "You know that Jerry's job is to take you back to New York to stand trial."

"I know."

"Is that the deal you have in mind?"

A sad, wistful smile appeared on the older man's tired face. "No, but it may be part of it. After all Jerry's the one to dictate terms. We're licked and we know it. We'll play ball."

"Did you come here alone?"

The sudden ferocity with which this question was flung at him jarred Judge North. Panic guttered in his eyes; they flicked involuntarily to the window, again they slithered away. "I—I don't know what you mean," he said at last. "Of course I'm alone."

The Parson grinned suddenly. "There's just one more thing. Last night…" He waved a hand airily. "You know what happened last night. There was quite a rumpus. Shooting and yelling and things like that. And one guy sapped me. Do you know who that guy was?"

North nodded wearily. "That was Hugg, Tobe Hugg they call him. He's Frankie Moore's hot trigger."

"Frankie Moore?" the Parson repeated gently. "I didn't see him after the sapping. So he was there last night, too."

"Yeah. He and Tobe Hugg nearly wrecked everything."

"Frankie Moore took over Cig Wolfe's numbers racket, didn't he?" the Parson said lazily. "The Dutchess sold the business to Frankie, didn't she?"

North stood moistening his dry lips, staring at the Parson.

"Well, didn't she?"

"Yeah." North's voice was tired and soft. "She sold it to him."

"How much did she get?"

North went on staring.

"I said how much did she get?"

"About a half million."

The Parson nodded. "So that was why." He pursed his lips. "All right. Let's go."

AS THEY DROVE in the little Austin through the crowded streets to the other side of the island the Parson imagined they were being followed, but when he glanced about, he could not be sure. He drove with a steady hand and from time to time he even smiled as if at a private, and very droll, joke.

The cottage which Jerry Lord occupied stood almost alone in a street that fronted the estate region of Cariba. There were flowers in front of it in huge yellow and blue ceramic pots, a small terrace. There was even a lawn. It was a poor lawn, however, with a wretched stand of grass, blighted by the limestone, which crops out in gray masses like dirty snow from the thin topsoil of the West Indies island.

Ching opened the door to the Parson and when the Parson walked in on Jerry Lord, he looked up with surprise, said: "Round trip, Parson? Forget something?"

"No. I brought you a visitor." Judge North walked into the room. Lord's smile receded slowly, leaving his face hard, purposeful. He was up on his feet, saying through clenched teeth: "Damn you, Parson! I thought I told you to keep me out of this. You know I can't—"

The Parson shook his head. "This is not a pinch. At least you don't have to make it here. The Judge says he wants to make a deal with you."

Lord's eyes snapped. "A—a deal?" he said waveringly. Then again he roared, pounded the table hard. "To hell with a deal! I gave you orders—"

"Aw, push your tongue between your teeth," the Parson said, and reversing a chair, sat down. "Ankle out, Ching."

The Chinese boy stood with his hands folded in his loose black sateen sleeves and did not stir. Lord shot an angry glance at the boy, barked impatiently: "Well, get out! Get out!" And when the door had closed, "This is sweet, boy, sweet! Fine mess you've thrown me into."

"It's not a mess," the Parson said patiently. "It's a deal. Maybe we both stand to make something big out of it."

Ford put his hands on his hips and stared fixedly, venomously at Judge North. Then his shoulders shrugged helplessly. "O.K., since you're here. What's the deal?" He swung across the room. "Wait until I lock this door."

He stopped short. The door opened and two men crowded in, pushing Ching before them. Both had huge .45 automatics leveled. They were rather young men to judge by their clothes. But their faces were old, hard. One was tall, even good looking in a hard-faced, thin-lipped way, with slaty, murderous eyes and vigorous, determined features.

The other was short-statured, furtive, with long arms ending in powerful looking hands; his eyes, cold as a reptile's, slid over the room, went carelessly past the Parson, then came back to linger at leisure on him. It was the man who had sapped the Parson the night before in the house in Puerto de las Damas.

"In reverse," the taller man said.

"What? Who?"

"In reverse, you."

Slowly Jerry Lord stepped back. His face was the color of smudged paper; his eyes jiggled nervously in his head; his upper lip twitched with the movement of his eyes, while the rest of his face was frozen.

"Hi, Judge," the tall man said, flicking a hand in mock cordiality in the air.

Judge North swallowed but he did not seem especially frightened. There was a fine dignity to the way he held his white-haired head.

"Hello, Frankie," he said.

"Who's the gent in black?" Frankie Moore asked.

"The Parson," North said almost indifferently. "That's what they call him."

"This runt? This little guy? He's supposed to be tough. I've heard of him. But he's built more like a divinity student. Hey, Tobe. This is rich. Rich!" Laughter gurgled in his throat. "Whatta you know—this is that famous guy, the Parson!"

Tobe Hugg grunted. "Hell, I can take him, Frankie. I took him last night."

Hugg moved suddenly. One step, one swing with his left. The Parson crashed to the floor with the chair he had been seated in. He scrambled to his feet. There was death in his eyes. His hand streaked for his shoulder holster, but at once, almost at the same instant, he let it drop to his side and put it behind his back. But the light in his eyes did not die out, though they were now almost calm.

"See?" said Hugg. "I can take him."

"That was a dumb thing to do. Hugg," the Parson said softly. "You'd better kill me, finish the job. That will be your easiest out." That was all he said. His glance was locked with Hugg's.

Hugg, holding the gun, dropped his eyes first. The Parson stood there, leaning slightly forward on the balls of his feet, with infinite purpose expressed in every line of his face, his body. It was as if Hugg suddenly realized that the Parson did everything and said everything behind the eternal mask of that mildness and obliqueness which had given him his nickname; and that behind the mask was concealed cruelty, steel-hard ruthlessness; a quite blind, but leashed, and terrifying power.

"Ah-h!" snarled Frankie Moore. "Don't horse around. We got business, Hugg. Let's get on with it."

Something of the Parson's unruffled confidence seemed to have communicated itself to Jerry Lord. He drew himself up.

"I can tell you that whatever your business may be, it will

be better done without guns. I ask you—I insist you put your guns away."

"Aw, take a walk on the ceiling! Shoo, fly!" Frankie's low, rough laugh was ironic, cutting.

"Nevertheless, I insist you put your guns away!"

"Insist then!" Frankie turned to Hugg. "Fat Face insists, Hugg, old tomato. He won't play it our way. He insists. He thinks we're still listening to him."

A covert look passed like a darting visible flame between Jerry Lord and Ching.

"All right, you're inviting trouble," Lord said doggedly.

"We're inviting trouble!" Frankie guffawed. "Listen to Fat Face! Boy, oh boy, if you ain't the icing on the cake! Keep 'em covered, Hugg."

He was crossing over to Judge North, but stopped short in sudden, sharp alarm. "Hey, ain't that footsteps I hear outside that door?"

Hugg and Frankie turned their heads for but a split watch-tick. Ching's folded hands came undone and from the folds of his sleeve appeared a small-bore Smith and Wesson.

"Geez!" yelled Hugg. "Lookit the Chink!"

Ching's gun went off, and the bullet tore Hugg's hat from his head. It slammed against the wall, seemed to float lazily to the floor.

Frankie Moore shot Ching.

Ching whirled, spun as if by a centrifugal force with one foot raised slightly off the floor. There was something undignified and silly about it, as though he were executing a dance step. Then he crashed down with one hand under him and blood seeping from between his fingers.

The sight of the blood, the feel of the hot gun in his hand did something to Frankie Moore. He was grinning vapidly, breathing hard, like a drunken man. He was kill-drunk.

He said, "I've got five more bullets. Any takers?"

No one in the room stirred. Frankie bent his gaze on the Parson. "What about you, toughie?"

The Parson shook his head slowly, dreamily.

"O.K. You're goners. All of you. Shell out your hardware while you still can."

No one moved. It was clear that the slightest movement would invite a bullet. It was very still in the room. Distinctly footsteps could be heard racing up the stairs; little, exceedingly rapid steps; someone seemed to be running.

But Frankie shook his head, still grinning. "I was made out a sucker last night—and in New York. You know about that, Judge. There was a bagful of dough last night. I didn't get it. I almost got it but I didn't get it. I'll collect in my own little way. Look at me, all of you. Look at me!"

"Geez! There's somebody movin' around outside," Hugg grunted uneasily. "There's someone outside, boss."

"Look at me!" chanted Frankie, disregarding Hugg's anxiety. "Look at me because you're going to die!"

"Look up here, why don't you?" a voice cut in softly.

There was a jarring, tearing sound.

A TOMMY GUN'S ugly snout ripped through the copper screening of the window, thrust into the room. Behind the gun was a face the Parson had last seen standing beside the Dutchess, soothing a sobbing little child.

Apparently nothing could change the expression on this face.

It was as elegant, as dignified, as unfeeling as it had been last night. The eyes, too, were the same—stern, thoughtful, preoccupied. The man said, "You two with the heaters—slide 'em to the floor. And don't be sloppy about it."

Frankie Moore's grin stayed congealed on his face. He seemed stupefied. Then suddenly his .45 spat viciously.

The Parson melted to the floor as the Tommy gun laid down a barrage. Frankie Moore screamed, twisted and fell on his side. Blood oozed out of his ears and nose.

Hugg, from an angle, smashed two bullets into the copper screen. The Tommy gun wavered. It was evident that Carl Blue had been hit. No fire was returned from the Tommy gun.

A gun behind the Parson began to cough. The bullets sang wide over his head. But they were not intended for him. Judge North took three of the bullets in the chest and neck and went down.

A bullet that was earmarked for the Parson dug splinters out of the floor inches from his head. His head jerked about and he saw Hugg shooting at him. He went over backward, hooked himself around a chair and somehow was unhurt. His hand snaked in, brought out his Luger.

"Curtains for you, toots," the Parson muttered, and fired.

Hugg plunged forward and hit the back of a chair with an outflung arm to keep from falling.

"That was for the sap last night," the Parson muttered. "And this is for the sock you just handed me."

He fired again and Hugg went down without even a groan.

The machine gun was operating again, pouring slugs into the bodies of Hugg and Frankie Moore.

And then suddenly, above the choked roar of crashing bullets, there was a faint sound of a child's sobs, muted, distant but clear, unmistakably clear.

The Parson's head shot up, listening, like a creature of the wild.

The machine gun came to a sudden halt. Simultaneously, a woman yelled. And instantly the machine gun went back on the job, but no longer was its snout protruding into the room. It was being fired at some short distance from the window. Pieces of plaster chipped off in an even row along the wall, head high.

The Parson stayed down. He heard a car being started outside in the street. Then abruptly the Thompson was silenced. Footsteps raced away across the lawn. The car was roaring, exhaust bubbling, and then it gunned down the street, its clean getaway plainly underscored by the diminishing sound of swishing tires and whirring engine.

Gunsmoke swirled in clouds in the bright bars of sunlight that angled into the room. The Parson heard people shouting out in the street. Then he heard a little whimper close at hand.

It was Jerry Lord. "My shoulder. A hunk of bullet ricocheted. A lot of blood, but it ain't bad. Help me out."

The Parson lifted him up and towed him across the room into the hall. The cottage was very quiet. Lord straightened, "Guess I'm all right now. Touch of nerves in there. Pretty horrible, with all those bodies on the floor."

"Yeah. Death is something you gotta get used to. Listen. There's gonna be cops and questions. What's the story?"

Lord groaned, pushed at his face with his knuckles. "Are— are they all dead?"

The Parson nodded.

"Then we'll tell the truth. We got nothing to hide. We'll tell 'em how I came down here to sew up Judge North and bring him back. The D.A. Linton, will back me up. Then Frankie Moore and Hugg tried to save the Judge. There was shooting and that's all."

"And the chopper—Carl Blue?"

Lord shivered. "Was that Blue? I didn't know him."

"Leave him out," the Parson said decisively. "Listen. With North dead, you must bring something back. Why not the Dutchess, possibly Blue as well?"

Lord stared. "Right! Right as rain. There were footsteps from upstairs, weren't there? I mean it wasn't imagination?"

"No. I heard them, too."

Lord pulled out a handkerchief. "Here. Tie up this arm. I feel better already. I'm going up to have a look."

"Be careful."

"Where's the need?" Lord asked cheerfully. "We came through alive out of that shambles in there, didn't we?"

"Yeah. We're the only ones who got down on the floor while we were still in one piece."

"What a horrible experience!" Lord said vexedly. "I wish I could understand all this."

"It's simple. Frankie and Hugg were at that house in the Puerto last night. They nearly killed the Dutchess. So her new husband trailed them today and when they came here he took his revenge and killed them."

"Yes, but Judge North. You said he had a deal to make with me."

"Uh-huh. I don't know what it was. Probably a deal to turn State's evidence if he consented to go home with you quietly and submit to formal arrest. We never got around to discussing it, you know."

"Not with all *that* happening."

"Say… that Ching. That was a fast one he pulled, plucking a gun out of his sleeve. It was a good trick even if it failed."

"Ching was very devoted to me," Lord said solemnly. "I am very sorry he had to die."

"So am I." There was a pounding at the door. "Cops. You do the talking. Just grease it thick and I'll supply the amens."

DUSK PLACED A gossamer, inky blanket over Cariba and as if through tiny rents stars began to appear. Lights began going on here and there among the cottages. Huge drop-lights illuminated the dining terrace of the main building of the Queenshaven. The Parson had been sitting in cottage number two all the afternoon. His coat was off and his tie was loosened. A tall iced drink had been riding at his elbow throughout the day. From time to time it had been replenished by the leonine-headed man he called Linny. The Parson was enjoying himself.

"Everything depends on catching up with the Dutchess now!"

The Parson made an expansive gesture. "Don't worry. She can't get out of Cariba."

"I wish I were as certain as you. I wish Clancy would phone."

"He will. Just hold on to your pants and subside."

Linny nursed his jaw. "Too damn bad about Judge North. All the guys who can talk knocked off. That helps, doesn't it? That helps loads!"

"What's the odds?" The Parson shrugged. "Besides, you know how he came to die."

"Oh, hell. If you'd brought him here instead of down to Jerry Lord, the whole picture would be different."

"Maybe. But there would have been nothing in it. I took a chance, I'll admit that. But it seemed the right thing to do. I wanted to play the string out. You can't blame me because Frankie Moore and his stooge showed up and dead-pan and his chatter gun. It was a circus setup and I took a header. Before I could get organized, it was all over."

The other man sank down into a chair. "I'm not blaming you, Parson. You're fine. But I'm worried. All these people dead and nothing to show for it."

"There'll be plenty if you'll only wait."

"I'm waiting! Hell, I'm sick and tired of waiting."

"Everybody's tired of waiting. Judge North was and he got the shroud." The Parson's eyes twinkled. "Boy, if you'd seen the faces on those British cops when they walked into that room. Four corpses! No less than four!"

They were silent a moment and then the Parson said, "You know what to do when Clancy phones, don't you?"

"Sure. I'll be at my post just as we arranged."

"Good. I'd like the act to go over smooth this time."

The Parson finished what was left in his glass, took out and inspected his Luger. Satisfied, he slipped it back, folded his hands over his stomach, seemed to doze.

The phone rang some five minutes later. Instantly alert, the Parson snatched it up. "Yes?… When?… O.K., Clancy, I'll be over in ten minutes. Just keep an interested eye on them but don't make a grandstand play. Swell."

He hung up, swung about. "Just as I figured, Linny. Clancy just lamped them at the seaplane base. I knew it was either a plane or the *Santos Prince,* the only boat sailing from Cariba tonight. My dough said the plane all the time."

"You sure figured the angles right this time, Parson! I hope nothing goes wrong!"

"It won't," said the Parson decisively.

"Just do your part."

"I'll be under the window looking in, just as you said."

THE PARSON PARKED his car in the cinder-spread parking area at the seaplane base and walked to the bright lights of the concrete, modernistic waiting room. Clancy met him near the door, said laconically: "They're inside. They've been buying the kid ice cream."

He fell in behind the Parson, strode with him across the cork-lined floor. The Parson saw them seated across the room with the little child between them. Three bags were on the floor at their feet. One of them the Parson recognized as Tex Kent's bag.

Neither the Dutchess nor Carl Blue moved when the Parson came up to them. He did not draw out his gun. His voice was soft, easy when he spoke. "We've got a date, folks. Let's go."

Carl Blue gazed fixedly at the Parson, but his expression did not change, "You're making a mistake. We're leaving on the plane."

The Dutchess put an arm about the little girl, drew her to her protectively. The child gazed with solemn, round eyes at the Parson. He leaned over and chucked her under the chin. She did not smile. There was something sinister, deadly about the Parson's lean, sharp-featured face. The child seemed fascinated by him.

He said, "Don't ever say I'm making a mistake. This is the show-down. I wouldn't touch either you or the Dutchess. The kid would be the first thing I'd shoot for."

Wide-eyed with fright, the Dutchess was saying: "You wouldn't! You wouldn't!" She looked deep into the Parson's eyes. Shuddering, she turned away, tugged at Blue's arm. "We'd better go," she said wearily. "He's not bluffing."

"That's sensible. Pick up the bags, Blue. All of them. You can hold the girl by the hand, Dutchess. Now march and act nice."

Blue bent over, took up the bags, one under his arm, two in his hands. Clancy walked at his elbow. The Parson walked a little behind the Dutchess and the child. Outside, at the car, he said:

"Search 'em for guns, Clancy. You'll drive. Blue will sit next to you." And to the Dutchess: "You get in the back. I'll hold the little girl on my knee. That's so you won't go getting ideas."

The little Austin purred down Cariba's boulevard, bright and colorful with evening promenaders. "What do you intend doing?" Blue asked.

"We're going to pay a call on an old friend," said the Parson. "Say, what's the little kid's name?"

"Alice. Parson, you can't get away with this. You can't take me where I don't want to go."

"Relax, pal. This is my party."

"Be quiet, Carl," said the Dutchess. "Oh, please!"

The car rolled through the main artery of town, hit Upper Leeward Road and followed it to Victoria. A mile or so on and it pulled up before a solitary house.

"But this is Jerry Lord's place!" the Dutchess exclaimed.

"Exactly. There are lights in the lower-story windows, so he must be at home. Now listen, all of you. There's going to be no break here for a getaway. Unless, of course, you want little Alice killed. I wouldn't like to do it. Honest. But if you force me…. So act nice. You take the bags and go first, Blue. Wait right there before the door. Keep him covered, Clancy. Now you, Dutchess. I'll carry Alice. Gee, she's just no weight at all. Now that's sensible all around."

Suddenly the child began to cry. Tears rolled down her cheeks. "I don' wanna go. I don' wanna. Bad mans!" she said suddenly to the Parson.

"Sh! You're all right, babe. Cripes, I won't hurt you." There was unexpected, soothing gentleness in the Parson's voice. And to Clancy: "Open the door."

Clancy took hold of the knob and pushed the door open. Carl Blue stepped in, still loaded down with the bags. Clancy prodded the Dutchess in, followed her. The Parson walked in last, carrying the wide-eyed child.

The house was utterly silent. The Parson saw Blue stop short at the threshold of the room in which the shooting had taken place that afternoon. The Dutchess also stopped. Only her profile was visible but he could see her lips tighten, her face muscles grow rigid. Clancy stepped closer, cried out bitterly:

"It's the Chief. He's been killed!"

The man the Parson had called Linny lay on the floor on his side with a hand pressed to his ribs. The Parson began to see that the copper screening had been removed from the window, which stood open. The Dutchess caught her breath as she looked down at the figure on the floor, exhaled slowly, said:

"Isn't that District Attorney Lew Linton?"

The Parson nodded. "Come in, everyone. Keep 'em covered,

Clancy." The Parson knelt down beside the inert figure. Very faintly he could hear breathing. His eyes flicked up at the others. "He's been stabbed. Just as Tex Kent was stabbed. But he's still alive. Knife didn't touch his heart. There! He's coming to."

Linton's eyes opened slowly. Slowly recognition came into them. "Hello. Parson," he whispered.

"Are you hurt bad?"

"S-scratched. Hit my head on the floor when I fell. I'll be O.K."

"Who did it, Linny?"

Linton tried to speak. But the words did not come. Again his eyes closed. The Parson felt his heart. The pulse was regular, strong enough.

He straightened. "He'll be fine in a little while. Sit down, folks." His voice dropped lower: "Sit down, Dutchess. You too, Cig."

The Dutchess broke in. "You can't—"

"Button up," the Parson silenced her dryly. "I'm talking to Cig. Cig Wolfe. How about it, Blue? You're Cig Wolfe, aren't you? Aren't you?" Again his voice lowered: "You see, Cig, the masquerade is over."

CARL BLUE TURNED his face to the Parson, his eyes wide, pupils dilated, but still his face was cold, expressionless, without movement of a muscle. He looked at the Parson without fear. His voice was quiet. "How did you know I was Cig Wolfe?"

"I knew almost at once. Your face. Always calm. Never a smile, never a frown. Lifeless, cold. And the too perfect features.

No nerves in it. I remembered what Tex Kent had told me. The chopper was good. Twenty dumdums went through the face of the man they thought was Cig Wolfe. Twenty dumdums so that no one could recognize it. You were that chopper, weren't you, Cig? Who was the man you killed so that they could bury him under your name?"

"Just a guy off a park bench. No good to anyone, not even himself. I sent his mother ten grand. That's the way he wanted it. He looked enough like me—hair, features, build—to pass, if the face wasn't examined too closely."

The Parson nodded, eyes lowered for a minute. "And then you got this new face. Plastic surgery. It's a beautiful job. But you can't smile or grin or look angry or show any other expression. They cut up your nerves to make over the face. They gave you not a new face but a mask. A perfect mask. Why did you do it, Cig?"

The man's head jerked back. A light flamed in his eyes, then instantly died away. He glanced sidewise at the Dutchess and it seemed, almost it seemed, that he smiled. But actually his features were as rigid as ever. His words, though, showed his intention.

"Don't take it so big, honey. This isn't the end yet." He looked back at the Parson. "Why did I do it? Alice. There's your answer. When the Dutchess had that kid, everything changed for us. We hid her from the world on a little farm in the White Mountains. But that couldn't keep up forever. Someone would have found out, hit out at us through her. And I couldn't quit as Cig Wolfe. There were too many—commitments. So we thought up this plan. I didn't want to be in the rackets any more. We had some dough. I wanted to live like other people, do things like other people, have my daughter grow up to be proud of me."

The Parson looked keenly at the impassive face of Cig Wolfe. He suddenly felt sorry for him. Cig was just a man who wanted to be a husband and a father. There was something touching in the way his voice broke, in the way his eyes strained, darted about; but something terrible, awesome in the way his face remained cold, expressionless.

The Parson said, "But you didn't break clean enough. Your kickback was when the Dutchess sold the numbers racket to Frankie Moore. Two weeks later Linton cracked down and Frankie never got to see any profits. He was dumb but not dumb enough not to know he'd been tricked into buying something worthless. That's why he followed the Dutchess here."

Cig Wolfe nodded diffidently. "We needed more money. We had to take the chance on Frankie. Listen, I never begged for a break in my life. But I've handed them out in my time. Look, I'm not a tough gunman now; I'm just a guy who's a father. I'm begging for a break. Not for me. For the Dutchess and the kid."

"You should have thought of that before you killed Frankie and his stooge, Tobe Hugg. The Cariba cops want you and the Dutchess now. You didn't have to come here and do a lot of typewriter work."

Cig shook his head. "That's where you're wrong. When a guy, who has no business in the mix-up, hooks up with a mugg like Frankie, knifes your best pal and then, when the shooting starts, sneaks off your little girl—what would you do? Exchange a bag of money for the kid and forget it?"

"You got the dough and this guy got the kid in that mix-up in the Puerto," the Parson interrupted. "Is that the way it went?"

Cig nodded.

"Then why didn't you pay out the sugar if the kid means so much to you?"

"We intended to. That was supposed to be the deal Judge North wanted to swing. The money for the kid. Then we saw Frankie and his gun and we knew it was no go. So we took the kid the hard way."

The Parson moved across the room to where the bags had been deposited, knelt before Kent's bag, unstrapped and snapped the lid open. The money was there in neat little piles as he had seen it last.

"Tex Kent brought this with him from the States, eh?" he said. "And the Judge brought the kid."

The Dutchess said, "Yes!" Her handsome face was very lovely, grave, stoical. "Maybe it's no use, but we've lived hard, we've tried to live it down, make a new life. You've got to give us our chance. You can't snatch our chance away from us. Here! We don't care about the money any more. It was the last of the numbers money cached away. We should never have touched it. You take it. It's yours. Let us go. There's still a few minutes to make that plane."

The Parson looked at her. "O.K.," he said quickly. "You can go and take the kid with you. Cig and the money stay here. I'll help you but I wouldn't lift a finger for him, even though I think he's a right guy."

"No! No! Oh, you can't do that! I won't leave him. You think I've gone through all this just to run out on him?"

"He's right, honey," Cig said. "I'll take my dose. After all, I can't kick. I guess I got this coming. You blow with the child."

There was no abjectness in his manner and no heroics.

Perhaps the abnormal passivity of his face lent particular dignity to his bearing. The Parson could not be sure.

"I won't go!" the Dutchess said with a quietness to match his own. "Nothing you can say will make me."

"Well, if that's that, Clancy," the Parson said, "you'd better get a move on. Linny needs help fairly fast." He snapped shut the lid of the bag of money. "Take this down to police headquarters. No, don't phone," he added as Clancy made a move in that direction. "Go there yourself and bring back a squadron of cops with you."

CLANCY WALKED TOWARD the Parson to take up the bag, but he never got his hand on it. The closet door opened and Jerry Lord stood there with a .45 automatic in his hand. He was breathing heavily. His coat was off. The armpits of his shirt were dark with sweat.

"Put down that bag," he said thickly. "Gosh, it was hot in that closet." His eyes were wild in his head.

The Parson put the bag down gently. "Hello," he said cheerfully. "Is that a gun? I thought knives were your specialty."

"Put up your hands, all of you," said Lord. "If any of you make a grab for me, it's the works."

He started moving toward the door, making his way closer to the bag all the time.

"You can't get far, you know," the Parson drawled quietly. "Not loaded down with the bag."

"What's in it will give me wings, take me ten times around the world. Far enough for me."

The Parson spoke again, still lazily. "Linton forced your hand, didn't he? He was supposed to be outside that window looking in while Clancy and I faced you with Cig and the Dutchess. Linton wanted proof of your crookedness, Jerry. He got it, didn't he? More than he expected. We were going to stage a little tableau, Clancy and me. But that isn't needed now. You surprised him looking in your window."

Lord's breathing was slow and thick. "Don't you dare move. I'll plug you. Parson."

"I'm not moving, Jerry. But I just wanted to tell you how it was. Linton knew there was a leak in his office, bribery, corruption, a guy who had 'protected' Cig Wolfe and was tied in with his successor, Frankie Moore. He wanted to root it out. He suspected you were it. When Judge North escaped the Grand Jury and came here, Linton gave out a story that North had been Cig's protection. The protection was you, but Linton couldn't prove it. So he sent you to round North up. That's what you thought. Actually he sent you to me. It was up to me to pin the goods on you. You thought I was a sap. You didn't think I knew that when you sent me to Tex Kent, it would dynamite Kent into running to North with his bagful of dough.

"Linton knew about that dough. He had followed Kent here. And when I phoned you about my talk with Kent, you weren't on the phone. It was Ching, covering for you. There was just enough difference in his voice to tell me. You and Frankie Moore and Hugg were on Tex Kent's tail. You followed him—and me—to the Puerto. You stuck a knife into Kent and you got the bag. But that wasn't all Frankie wanted. He wanted to blast Cig and the Dutchess. You got tripped up, lost the bag. In the mix-up, you took second best—the child.

"When I got here with North to lay his deal before you, Ching was waiting with a gun up his sleeve. That gun was meant for me. Frankie busted in. He had been upstairs with Hugg. They sneaked down the back way probably. Frankie was riding high. You got scared. Frankie fully intended to kill North and me. You caught Ching's eye. You wanted him to wipe out Frankie, a dangerous confederate. But Cig spoiled that party and saved my life, even though he couldn't save North. You shot North over my head. The bullet came from behind me. I knew it came from your gun but I couldn't do anything about it—then."

Lord had stopped, standing on the balls of his feet. He said very coldly: "Is there any more?"

"Yeah," said the Parson. "This: I'll bet I can draw out my gun and shoot faster than you with a gun already in your hand."

Cig Wolfe laughed. It was something to hear not see. Nothing showed on his face. He threw himself in a pantherlike spring that carried him six feet to crash into Lord. The gun in Lord's hand barked aimlessly.

Lord went hurtling into the wall, went down on one knee, face panicky, gray, the gun wavering in his hand. Again that dry, hard laugh of Cig Wolfe's was heard. He lifted himself from the floor and leaped at Lord a second time. It was practically tossing his life away.

Lord fired and Wolfe was hit but not stopped. He kept on coming with a slow, dragging step, while blood pumped out of his cheek in a gushing rivulet. His mouth was filled with blood and he spat out a dark wad of it and a tooth.

Behind him Clancy began to fire with nervous haste, chipping the wall. The Dutchess cried out once and covered her little girl with her body. The child's frightened screams blended with the roar of gunfire.

Lord jumped toward the door, tripped, almost fell headlong, then caught his balance and pumped two bullets into Cig.

The Parson's body had jerked to one side and out of the jerking had appeared his gun, large and ominous in his hand. But he had held his fire. Cig had been in his line. Now Cig went down on his face. The Parson fired. He did not want to kill Lord. He wanted to hurt him.

Lord screamed as the bullet smashed the delicate bones of his hand. His gun fell down out of the bloody mess, bounced on the floor.

Cig kept on coming, crawling, dragging along on the floor. Lord, screaming in pain and hysterics, pushed at him. Cig got a hand on his trouser leg, pulled him down. Lord frantically snatched up his gun with his left hand, dug it into Cig's eye.

The Parson fired again with delicate, precise aim. A small round hole appeared magically high up on Lord's beaded forehead. At once three small drops of blood trickled slowly out, mingled with the sweat, trickled into Lord's glassy eyes.

Linton slowly, painfully raised his head, as if roused by all the shooting, gazed about dazedly.

The Parson stood quietly, a short undersized figure in black, unruffled and calm. He walked swiftly across the room to where Cig lay on the floor, squatted down beside him.

"How is it, Cig?"

Cig spat blood. "It doesn't hurt."

"Why did you do it?"

"I gave you your chance," Cig said brokenly, hoarsely. "I gave you your chance to get him. He'd have killed you otherwise. It wasn't throwing my life away. I was a goner anyway. If I stuck around, the Dutchess would stick with me. She would never leave me no matter how I argued. Some dames are stubborn, huh? So I gave you your chance. You won't forget a favor. You'll give her a break. And my kid. Now she's got to go, doesn't she? She can't stick with me now, poor kid. She's got to go...."

The agonized eyes peered at the Parson but the nerveless face was set, expressionless, cold like a mocking mask.

SOFT BREEZES STIRRED the pennons and rigging of the magnificently white *Cortania,* but still it was hot. Cariba was always hot. Linton, perched moodily at the rail, watched the shimmering lights of the little city. He drew on his blackened pipe, said: "You saw her off?"

The Parson nodded. "She took the plane for Buenos Aires. She'll get a new start there. A dame with her brains and looks won't find the going tough."

"All I can say is I hope she has her lesson learnt by heart."

"Oh, she'll go straight. There's her kid, after all. You know, she fell in love with Cig and married him before she knew how he made his dough. She was just a babe in arms then. Barely eighteen. And when she found out, she didn't quit. Some dames are like that. She stuck and tried to talk him into giving up the life he led. The reason why she plunged into the racket the way she did was to shame him; show him she was being dragged down too. Then the kid came along and Cig really decided to ease out."

"So Cig hauled off and got himself a new face?"

The Parson's eyes dreamed. "Yeah. And if he hadn't crossed Frankie Moore he'd have gotten away with it."

Linton sighed. "Poor Cig... so close to his goal. But he'd never have reached it really. Somehow, somewhere the backwash of his past life would have caught up with him, engulfed him. Still, that was a pretty noble thing he pulled on Lord."

"Well, he had it figured right. He was never yellow. He wasn't afraid to die. He knew he'd never get clear. He wanted the Dutchess and the little girl to get their chance."

A voice bawled, "All ash-oah that's go'n ash-oah…."

The ship's whistle throbbed. People started to wave handkerchiefs, hats. The ship's band tootled, "Auld Lang Syne."

Linton thrust forth his hand. "Well, it's good-by again, Parson."

The Parson, wrapped in thought, took it, shook it briefly. "Good-by, Linny. If you should happen to pass by the old Five Corners where we played as kids, just give it a look-over for me."

"Wouldn't you like to go back? Aren't you tired," Linton waved a hand toward Cariba's lights," of all this?"

The Parson shrugged. "One place or another, they're all the same after a while. And I'm beginning to like it here, to be truthful."

He was on his way to the gang plank when Linton ran over and caught his arm. "One more thing, old kid. If I remember correctly there was a suitcase mixed up in the case somewhere. Somehow when we got around to it, it had disappeared and I didn't want to make a fuss in front of those stiff British colonial police."

"Suitcase?" asked the Parson innocently. "What suitcase?"

"A suitcase full of money which Tex Kent had brought with him from New York."

"Oh, that. A trifle, you know."

"Seriously, Parson, how much was in it?"

The Parson faced him. "A hundred and twenty grand."

"Wha-at! What did you do with it?"

"Well, I kept twenty. I thought I had at least that much coming to me."

"And the rest?"

"Went with the Dutchess. Only she doesn't know it. Maybe she does by now. I helped her pack her bags."

Linton squeezed his arm affectionately, grinned. "You're the berries, kid. No fooling! And you're a white man, too!"

"What's up? What went wrong?"

Linton exploded into rich laughter. "Nothing's wrong. But the Dutchess—now don't break down, boy—the Dutchess returned that money to me just before her plane took off. She didn't want any part of it. You see, it was blood money to her. She wants to start clean. I've got it now in the ship's safe. A cool, clear hundred grand."

The Parson's eyes snapped. "And I was sucker enough to hand out good dough to a dame only to have her turn around and hand it right back! That's gratitude!"

He looked at Linton for a half a second. Linton was grinning broadly, and presently the Parson, too, was grinning.

"Anyway," he said, "I got my twenty grand. That's no gag. And you're not getting any part of it back."